Isabel finished the last stitch and made a secure knot.

She rubbed a salve liberally over the wound, her fingers lingering over the smooth, taut skin, then fetched lengths of clean, dry linen and wrapped it a few times around his broad chest, which of course brought her tantalizingly close to him.

His lips were only a fingerbreadth apart from hers, and as his eyes dropped to her lips, she licked them without intending to.

Oh dear... Her stomach flipped on itself and her breath hitched, stuck in her throat. They both stared at each other for a moment, neither of them moving. There was a question in Will's gaze, a question that she was only just beginning to understand. He wanted to kiss her and, to her shame, she wanted him to...very much.

He edged near, his lips hovering just above hers, his breathing coming in shallow breaths.

"I shouldn't, Isabel," he muttered, his voice a low rumble.

Her heart was pounding against her chest. "I shouldn't allow you to."

Will cradled her cheek with one hand, running his thumb across her bottom lip. "No...you mustn't," he whispered as he dipped his head, pressing his lips to hers lightly.

Author Note

The First Barons' War began in 1215 in England, after King John reneged on the Charter of Liberties (Magna Carta). It lasted two bloody and bitter years, yet much of the troubles and deep divisions in the country had been brewing for most of King John's reign.

However, the king's timely death in October 1216 and the decisive win for the men loyal to him at the Battle of Lincoln a year later meant that the country could start to heal under the stewardship of William Marshal—the Earl of Pembroke and Lord Protector of England (the newly crowned Henry III being too young to rule).

In the aftermath, old wounds were still raw. As was the case for Sir William (Will) Geraint, the hero in this book.

It was a time when young noble girls could be sent to live with their betrothed's family to strengthen ties. Which was what *almost* happened when Lady Isabel de Clancey, the heroine, was a little girl.

Will and Isabel embark on the most important journey of their lives, but can they discover a treasure that guides them home? Or do they find more than they bargained for?

I hope you enjoy their story!

MELISSA OLIVER

———

Her Banished Knight's Redemption

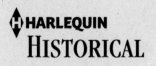

HARLEQUIN
HISTORICAL

HARLEQUIN®
HISTORICAL™

Recycling programs
for this product may
not exist in your area.

ISBN-13: 978-1-335-50603-0

Her Banished Knight's Redemption

Copyright © 2021 by Maryam Oliver

For questions and comments about the quality of this book,
please contact us at CustomerService@Harlequin.com.

Harlequin Enterprises ULC
22 Adelaide St. West, 40th Floor
Toronto, Ontario M5H 4E3, Canada
www.Harlequin.com

Printed in U.S.A.

Melissa Oliver is from southwest London, UK, where she writes historical romance novels. She lives with her gorgeous husband and equally gorgeous daughters, who share her passion for decrepit old castles, grand palaces and all things historical. When she's not writing, she loves to travel for inspiration, paint, and visit museums and art galleries.

Melissa Oliver won the Joan Hessayon Award for new writers from the Romantic Novelists' Association in 2020 for her first book, *The Rebel Heiress and the Knight*.

Books by Melissa Oliver

Harlequin Historical

Notorious Knights

The Rebel Heiress and the Knight
Her Banished Knight's Redemption

Visit the Author Profile page
at Harlequin.com.

To my three treasures—Bella, Scarlett and Sofia.
Always and forever.

Prologue

AD 1206—the remote outskirts of La Rochelle, Poitou region, Aquitaine. A region still part of the English Crown.

She was going to die today. Now, at this very moment...

Isabel opened her mouth to scream, but no sound came out. It was as if her voice had frozen, owing to the unspeakable horrors she had just witnessed. She wanted her mother to comfort her, soothe her and make this all go away, but that was not possible.

Mama was far away from here.

Her whole body shook violently as she lay on the ground, gawping at the bad man hovering over her. He had caught her easily as she had run away into these woods, trying to get away from the carnage that he, along with the other bandits, had inflicted. It had all come to this: staring death in the face. Isabel drew in a shaky breath and screwed her eyes shut, thinking that she had let her father down, through no fault of her own.

Oh, please, God in heaven, let it not hurt...please let it be over quickly, she said over and over again in her head like a prayer, as she wrapped her small hand around the pendant dangling from her neck.

But nothing happened. Instead, the man made strange, unexpected noises. Isabel slowly opened her eyes and saw the bad man swaying from side to side, his eyes rolling to the back of his head before he fell with a thud on to the ground. It was then that she saw him…a boy, several years older than her, eyes wide and holding the blade of a sword, the hilt pointing down. He must have surprised the bad man and struck him from behind using the heavy metal hilt. The boy had hit him well because the man was lying motionless.

'Are you all right, miss?' he said gently. 'My name is Will Geraint and I'm here to help. He didn't hurt you, did he?'

It was a nice voice, with so much warmth that she was instantly put at ease after what she had witnessed and almost endured.

Not that she knew whether the voice belonged to someone that she should readily trust. Isabel cautiously shook her head as the boy moved forward to help her on to her unsteady feet.

'You're safe now, but it's best if you don't look back there,' he said, pointing towards the smouldering wagons, which were shrouded by an eerie silence. All the people she had been travelling with were now dead, as she would have been, if it had not been for this boy.

'Do you know what happened here?' He was watching her. 'Who did this?'

He seemed to be about the same age as her eldest brother, twelve or possibly thirteen, and his eyes were the bluest she'd ever seen. They were kind eyes.

But she couldn't answer. She dared not.

'Was it an ambush?'

She nodded slowly, suddenly shaking uncontrollably. 'Can you tell me your name?'

Again, she said nothing as she tried to compose herself.

He exhaled as he dragged his fingers through his matted hair. 'Very well, but you can't stay here. You'll have to come with me and I will ask Sir Percy what is to be done with you.'

She stilled before taking a step back. She couldn't go with him! Who was his lord? For all she knew he could be another enemy of her father's.

As though he sensed her apprehension, he tried again, 'Whoa, easy now. Sir Percy is a good man and he'll help, I know he will. Besides, you really can't stay here. It's not safe.'

No, she really couldn't stay in this place, with the carnage all around her, the repugnant smell of burning flesh. Oh, God, it was all too much. She turned and retched violently, emptying the contents of her stomach on the ground. The boy patted her gently on the shoulder.

'I'm so sorry, but there's nothing for you here any more, miss,' he whispered. 'Come, I'll take you to safety.'

She hesitated for a moment before grabbing her satchel, which had fallen beside her, and tentatively took his outstretched hand. His lips curled into a friendly, placid smile. He nodded and led her through the woods to his horse, which had been tethered far away from it all. They mounted the huge animal, riding away from that horrible scene. She nestled against his shoulder, feeling a huge sense of relief as anxiety slowly drained from her body to be replaced with overwhelming exhaustion.

The drum of his beating heart and the pounding of hooves against the ground lulled her into a deep sleep, one that she did not wake from until much later.

It was dusk and Isabel was no longer on the back of a horse, but instead lying on a hard, lumpy pallet.

She opened her eyes and sat up, looking around the small crypt to see a fire crackling in the hearth. She rubbed her eyes, her vision adjusting to the darkness and it was then she saw him—the boy, Will. His back was to her as he stood at the doorway, leaning against a stone wall, talking to someone, but he turned, as if sensing she was no longer asleep. He took two big strides into the room and knelt beside the pallet.

'I waited until you were awake to take my leave and wish you well before I go.'

No, please don't leave me here!

She threw herself against him, clutching on to him as tears streamed down her face.

'You must be brave, little maid, and stay here with Father Clement. He'll take you to a convent nearby where you will be looked after and...'

Was she to be abandoned again? She thought she could trust the boy, she thought she was safe but, no... she had no one to rely on except for herself. She sobbed desperately as Will Geraint grimaced.

'Come on, miss, I'm sure you will do well here.'

Isabel shook her head, unable to get the words out.

'You could tell me your name?' He raised a brow. 'We could then find your kin and send a message so that they could come for you?'

She opened her mouth to speak, but shut it firmly. No, she couldn't tell him her name. She had promised Papa not to tell anyone about who she was and where she was going, no matter what the circumstance. Father had made her swear on the holy bible.

Will Geraint's eyes widened. 'Oh, God, unless they were the ones who perished back there.' He pulled his fingers through his hair, looking uneasily at her. 'I'm so very sorry.'

They might not have been her blood relatives, but the people she had travelled with had all been part of her father's household retinue, accompanying her to France, where they had met their grisly demise.

She shook her head again, wordlessly pleading with him as she tightened her grip on his arm.

'I cannot take you with me, miss. Sir Percy only allowed a little time for me to bring you here,' he said, scratching his head. 'And anyway, I'm only a squire, but I am training hard to be soldier and, one day, God willing, a knight.' He smiled at her. She stopped crying and sniffed as he untangled himself, pulling her up to her feet. 'I must go, but promise me you'll be brave. As much as I will have to be.'

She nodded slowly as more tears dropped on her cheek. He brushed them away and sighed.

'Have faith and courage, miss. One day you will overcome this. I know it. And don't forget that you will always have a friend in me,' he said, thumping his chest. 'In William Geraint.'

Please don't leave me here! she wanted to scream.

Isabel knew there was nothing she could say or do to stop Will Geraint from leaving her here, unless she informed him of who she was. Yet she had made a vow to her father and he would be so disappointed if she let him down again. She hated that she always seemed to disappoint him…

Papa had specifically told her not to trust anyone.

'There are too many enemies circling around us. Trust no one. Do you hear me, girl?'

'I do, Papa.'

'Good, now don't forget. A vow is a solemn promise. One that can never be broken.'

Her shoulder sagged in resignation. Yes, it seemed her destiny was to stay here, wherever that was. Anyway, her father would likely come looking for her and then she could go back home.

Oh, to be back home…

Isabel looked about the sparse, cold room. How everything had changed for her in a matter of days, in a matter of moments. The boy was probably right and she would be safe here, but before he left there was something she wanted to give him.

A symbol of her gratitude.

As he turned to leave, she quickly unfastened the leather cord from the back of her neck and allowed the heavy pendant to fall into her lap. She pulled the sleeve of his tunic a couple of times and dropped her silver and ruby pendant into his hand.

He shook his head. 'You really don't have to give me anything.'

No, but she liked giving things to people. And he did have kind eyes. Besides, it was dangerous to keep the *two* identical pendants together and, since she had found the other one in her satchel earlier, this one could be given away. She hoped her father would be proud that she had thought of it all by herself, but he was so difficult to please. She wrapped her small hand around Will's and squeezed it, nodding in encouragement when he hesitated. He had to keep it. The pendant was her present and no one ever said no to a gift. Mama would say that it was bad manners.

Mama... Oh, Mama...

She gulped and sniffed, hoping she would not start crying again. Her brothers always used to get annoyed if she cried.

'Very well, if you want me to have this,' he said dangling the pendant from his hands, 'then I will thank you and always treasure it. I must leave now. Good luck, little one.'

She kept her eyes fixed on the stone floor, but knew that the boy had quietly left the chamber. With no one now there, she covered her face with her hands and started to weep once more.

Chapter One

Spring 1218

Will Geraint spotted him the moment the old peacock stepped inside the tavern. The older man was not the usual customer who frequented the dirty, dubious establishment that Will liked to call his home away from home.

Instinct made Will lean back and sink into the shadows, clasping the hilt of his dagger underneath the wooden table as he watched the man scan the room. His beady eyes settled near the area where Will was sat and he gave a decisive nod before walking over.

Who the hell was he? And, more importantly, what did he want?

Will tightened his grip around the hilt as the man flung his feathered hat on the table and sat opposite him, his eyes studying Will closely. There was something about the man's presumptuous manner that he didn't particularly like.

'Mind if I sit here?' The stranger spoke French, but Will realised instantly that he was English. A fellow countryman—a courtier, no less. His senses were further alerted to the man's every movement, aware that he might not be here alone, might have any number of accomplices waiting somewhere outside.

The fact the older Englishman had come to this god-forsaken tavern in a remote part of France made it obvious he had meant to seek Will out, especially since the tavern wasn't particularly busy and he could have sat anywhere else.

Will ascertained the various ways he could leave expeditiously without using the front entrance and without the man being able to follow him in any capacity.

He shrugged without betraying any of his internal calculations. 'I don't care where you sit, stranger, as long as you don't disturb me.'

'That is not my intention. However, I was told that I would find a man here whose talents with a sword were—and still are—legendary,' he said, brushing non-existent dirt off his shoulder. 'A man whose reputation precedes him, even if he does seem to prefer living in such obscure places, as he has these past two years.'

'There is no man of that description. Not here.'

'No? What if I could give this man a chest full of silver and a pardon so he could return home to England?'

Hell's teeth!

Will had to tread carefully here. He had been living in France as a mercenary, a sword for hire, in the shadow of exile for the past few years. The truth, however, was that since King John's death he had worked tirelessly for England's new regent and Lord Protector, William Marshal, gathering important information for the Crown under the guise of being a disgraced man. A disgraced rogue knight. Not that many knew. Not that this man knew.

'And what would you want with such a man? If one were to exist.'

'I'd need him to find something—rather, someone. Urgently.'

Will smirked dismissively. 'I cannot think of who you would mean. You have the wrong place.'

'No, I don't think so. I have been making a lot of enquiries, both here and in England and I'm certain I am in the right place, talking to the right person. You are Sir William Geraint,' the man said as his lips curled into a sneer.

Will tightened his grip on his dagger and spoke in a low voice. 'If I were you, stranger, I'd leave and go back the way you came. That is, if you want to hang on to your life.'

'Peace, Sir William, peace.' The man held out his hands, palms facing outwards, and swallowed. 'You have not been at court and so have not been privy to the whispers and rumours about how you, along with the knight you squired for, Sir Percival of Halsted, saved a young girl's life more than ten years ago.'

'What of it? It was our duty and not of any consequence.'

Except for the lasting memories of the young girl, of course…

Will had often thought of the frightened little girl with unusual eyes whom he had once helped rescue when he was still a young lad himself. He had wondered from time to time since that fateful day what had happened to the girl. He remembered her looking so desolate, so hopelessly alone and so reluctant to stay in that cold, foreboding place. He'd felt sorry for her and hoped the intervening years had treated her kindly.

Although the incident had been harrowing, Will had

been commended and rewarded by Sir Percy for his perceptive quick thinking in the situation. It had led to a time when life seemed like an endless adventure, full of possibilities.

Not like the shadowy, dark world he inhabited now.

Will dragged the leather cord out from under his tunic and absently wrapped his fingers around the silver and ruby pendant that dangled from his neck. A pendant the little girl had gifted him and which he had always worn since.

The other man's eyes narrowed and he murmured something under his breath, no doubt recognising the jewel. Damn, that was short-sighted of Will, but he could hardly hide it now.

The man pressed his lips into a thin line before speaking again. 'Neither of you ever knew the girl's identity—not that I'm surprised. Her family were out of favour with King John and never came to court. With Sir Percival having only just returned from the Holy Land, my mistress has only now learnt of this girl's existence, when she had been presumed dead all this time.'

'And who are you and who is your mistress?'

'Eustace Rolleston at your service, Sir William.' He inclined his head. 'And my mistress is Lady Adela de Clancey.'

'So, Eustace Rolleston, let me comprehend this. You want to commission me to find a girl, who is, if she is still alive, a fully-grown woman?' He smirked, shaking his head. 'Apologies, but you have the wrong man for this.'

'Oh, I have the right man. Sir Percy confirmed it as much but his memory is hazy now and he cannot remember anything about the incident other than your

gallant rescue of the girl somewhere outside of La Rochelle.'

The fact that the old knight Will had once served had
told this man the barest of information about the incident, however hazy his memory, sent darts of warning
through him. Sir Percy was sending him a message of
caution regarding the man sat opposite him.

Will narrowed his eyes. 'No, I don't believe you understand, stranger. I am hired for many reasons, but
finding lost people is outside my remit, especially when
I have no idea where they may be.' He leaned forward.
'And no amount of silver would tempt me to stray from
that.'

That was not strictly true, but Will wanted to ascertain how far he could bargain, how large that chest of
silver was…and how desperate this man's cause.

'I thought you might need a little convincing,'
Rolleston scoffed. 'I carry with me a sealed document
from the Lord Protector himself as well as a letter from
Lady de Clancey regarding the particulars of this commission. As for the silver, I'm sure we can negotiate a
sum that would satisfy even you. Besides… I *know* you
can find her.'

Will ignored his last comment. This was not a situation he wanted to embroil himself in. 'As I said to you,
this is not the sort of work that I accept.'

Rolleston raised his brow. 'Find the girl, bring her
back and get a full pardon for what happened at Portchester, your honour restored. The silver you'll be paid
could help re-establish you and your family. Your sisters, your widowed mother. Even your young appren-
ticed brother. Find the girl and get your life back.'

A muscle leapt into Will's jaw. God, but the man was
insidious! He had certainly investigated Will's past. Yet,

interestingly, Rolleston had not been informed by William Marshal, the Lord Protector, that his honour *had* been restored, his pardon *had* been given. It had been at Will's behest that it was not acknowledged publicly, of course—a mutual agreement that had suited them both—yet this man who claimed to be here in the name of the Lord Protector's didn't know. He had not been taken into Marshal's confidence.

Another note of caution…

'You want me to find a lost girl—a woman who could be married with children at her feet for all you know.' He sipped ale from his cup. 'Presumably you'd have me drag her away to hand her to you?'

There were endless other possibilities of what had happened to the girl and none of them were good.

'Yes, Sir William. We are prepared to deal with any possible situations, if the lost girl is whom we believe her to be.'

'And who is that, Rolleston?'

He watched Will for a moment before he answered. 'The heiress of Castle de Clancey and its environs. Her father and her brothers have passed, God rest their souls.' The man made a sign of the cross. 'So, it's imperative that the girl is found and brought home to her mother. If the girl is whom we believe her to be, then she will rightfully take her place beside Lady de Clancey. And at this difficult time, Lady de Clancey is greatly helped and supported by Geoffrey Fitzwalter—her cousin by marriage.'

Will waited a moment, tapping a tattoo with his fingers on the wooden table, watching the other man. 'You didn't answer me, Rolleston. Who is the girl?'

'Didn't I say…? She's the lost heiress—Lady Isabel de Clancey.' Rolleston nodded at the pendant dangling around Will's neck. 'And that is an important family heirloom. She probably meant for you to take it back to them and it's high time you did, Sir William.'

Chapter Two

Sometimes, just sometimes, Isabel could happily throttle Heloise! It was one the biggest and most important feast days of the church year with much to do in the village of St Jean de Cole and yet her sister had spent the whole day preening herself for the evening festivities instead. Leaving everything, as always, for Isabel to do. She wiped her forehead with the back of her hand as she settled the big basket of her mother's warm bread rolls and sweet honeyed breads on the ground and took a deep breath.

Isabel absently crossed herself and pushed such thoughts out of her head. They were inappropriate, especially on a holy day, but really…sometimes Heloise's behaviour was intolerable.

The truth was that there was still so much to do and she could do with another pair of hands to help, but it was useless to think that they could belong to her sister.

Ever since they had been little girls and plucked from a local convent by her new family, the Meuniers, their roles had been clearly defined. Isabel was the one who was sensible, assiduous and conscientious, whereas Heloise was…well, she had been a beautiful little girl then and was an acclaimed local beauty now. She was indulged and indolent, but exceptionally beautiful with it.

The girls had been adopted into the family to help Madame Meunier, as her eyesight had been getting progressively worse and she needed help with tasks around the mill. They had only the need for one girl, but Heloise had kicked up such a fuss that the couple had acquiesced and taken Isabel as well, which she was thankful for.

She loved her life at St Jean de Cole. Every little thing about it.

Except this. Except today.

Isabel strolled across the small humpback bridge over the River Cole that separated the mill from the main part of the pretty village tucked away in the north of Aquitaine, exchanging greetings with a few of the villagers she passed.

'Good afternoon, Blanche, how do you fare?'

'Much better. Your salve was wonderful, very soothing.' She leaned forward. 'And it worked. My skin no longer feels itchy!'

'I'm so glad. That would be the calendula, chamomile and mint to help soothe the skin.' Isabel noticed the woman's awkwardness. 'But, of course, we did say prayers as well, so I'm sure that helped, too.' This was added quickly, with an understanding of the piety and superstition that most people held on to.

'Well, be sure to pass on my thanks to Sibylla, my dear.'

'I shall and I hope to see you at the feast later.'

Sibylla, the local wise woman who was instructing Isabel on the healing properties of plants and herbs, would be thrilled to know that her protégée's salve had worked. Apart from the back-breaking work Isabel did at the mill, mixing salves and ointments was what she truly loved.

And to heal people.

Isabel wondered, as she sometimes did, what her life would have been had she arrived safely on that fateful journey she took when she was just a little girl. But her new life in St Jean de Cole was nothing short of an unexpected blessing.

Her life was simple and uncomplicated compared to what it could have been. And even though she had to work hard, it was a blessing that she could enjoy the relative freedom she had. But it was more than that...

She felt safe here.

Initially, Isabel had hoped and prayed that her father would eventually come for her at the convent of Abbaye aux Dames all those years ago. He had promised to do so if something had gone awry on the journey, as it eventually had. He had said that he would come, find her and take her home, but he never had. She had been abandoned, her prayers never answered.

And while her father hadn't come for her, neither had the people who still plagued her dreams after all these years. People who had wanted her dead, and possibly still would, if they knew she was alive.

Ah, but it didn't matter now. Life was good in St Jean de Cole, where she did indeed feel safe and confident no one would find or hurt her again. She had made sure of that. Even going to the trouble of concealing her given name from everyone she met, including her adopted family.

She lifted her head and smiled when she saw a tall, handsome young man hobbling towards her. 'Good day to you, Ralph.'

'Well met, *Adela.*' He grinned as he came up to her. 'Can I help carry your basket into the village square?'

Isabel shook her head slowly and returned his smile, knowing as always that it was for her own protection that she had used her mother's name instead of her own…even after all this time.

'Goodness, no. What would Sibylla say if she knew that, after all our hard work, you'd now overexerted yourself on this particular day?'

A spark of annoyance crossed his one good eye, the other still bandaged. 'I'm getting stronger and, while I am for ever in your debt for your ministrations and your care, I'm not an invalid.'

Isabel pulled his sleeve gently. 'You know that I'm only teasing you.'

Ralph rubbed his brow and sighed. 'Forgive me, that was uncalled for, especially after everything you have done for me, but sometimes, ah, but sometimes… I'm frustrated at how slowly everything is progressing. My damned inadequacy.'

Isabel thought back to early spring, when a few locals had found the lone injured man, unconscious in the forest. It hadn't been easy, but together with Sibylla's knowledge and Isabel's care, perseverance and dogged determination, they had patiently nursed him back to health. Having suffered such a severe head injury, his memory had been patchy, only retaining scant details, such as his name and knowing that a faded purple ribbon, which he had in his possession, was of great importance to him. His face, too, had been badly scarred on one side by some weaponry or another.

'Time, Ralph, and patience are what is needed. I'm hopeful that all will be well for you soon.'

'I like your optimism.' He leaned forward and kissed

her cheek. 'And I thank you for it, Adela. You've been a good friend to me. I hope to see you at the feast later.' He nodded his farewell and walked on, leaving Isabel speechless. She dropped the basket on the ground, her finger tips grazing her cheek.

The truth was that Isabel had revelled in the challenge and difficulty in helping heal Ralph's injuries. Her natural obstinacy wouldn't allow him to fade away as he very nearly had.

He had to live.

He had to be saved.

Just as a young boy with friendly blue eyes had once saved her... A young boy whom she had always given thanks for at prayers, even after all these years. Isabel hoped, as she always did, that the pendant she had gifted him had brought him some measure of protection and that he had made a success of his life.

Isabel had been glad that she in turn had been able to help save another, just like her blue-eyed saviour. Well, not save exactly, but certainly help in his recovery.

She touched her cheek again and sighed.

Now, if she could get her many errands done expediently and get ready in time, she would get to enjoy the feast. This was possibly shaping up to be a good day after all...

And, possibly, it was not!

Isabel's assistance had been much in demand, from helping set up in the market square to cleaning the church before Vespers. Now, after getting ready in haste, hoping she looked presentable, she was finally heading towards the market square, long after her family had gone. Oh, for goodness sake, if she didn't hurry, she'd miss the whole thing!

She rushed down the narrow, cobbled street, greeting and smiling at passers-by, holding on to the floral headdress and sheer veil attached loosely to her head, hoping not to lose all of the flowers she had haphazardly woven through her hair.

Isabel finally emerged out of the shadows into the big expanse of the village square. Ah, but it looked beautiful with the sun setting beneath the hillside, casting a warm amber glow over their festivities. Sky-blue shutters opened invitingly, with vibrant coloured geraniums peppered across the windowsills and creepers with small white flowers trailed up the stone walls of the buildings enclosing the open space.

To one side was the covered market space, which had been temporarily transformed with a long line of trestle tables groaning with the bountiful harvest of late summer. The outside stone columns holding up the large roof were festooned with garlands of bright summer blooms draped from the top to the other side of the square, creating a sublime, colourful canopy of flowers.

It seemed her efforts had been worth it after all. The whole village was there, laughing, chatting, eating and enjoying the merriment. Soon there would be music and even a little dancing. Perhaps the estampie dance that was gaining in popularity and hadn't—thankfully—been frowned upon by the church.

Isabel smiled as she caught a glimpse of Ralph sitting with Heloise and her many other admirers. She sighed and bit her lip. Really, though, it was hardly Heloise's fault that she attracted the attention she did.

Ralph caught her gaze, and returned her smile as he got up to limp towards her.

'Well, it seems you have finally arrived,' he said as he reached her side.

'It seems I finally have,' she chuckled. 'Although you make it sound as though I chose to be this late.'

'Adela, I'm fully aware of your contribution to this feast, unlike some who merely just attend.'

'Ah, but some of us live to work while others are born to…to…'

'Be idle?' he concluded, raising his brow. 'Well, I'm glad you're finally here.'

'Me, too.'

Isabel scanned the area, taking in the happy convivial mood, when something—or rather someone— caught her interest. It was not just that the man who stood in the shadows in the corner of the square was a stranger. No, it was also the way the man was staring at her sister. Where had he come from and what did he want here in St Jean de Cole?

'Ralph, do you know who that man is over there?'

He turned around and narrowed his eyes. 'No idea. He's probably a reveller who has heard how good the feasts are here. Come, let's go and sit with Heloise and the others.'

'You go on. I'll be there in a moment.'

Isabel moved towards the covered area, grabbing a juicy red apple on the way, but all the while keeping a close eye on the stranger. There was something about him that was oddly familiar, yet she knew she had never laid eyes on him before. She watched with curiosity as the old bald man he was speaking to presented him to her parents. Her interest getting the better of her, Isabel meandered close, but remained inconspicuous, wondering what on earth the handsome yet exceptionally sullen man wanted.

Whatever had been said must have been of some significance as her parents looked somewhat anxious.

Even more astonishing, Heloise had been hastily fetched to their side.

How strange that Isabel had not been called to join with their discussion, but then, whatever it was might not actually concern her. The stranger spoke to Heloise, who lifted her fingers to her lips in shock, but seemed delighted at whatever had been said.

Ah…another suitor. That explained everything.

Isabel smiled, shaking her head at her silly worries, and was about to move away when she noticed something that almost made her stumble and fall.

The stranger was still in discussion with Heloise and her family and had pulled out a leather cord from under his clothing. A leather cord that had a diamond lozenge-shaped silver and ruby pendant dangling at the end of it.

She recognised it immediately.

It was the same pendant that she had given to the young boy who had saved her life twelve years ago. The same pendant that she had a duplicate of, but never wore in St Jean de Cole for fear of exposure. It was her family's heirloom, which meant, of course, that the stranger, the man who was at that moment talking to her family, might possibly be William Geraint. Unless, of course, he was an enemy? Someone who had taken the pendant from William?

No, it had to be him…no one else knew she was still alive nor that she could possibly live here.

She had to be cautious…

It could be that her father had finally wanted her back or that he was intent on sending Isabel to her betrothed again, as he had planned all those years ago.

When she had been sent at such a tender age to live with her betrothed and his family, she had not expected to marry the man until she was older. Well, she was certainly old enough now. And the one man who could possibly find her after all this time was here—if it really was *him.* Either way, she had no idea whether he was friend or foe.

Her instinct was to find out if the stranger was William Geraint and welcome him here, since she could never forget what he had done for her. But no, that was not a good idea.

Isabel watched with incredulity as she realised that the man must have assumed that Heloise was in fact *her.* It was frustrating that even when people were sent specifically in search of her, she was still overlooked. William Geraint, or whoever the stranger was, really wasn't to know, but was Isabel so inconsequential, so invisible, just as she had been as a child to her real family, to her real father?

Well, just because her father suddenly wanted her found to resume her duties after twelve long years, it didn't mean she had to go back, did it?

No…

She certainly did not want to give up her precious freedom, but, more importantly, she dreaded having to face the dangers from her past. A past that she hoped would never find her.

Yet it, apparently, had.

Isabel could not leave the feast yet as her early departure might be remarked upon. No, she had to behave in her usual, customary manner and not give rise to any suspicion and pray that this stranger would leave once he was satisfied that she was not here. The stranger who was possibly William Geraint…

The boy who had once saved her life.

* * *

Will pinched the bridge of his nose and expelled a breath in frustration.

Not again.

He seemed to have reached another impasse. There was something wrong here, just as there had been at every place the trail had led to, where every other young woman had tried to convince him that they were indeed the lost lady.

Just like this woman before him.

He didn't know what it was, but something about Heloise Meunier didn't feel genuine.

Damn!

He had been so hopeful that in this little village he would finally find Lady Isabel de Clancey after months of searching, but again he had hit a wall. A very beautiful and attractive wall...but a wall, nevertheless. And yet he was obliged to find out for certain.

'Forgive me, but if you are the Lady Isabel, why do you not remember anything that happened when I rescued you?'

'It was all such a trying experience. I must have blocked it out,' Heloise said, sniffing and placing her hand over her forehead.

'I would have thought it was a little more "harrowing" than "trying",' he said, narrowing his gaze. 'Surely you remember something?'

'My memory is not so good and, as you say, it had been such a harrowing experience!'

'Indeed,' he said in a flat voice.

'All I remember was your kindness, *messere*, in taking me to Abbaye aux Dames and that, after a few years, I came to the local priory here and from there to the family who looked after me—the Meuniers.'

'I see.'

'But I have always known that you'd come back for me, *messere*. I have always known that I was special,' Heloise said, fluttering her eyelashes. 'That I would lead a life different to the one that was thrust upon me.'

Hell's teeth!

No. This girl could *not* be the little girl Will remembered. She was another pretender, just like the others.

He shook his head absently. God, but he was tired after the long journey in search of Lady Isabel, which was frankly going nowhere. This commission, which he hadn't particularly wanted, but was nevertheless drawn to, was beginning to take its toll after many long months in the summer heat. He had continually examined the reason why he had eventually agreed to take it on, because it certainly wasn't just the silver.

No, it was more than that. It was a way to appease his conscience about a scared little girl whom he had been forced to leave at a monastery many years ago, when he was just a boy. He had often thought about her in the intervening years, hoping that she had somehow survived against the odds.

The search had been arduous, but he'd also had to endure the ignominy of being followed from La Rochelle—in all likelihood by Rolleston's men.

Damn their impudence but, whoever they were, Will had made sure that he lost them.

It wasn't like Will to admit defeat, but he had to concede the lost heiress might possibly have eluded him. He had visited the Abbaye aux Dames, the convent that Father Clement had said he would take the young girl to, but they hadn't kept any record of the girl and his aimless search for her had continued with only false leads.

This, apparently, was another.

The mother was still talking. 'Yes, *cherie*, very special. That's why we took you…well, both of you,' she said, nodding her head.

Will lifted his head. 'What did you just say, *madame*?'

'Well, that we…we took both girls.'

That got his attention. 'Both, you say?'

'Yes, both Heloise and… Adela.'

Adela? Adela was the name of Lady Isabel de Clancey's mother.

Interesting…

'And exactly where could I find Adela? Is…is your other daughter here tonight?' he said impassively, not betraying his curiosity.

'I believe so, although my eyesight is extremely poor. Heloise, have you seen your sister?'

'No, and I'm not sure I understand your interest in my sister, *messere*.'

'Quite.' Will darted his gaze back to the busy square, which was now crowded with many more people. He turned and inclined his head. 'I bid you a good evening and I hope we can continue this discourse on the morrow.'

'I look forward to it, *messere*,' the girl said and inclined her head in return, but Will had already walked away.

Well, now… Adela?

Could it be her…? Could it be Lady Isabel de Clancey?

He knew it was wishful thinking on his part—he wanted to be done with this commission so he could get back to his solitary life—but this seemed more than just a coincidence.

He shuffled along, nodding and smiling at the villagers who returned his greetings reservedly. Will stopped next to a young girl leaning against the edge of the stone column, clapping along to the music that had started to play. She turned and gave him a pensive smile.

'Apologies, little one, but have you seen Adela? Only her mother doesn't know if she has arrived at the feast and wouldn't want her to miss it.'

'Oh, yes, she's arrived.' She giggled. 'Adela is there dancing.'

Will swung around in the direction the little girl had pointed.

'My thanks, little maid.'

He walked towards the group assembled in the dance and watched on the sideline of the area, surveying each young woman who passed him.

He hoped that this time he'd found her. That one of the women among the dancers was her…

Will edged closer and closer to them before an opening for him was made. He was ushered to join them, since they were a man short for the estampie dance. Good. Now he could interact with each of the dozen or so young women and find out if 'Adela' really was, in fact… *Lady Isabel de Clancey.*

Good grief!

It was an unmitigated disaster to have remained at the feast. Isabel should have left the moment she had laid eyes on the stranger and now *he* was dancing the estampie with them. She hoped that if she kept her head low and avoided making eye contact with him, he would move on somewhere else. But every time she caught his gaze, he was looking at her in a shockingly open manner, scrutinising everything. She felt her cheeks getting warm.

Isabel tried to diffuse the tension in her body and act

nonchalantly, even nodding at him with civility, but she was all too aware of him: his height, his broad shoulders, his powerful presence and raw masculinity. There was something about him that sent a frisson of awareness through her.

She circled around him, noticing that his demeanour and physical bearing of a honed and skilled warrior seemed at odds with the fluid, graceful moves of the group dance. She pushed down her apprehension as she moved next to him again. The best thing to do was to continue the dance without giving a hint of whom she was and then to slip away afterwards.

Yet, the more he studied at her the more the fear of discovery gave way to annoyance. She knew she should keep her mouth shut and not allow this man to rile her, but eventually she couldn't help herself. 'You are staring at me, sir, in a wholly inappropriate manner.'

'Apologies, I had not realised there was a more appropriate way to do so.'

Isabel blinked at his outrageous response. She was trying to think of a rejoinder, but cautioned herself at being taken in by his brazen behaviour. If there was to be conversation, it would be better to keep it sedate, dripping with uninterest.

'You are not from around here, *messere*?' she said casually, hoping she sounded indifferent.

'No, I am not.' He swerved around her so they were back to back, rising on one foot and then lowering down again, taking a step back to his partner.

Soon enough he passed Isabel again. 'And you have come among us here in this village to improve your dance technique?' She knew she was now being uncivil, but really, the stranger made her feel uneasy about things she would rather forget.

'I don't believe I have any need of improvement there.'

'You're very sure of yourself, *messere*.'

And to prove her point, he switched partners with such an air of presumption and self-assured ease—standing beside her, holding one of her hands gently in his, as if she had always been his partner—that something inside her snapped.

'You are very forward, *messere*! And I would ask you again to refrain from staring at me in that impertinent way.' she hissed under her breath, as she moved past him with a fluid click-heel step.

He raised a brow. 'Apologies, I do not mean to make you feel uncomfortable.'

'Do you not?'

He smirked. 'No.'

Isabel had to admit that there was something quite appealing about him when he smiled like that, with a sudden, unexpected spark of humour in his azure-blue eyes.

'Well, what were you doing then, *messere*?'

They moved past each other in the circle and looped around the other couples before pivoting around to stand side by side, the length of her arm against the solid warmth of his. She felt slightly breathless being in such close proximity to the man.

'I'm trying to ascertain whether you are someone I met briefly a long time ago.'

'Oh? But I have never seen you before in my life,' she said too quickly as they parted again, thankfully, and danced a few steps with different partners before returning to face each other.

'I'm not so sure. There is something about your eyes that looks familiar to me.'

Dear God!

Her hazel-green eyes would have to give her away. They had always plagued her for being so strange... so uncommon and different. One eye had a dark patch across it, which meant that people always believed her eyes to be of two separate colours, even going as far as to call her names. Even her own father believed she was cursed because of this affliction.

'I don't think so, sir.'

He tilted his head as he watched her. 'Pity, since I am starting to think differently.' He took her hand and swung it up and above her head, allowing her to twirl around and under their joined hands.

For goodness sake. 'Pity, since you are mistaken.'

'I don't think so. The more I look at you, the more I believe that it is you.'

They parted again and moved to the opposite side of one another, weaving around one couple and then coming together in a large connected circle.

'Who are you?' she demanded, frowning.

'William Geraint at your service, but my friends call me Will.'

'You and I are not friends, *messere*.'

'Cruel heart,' he said, shaking his head and smiling. 'You wound me.'

'Do I?' she said through gritted teeth. 'How very thoughtless of me.'

'Indeed, yet it begs another more puzzling question about you.'

'Oh, and what might that be?'

'Your apparent disinterest in why I might have come to your village.'

They held hands in the air, far too close for Isabel's comfort. 'My disinterest is very real, believe me.'

'Ah, well, I cannot account for your look of trepidation then.'

'Since I know you to be mistaken about any previous acquaintance, however brief, there really isn't any interest. Why would there be?'

'Why indeed? Yet for my part, I would have to disagree again, I'm afraid.'

His teasing tone was beginning to make her exasperated. It was as though he was purposely provoking her to reveal more. 'You may do as you choose. It has really no effect on me.'

'In that case, would you humour me?' He raised a brow as she moved around him. 'You see, twelve years ago I rescued a girl surrounded by horrific carnage.' He paused to watch her a moment before continuing. 'The girl was naturally frightened, but she was left in the security of a local convent… She gave me this,' he said, pulling out the pendant from under his tunic. 'In thanks, and in…friendship.'

Isabel swallowed and licked her dry lips. 'That was a kind thing to do, and I'm sure the girl, who must now be a woman, if she is alive, was incredibly grateful if she gave you something so precious. However, I fail to see what it has to do with me.'

'Do you not?' he whispered in her ear as they passed each other in a circular flourish. 'You see, I believe that girl was you…my lady.'

She almost faltered.

'What?' she scoffed. 'I assure you, *messere*, I am no lady.' She realised her mistake as a slow smile spread on his face. 'I *meant* that I am just a miller's daughter and not the kind of lady you're looking for.'

His smile deepened. 'Oh, and what kind of lady would that be?'

Isabel felt like stamping on his feet. 'I'm sorry to disappoint you, but I'm not the kind of woman who would inspire a man to traipse all the way to a remote village in Aquitaine in search of some long-lost lady, whom he saved when she was eight years old.' She lifted her head as the music slowed.

His eyes glittered with bemusement. 'I don't believe I mentioned how young the girl was.'

'Didn't you? How remiss of me to guess then,' she ground out. 'Now, if you'll excuse me, I believe this dance has finished.'

Isabel yanked her hand from his and strode off in a different direction. Anywhere but near this man who had, in a matter of moments, managed to shake the foundations of her carefully constructed existence.

He thought he knew who she really was.

Well, he was wrong. That part of her life was gone and she did not want it back…did she?

Isabel loved being *Adela*, the ordinary daughter of a miller, who toiled all day so she could have a moment or two to learn everything there was from Sibylla. Oh, God, how she loved her simple, uncomplicated existence. She chose it, she lived it and she cherished it.

She liked the pretty peaceful village, enjoyed her adopted family—even Heloise—and appreciated her friends, especially Ralph, who would not always be here and would eventually move on, but still…

Still…she did not want to go back to being Lady Isabel de Clancey and once again be a pawn. To be used for whatever gain her father sought. She didn't want to be bartered and trussed as some proscribed paragon of deferential noblewoman.

Yes, Isabel missed her family—she missed her real mother desperately and even her older brothers—but that family had sent her away, abandoned her and had all but forgotten her. She had had to learn to suppress those feelings.

The hurt.

The loss.

She was obviously too inconsequential and unimportant because they had never come looking for her... until now.

Isabel had cried herself to sleep night after night as a child, alone in the world and longing to be home, but determined to keep her promise to her father. And she had—she had never revealed her true identity to anyone, frightened by what would happen to her if she had. Fearing her father's wrath and fearing the unknown entity that had threatened her life on that day so long ago. But gradually, those tears had dried up as she remembered pieces of her old life that made her feel uneasy. And eventually, with the passage of time, she had gained some peace.

She had made a new home, with a new identity, and forgot about the old. She became stronger—and, yes, happier.

Was it now going to be snatched from her?

William Geraint had saved her a long time ago, gifting her the chance of the hard-fought-for freedom she now had. Now, after all these years, it seemed as though he was going to try to take it away.

Well, she was not going to let that happen.

Chapter Three

'Oh, for goodness sake, are you even listening to me?' Isabel expelled an irritated breath as she tried to catch her sister's attention. 'Heloise?'

Her sister threw a dismissive look over her shoulder as they walked along the pathway. This was bad. This was very bad indeed, especially as Heloise was simply ignoring everything she was saying.

Ever since the dance, Isabel's sister was determined to make William Geraint believe that she was the Lady Isabel de Clancey. And Heloise was nothing if not single-minded when there was something she wanted.

Isabel tried again. 'This is nonsense. You cannot take the place of someone you are not.'

Me...you can't take the place of me, for the love of God.

'Besides, you cannot even be sure that this man, this William Geraint, is who he says he is.'

Isabel knew, however—she knew the moment he had started talking to her during the dance—that it was her long-lost hero. But Heloise didn't need to know that.

Isabel had been in a muddle since Will Geraint's arrival at the feast, which was why she had avoided him since. She didn't want this reminder of her past and had to try to get the man to leave their village. Either that, or be forced to leave herself, if only temporarily.

'Being a noble lady isn't all that you think it is, Heloise.'

'And how would you know? You're an orphan like me.'

Isabel grabbed her sister's arm. 'Yes, exactly. What of the family who have raised us? Who have done everything for us? You are just going abandon them?'

'They'll get over it, especially with the coin that Sir William has offered them.'

'What?' Isabel whispered softly. 'They would give you up so easily? For money?'

Did everything in life have to always come down to that? Money and greed? Did her father want her to resume her former obligations so badly that he would go to such lengths? Naturally, he would. But why now after all this time? Oh, how she hated that everything had changed since William Geraint's arrival in St Jean de Cole.

'Of course. Everyone has a price. Besides, I want to leave.' Heloise pursed her lips.

'You'll not be leaving if you cannot convince the man,' Isabel said, turning to catch her sister up. 'And I don't know how you shall. You don't know anything about the real Isabel de Clancey. And what about her family? They'll know you are not her.'

Heloise shrugged. 'I'll think of something by then. I don't really care as long as I can get away from St Jean de Cole. As for William Geraint—there are other ways to persuade him.'

Isabel exhaled slowly, hoping to regain some of her composure. At least they were alone in this secluded

part of the village. Thank God, or else the whole village would be shocked by their discourse.

'Oh, Lord, he's coming!'

Isabel swung around, frowning. 'What? Who?'

'The man himself, of course—William Geraint,' Heloise said from the side of her mouth as she straightened
her spine, smoothed her sheer veil and curled her lips
into a ready smile. 'How do I look?'

This? This was what Heloise was prioritising, at a
time like this?

But for her sister, her appearance when a handsome,
young knight was approaching was of utmost importance. Her confidence in herself was staggering.

'Good morrow, ladies,' he said in a pleasant tone as
he halted in front of them.

Isabel ignored him, but naturally her sister did not.
'Oh, good morrow, Sir William. I hope you are well?'

He scratched his head in a way that reminded Isabel
of the boy she remembered.

'As well as can be expected. My sojourn at the home
of local farmers means I am woken with alarming reg-
ularity.'

'How unfortunate for you, *messere*,' Isabel said, raising a brow. 'Although as a soldier I would have thought
you would be used to erratic, broken sleep. I thought it
would be deemed necessary training for you to be ready
for any eventuality.'

He smirked. 'Oh, I'm always ready for that.'

'What I meant was that if it was so bothersome, you
could always leave.'

He grinned. 'True, but not until I have completed my
task of facilitating the journey back to England...for
Lady Isabel,' he said, keeping his eyes locked on to hers.

His *facilitation* of the journey back to her real family

was more a coercion than anything else. Subtle, courteous, and well meaning, but resolutely and single-mindedly a coercion.

Since the feast, wherever Isabel went, wherever she was going, he was there, waiting and watching her, letting her know in every way that he was not fooled by her. It was grinding her down slowly, this intrusion into her inner peace, and she felt weary of it and weary of him.

Will Geraint's presence in St Jean de Cole had dredged up long-forgotten recollections of what had happened that day. Distant memories of muffled voices, all merged together with the grisly events of the ambush all those years ago. They played repeatedly in her mind. It made Isabel feel restless and her sleep had been disturbed these past few nights but from more worrying reasons than a few noisy farm animals.

Isabel had thought she had put the past behind her, she had thought she no longer needed to worry, but it was strange how the past could suddenly push itself back into the fore. Those distant memories of life in England might be fragmented, much of it overshadowed by what happened when she journeyed to France, but she could recall the reasons for that journey.

Her father had sought to forge new alliances after his fall from grace with King John and the only way to do that was to bring forward Isabel's arranged betrothal. Although she was a child at the time and too young to actually marry, she had been old enough to leave her family to live with her betrothed's. But, of course, it never came to pass and Isabel had spent the last twelve years forgetting about it.

That betrothal was most likely now broken, thank God, but it did not mean her father would not want to use her in another way once again. And this was what she wanted to know from the man stood in front of her.

Why now?

Why had her family not come for her before when she needed them, when she was a lost little girl in a strange land? Had she never mattered to them at all? Yet, she knew she couldn't ask William Geraint any of this. There was a part of her that didn't want to find out the truth, knowing it could hurt her again.

She gave a small shiver and lifted her head. 'Well, I'm sorry you have had a wasted journey to St Jean de Cole, *messere*.'

'He has not, since he's found *me*—Lady Isabel de Clancey,' Heloise muttered through gritted teeth.

'Indeed.' William Geraint kept his eyes locked on to Isabel's, with a ghost of a smile playing on his lips.

Just as when they had danced together, his piercing gaze made her knees feel a little weak. Made her feel a little breathless. He was certainly handsome, but there was more to him than just that, some unknown quality behind that penetrating gaze. He intrigued her, even though he really shouldn't.

Isabel wondered again whether he was really the same boy who had rescued her a lifetime ago. The memory of his kindness etched on to her mind had been replaced by this man's mocking tone. For the first time since his appearance at the feast, Isabel wondered what had happened to him in the intervening years since boyhood. What had happened to that young, caring squire she remembered or had she made far too much of the boy-hero? She could not have. William Geraint had, without a thought for his own safety, saved her life.

She gave herself a mental shake.

'As I said before, I'm not sure why you remain here

in our little village that sadly provides you with an inadequate place to rest and sleep, when your search had proved unsuccessful.'

'Oh, I wouldn't say that,' he said, raising his brow.

Again, that gaze of his was making her feel a little on edge. It conveyed that he didn't believe a word she said.

God, but every time Isabel encountered this man, she somehow reinforced and strengthened his belief that she was Lady Isabel de Clancey. And just as every other time, she had to get away. She couldn't stay and be reminded of what she owed her real family, her duty to them. Oh, yes, the doubt and guilt were slowly gnawing at her.

She took a step in an attempt to get away. Far away. 'If you'll excuse me.'

He caught her arm gently, the warmth of his fingers sending a shot of unexpected awareness through her.

'I do not mean to cause you any distress. I am only here for one purpose and one purpose only.'

'Ah, but consider, *messere*, that your purpose is the very thing that is the cause of my distress.'

He raised a brow. 'Why?'

'Not everyone desires to be found, Sir William, or for that matter welcomes their old life back,' she hissed under her breath.

'Again, I must ask why?'

She clenched her fists at her side. 'I do not have to explain anything. I am not answerable to you, or anyone else, for that matter.'

'Is that what this is about?' He narrowed his gaze as Heloise looked from one to the other of them.

They stared at each other for a moment longer, neither backing down before a new voice broke their silence.

'Good morrow, is everyone well?'

They all turned to see Ralph coming towards them, allowing Isabel a little time to calm her jangled nerves.

'Ah, if it's not the hero of this saintly village,' William Geraint muttered.

She rolled her eyes. 'What does that make you, *messere*? The villain?'

'No, my lady.' He leant towards her. 'I would rather hope not.'

She ignored him and smiled at her friend instead, grateful that he had come by when he had.

The situation seemed hopeless now it was clear there was no way that William Geraint was going to leave St Jean de Cole without her. Isabel had to think of something. She had to find another way. Although the annoyingly handsome knight might not be a villain, he was still intent on taking her back to her father, back to her family. And the thought of that made her apprehensive.

She remembered when she had pleaded with her father not to send her away from everything she had known and loved, how he had reprimanded her and scolded her for attempting to evade her familial duty. Despite her pleas he had sent her away all those years ago. Now, he wanted her back?

Well, it was too late.

Will sighed and looked to the heavens.

Oh, God give him strength! The woman was going to try to evade him again. She was going to continue her denial and frustrate his attempts of completing this damnable mission. And this time she would use the young man who had just joined them, judging by the pleading looks she had sent her friend.

Why?

The irony was not lost on Will that the woman whom he believed to be—no, knew to be—Lady Isabel de Clancey was reluctant to take up her birthright, unlike all the other pretenders he had contended with before. He had thought that if he were lucky enough to find the heiress, she would be happy and overjoyed at the opportunity to be finally reunited with her real family. Not so…

There was something deeply troubling about Lady Isabel. On the one hand, he could understand that she might feel anxious and even a little resentful towards her family. After all, they had readily believed that she was dead, without any proper investigation. But then, with wars, separation and the Baron's conflict that had plagued England during King John's reign, it was no wonder that her family had given up on her. Will sighed as he studied Lady Isabel further.

He had always been perceptive about people and was especially good at understanding them after careful observation. Their foibles, the little nuances, and the expression in their movement and conversation—all painted a picture about any given person. And more times than not, this always betrayed their inner fears, desires and thoughts. That was even before they started to speak candidly to him, which was another thing he was good at. Making people talk. Extremely useful when he was gathering information for William Marshal and the Crown.

But with Isabel de Clancey, Will had no need to do any of that. It hadn't been necessary. He knew immediately who she was, the moment he had danced with her at the feast. It was her eyes that had given her away. He hadn't realised that he would recall how unusual they were, but as soon as he saw her, he remembered. He recalled how expressive her hazel eyes were and how one eye had a streak of dark brown across it, making each eye unique and beautiful.

Her denial of who she was intrigued him, though. With closer observation Will realised that she was frightened about something, not necessarily of him, but certainly by the prospect of going home.

This, he couldn't understand. He had not even managed to relay the importance of why she was needed back in England, or the fact that she was now an heiress since her father and brothers were dead.

Will had wanted to tell her, but their conversations had never moved beyond her repudiating who she was.

Hell's teeth, she was rattled and it worried him. He never wanted any woman to have this reaction in his company, but it was his mission to find her and to return her home. He would do it, yet he couldn't help but feel uncomfortable about doing so.

He gave himself a mental shake, reminding himself that this was not his problem. *She* was not his problem. Whatever Lady Isabel's feelings, they were not his concern and he would do well to remember that. He had a job to do and he would see it through.

But first Will had to thwart whatever scheme she was about to employ to elude him.

Later, in the dead of night, Isabel paced around the chamber that she shared with her sister on the top floor of the mill house. She heard the clink of a pebble against the wooden shutter.

'Ralph? Is that you?' Isabel opened the arched window in the small chamber. She had been waiting impatiently after gathering her meagre belongings and now the time to put her plan in motion had finally arrived. She would leave St Jean de Cole for a nearby village where she had friends and wait until William Geraint left for good. Only then would she return home. It wasn't a great plan, but it was the best she could come up with, with only an afternoon to make arrangements.

'Yes.' She heard his whisper from outside and looked down to the ground below to see her friend waving at her. 'I'm going to throw this rope up at you, Adela, and I want you to catch it. Make sure you secure it to something sturdy that will take your weight,' he said.

She nodded and leant out of the window.

Ralph threw her the rope, but it failed to reach anywhere near the height it needed to. The second attempt fared better, but this time she floundered. However, the third attempt proved successful, as Ralph propelled the rope high enough for Isabel to grab on to it before it fell back down. She wound it around the brass handle of both sides of the coffer before tugging at it a few times to make sure it was secure. Then, with a heavy sigh, Isabel looked around the room and crept towards Heloise, who was fast asleep and snoring lightly.

'I'll come back soon,' Isabel muttered, more to herself than her slumbering sister. A promissory oath that she hoped to God she could keep.

She then grabbed her leather satchel, strode to the window sill, sat and swung her legs around so that they were suspended from the great height, then threw the satchel down. Clasping the rope tightly, Isabel curled her legs around it and let go of the security of the window sill. She started to climb down, but realised her descent wasn't progressing as well as it should.

Dear God, she felt she was about to plummet to the ground!

What on earth was going on? Ralph didn't seem to be

holding the end of the rope and it was swinging around, frantically. As was she.

'Ralph? For goodness sake, hold on to it firmly so I can get down. Ralph… Ralph?'

Isabel heard his muffled voice from below. 'Hold on. I won't let you fall.'

She didn't dare look down. The rope was swinging round so much that Isabel found it increasingly difficult to get a proper footing on it to climb down safely.

Oh, Lord, she really was going to fall! Her hands and feet were not gripping round the rope readily. And with the clammy moisture on her hands she slipped and tumbled down, descending with a thud…into a pair of very strong arms. She heard him take a huge intake of air with a *humph.*

Poor Ralph. She hoped she hadn't winded him. This physical exertion was really not good for his recovery.

But, of course, it wasn't Ralph who was holding on to her. It was another man, entirely…

'Good evening, Lady Isabel.'

Who else could it be other than William Geraint? The man positively plagued her!

'What the devil are you doing?' she hissed.

'Catching you, my lady. And by and by, I must say how fortuitous it was that I looked up and saw you falling from the sky.'

'Put me down, Sir William, if you please,' she said, her patience wearing thin.

'Not yet, I first need to establish a few things with you…although we must stop meeting like this.' His lips curled upwards while he carried her in his arms. 'You do realise that people might talk.'

Lord, but he was infuriating.

'What have you done to Ralph?' She crossed her

arms over her chest, refusing to hold on to his neck or any other part of his large and honed anatomy.

'Oh, he's all right, I made an oath on my honour that you had nothing to fear from me, so he's now on his way back to his pallet. But he might wake up with a sore head tomorrow.'

'*What?* What did you do? I swear that if you have hurt him or done anything that may set his recovery back, I will…' She covered her open mouth with her hand. 'Oh, my God, what if he falls back into unconsciousness again?'

William Geraint's brows furrowed as he gazed down at her for moment. 'Calm yourself, my lady, he isn't unconscious but with a slight bump to the head. In any case, I wasn't aware of his condition. It is curious, though, that you take such an interest in his well-being.'

'Not that it's of any concern of yours, but Ralph is a highly valued friend.'

'Is he now?' He raised his brow. 'I'm wondering whether *he* may be the real reason for your reticence in going back home where you belong.'

Oh, how her fingers itched to slap that smirk off his face.

'If you must know, I helped the local wise woman tend to him after he was left for dead in the woods near here. So, yes, I take a great…great deal of interest in Ralph's well-being,' Isabel said, trying to hide her annoyance at his implication. She reminded herself again that she didn't answer to this man.

'So, you helped save another's life just as I once saved yours? Interesting and, I must say, highly commendable.'

This was not something she wished to discuss with anyone—her motives to learn about healing others.

'Put me down, Sir William.' She wriggled around in his arms so much that he dropped her unceremoniously to the ground.

'Forgive me.' His eyes sparkled with mild amusement. 'I am only doing my duty and, as I said to you this morning, I am not the villain you take me for.'

She smoothed down her skirts and stood up. 'What, then? I suppose you think of yourself as the daring hero you once were?'

The amusement faded from his eyes. 'That remains to be seen, but for now you and I must talk about how we are to break through this impasse.'

She shut her eyes momentarily, hoping that once she reopened them, she would be back in her warm bed and this would all be a dream. 'That's easy for you to say, Sir William, but you are not the one being forced to do something you have no desire to do.'

She started to walk away, but he caught her arm. 'Trust me, my lady, there have been many things in my life that I had no desire to *do*, but I was still duty bound to do them.'

She tilted her head and studied him. What had he meant? There was definite anger and sadness in his words and Isabel wasn't the type of person who would take satisfaction from anyone's misery.

Again, she wondered what had happened to William Geraint all this time? What had happened to make him so impervious, mocking and detached? Now and again, a glimmer of humour would flicker in his eyes, but it was so fleeting that she wondered whether she had imagined it.

The man must have realised that he'd revealed something about himself that he hadn't meant to. He let go of her and took a step back, looking away.

Isabel watched him, allowing the silence to extend, before expelling a heavy sigh.

'What now, Sir William?' she said quietly. 'I take it you will still insist on dragging me back to England?'

'I'm afraid I must, my lady.' He leant back, and crossed his arms.

'Tell me, what have you to gain by this mission?' She frowned. 'But, oh…oh, how foolish of me. Of course, you're getting coin for finding and taking me back, are you not, Sir William?'

He looked slightly embarrassed. 'I would be lying if I were to contradict you, but understand this, Lady Isabel. I had… I have always wondered what had happened to you.' He moved a little closer to her and shrugged, reminding her of the boy who had rescued her. 'And I had always prayed that you fared well, despite the terrible brutality of that night all those years ago.'

As I did of you… she thought wistfully, meeting his gaze. The moonlight gave his eyes such a luminous clarity that Isabel felt herself staring for longer than necessary. Longer than she should.

He coughed, clearing his throat. 'But now that I have found you, and in good health, I find that I am puzzled by your refusal to acknowledge who you are.' He raised his eyebrows. 'Care to explain, my lady?'

And just like that, the moment between them was broken.

'Not especially, no.'

'Every woman I found tried to convince me that they were Lady Isabel de Clancey, yet you did the opposite. Why?'

'Has anyone ever told you how belligerent and annoying you are?'

Sir William grinned, setting her teeth on edge. 'Yes, quite a few. But you didn't answer me. Tell me…please.'

She opened her mouth to explain it all. Explain the conflicted emotions she felt regarding her real family. How she feared their disapproval and rejection…again. And also, the deep sense of trepidation and dread she felt in her bones about the prospect of going back home. Her eyes dropped to the pendant hanging around his neck. She frowned, trying to remember something from the past, but gave her head a shake. This was not William Geraint's concern. Her feelings and her muddled memory were inexplicable, even to her.

'I can't,' she whispered.

He nodded, in apparent sympathy. 'What you went through could not have been easy, my lady. I can understand that.'

'You can?'

'Yes, but think of your poor mother, after everything she has endured.'

'What do you, mean?' she said slowly. 'What has my mother endured, Sir William?'

'My lady, I…' he said, dragging his fingers through his hair impatiently as he exhaled. 'Please, let me escort you back to your mother.'

Isabel stared blankly, her mind reeling.

What had happened to her family? What had her docile and deferential mother *endured* all these years? Isabel had only considered her own feelings regarding everything that had happened. She had known from the day William Geraint had rescued her that she must do everything she could to survive. But she had never once thought that her family might have fared worse than her in the years since she had seen them. Her father might have been out of favour with King John, but that didn't mean that anything had befallen her family...did it?

Guilt suddenly coursed through her now as a long-ago abandoned emotion pulled inside her chest with such force that it both surprised and pained her.

He was not telling her, but she could only guess. Her mother was alive, but what had happened to the rest of her family?

She swallowed, looking at him, her eyes wide. 'What has happened, Sir William?' she whispered in the quiet of the night. 'What has happened to them?'

He couldn't look her in the eyes, but she knew... she somehow knew what he was about to say. 'I'm so sorry to be the one to have to tell you, my lady, but your father...your brothers...'

'They're dead...aren't they?' She sat on the small bench near the path, her unsteady legs unable to support her any longer.

'I'm afraid so, my lady.' He threw her an anxious look. 'You are now the sole heiress of your family's title, wealth and vast domain.'

Isabel felt numb, void of any feelings. She searched her feelings and, while she felt regret, there was little more that she felt for the loss of her father...but her brothers?

Oh, God...

'This explains the necessity of my expedient return. Do you...do you know how they...?'

'I don't know about your brothers, but your father died by accident when he fell from his horse.'

An accident?

'I see.'

Somehow, she had always been anticipating something as awful as this happening. But she had never thought her father or her brothers would be the ones to fall.

Sir William sat beside her and covered her hand with his, giving it a squeeze of reassurance. 'I'm sorry for your loss,' he said quietly.

They sat beside each other for a long moment. The breeze whipped through the air and caused the leaves of her favourite oak tree to rustle and dance in the night sky.

She broke the silence. 'Thank you, by and by.'

'For what?'

'Saving my life. I have always meant to say that and now I can finally do so in person.'

'You did by giving me this, remember?' he said, wrapping his hand around the pendant and pulling it out from under his tunic.

'Yes,' she whispered, 'that I remember.' Her memory of the pendants made her feel uneasy. It could be another reason why she had given something so precious to Will in gratitude all those years ago.

He studied her for a moment. 'What is it you're afraid of, my lady?'

'Everything.'

'Well, I want you to know that I will protect you while we journey back. You have nothing to fear.'

She blinked and looked back at the pendant around his neck. 'Do you propose to save my life again?'

'If I must. Who knows, you may end up saving me this time,' he said with a ghost of a smile. 'But know this, Lady Isabel, I shall be ready for any eventuality... as will you.'

She wanted so much to believe him.

There were too many things she just didn't understand. Her memories from that time in her life were broken into bits that had to be pieced back together again, if she were to make sense of it.

But for some inexplicable reason Isabel felt that, somehow, it had to do with the identical silver and ruby pendants…

Her mother had told her that the pendant would bring her protection, so Isabel had chosen to give that to her rescuer. She had almost forgotten about its existence—until William Geraint's sudden appearance back in her life.

No, she wasn't ready for any of this.

Chapter Four

Will and Isabel had been travelling on horseback for many long hours. Though for Will it might as well have been an eternity, since the duration had passed with barely a word spoken between them.

They had meandered through on the outskirts of St Jean de Cole, through open sun-drenched fields and eventually entered the woodland that would provide a welcome relief during the day with its tall canopy of contrasting trees, thickets and cool streams. The route for their journey back was fairly straightforward. They would need to navigate their way a little north before eventually riding west towards La Rochelle. But it would take over ten nights before they reached the port.

Heaven help him!

Will could understand Isabel's confusion, empathise with her situation and certainly share her misery, but, by God, he wished for some light discourse to break the heavy silence. Anything that would help make the journey pass a little easier.

It hadn't helped that Will felt strangely responsible, once again, for Isabel's brooding melancholy. No wonder she had found it difficult saying goodbye to her old life, clearly wishing she could somehow cling on to it.

The endless farewells with Isabel's adopted family, the wise woman and the many well-wishers from the village had, in itself, been emotionally draining. It had been obvious to Will that Isabel was not only attached to the village, but also to its people, and was still circumspect about the prospect of becoming Lady Isabel de Clancey once more, despite his assurances.

The only smile of gratitude Will had earned from Isabel was when she had thanked him for the assistance he had provided for her friend, Ralph. Will had offered information about whose banner he had most likely served under before his attack, judging from the motifs Ralph had remembered and put to parchment in ink. That exchange had been brief, however, and they had quickly descended back to an awkward silence.

Damn...

There was a time when Will knew exactly what to say to a woman to put her at ease, make her smile or even laugh heartily.

He could flirt, flatter, compliment and humour any given woman with a courtly verse or meaningful gesture. But no more. That side of his personality no longer existed and he hadn't wanted it to, anyway. Not until now—riding beside Isabel. He wished he could say something that would make her snap out of her disheartened manner, but could think of nothing.

And it hadn't helped that they had begun the journey with a disagreement about something as simple as engaging a handmaid to accompany them. Isabel had flatly refused, arguing that it would be highly embarrassing to employ someone from St Jean de Cole. She couldn't understand why she would need one anyway.

But she definitely did and it struck Will that, again, Lady Isabel seemed to have difficulty in accepting who she was. He must broach the subject once more, reiterating the importance of having someone attend to her. Surely she would now see how necessary that was for someone of her rank?

Will turned his head towards Isabel. 'We'll be nearing the village of St Romaine later today and I thought that we could possibly look for a woman who'd be happy to be your handmaid, if that meets with your approval.'

Isabel kept her gaze steadily forward, refusing to meet his eyes. 'I had hoped that this topic of conversation had ended.'

'Whereas I had hoped that you would now see sense in what I advised earlier, my lady.'

'It seems my assumptions about you have been correct, Sir William. You are belligerent—extremely so.'

'I aim to please.' He inclined his head a fraction, earning a scowl.

'That,' she said wryly, 'is a blessing, Sir William. But as I said to you before, I'm sure that I cannot be comfortable having a handmaid accompany my every move.'

'But I'm sure that I shall, Lady Isabel.'

'Are you suggesting that I cannot trust you or, dare I say it, feel safe with just your esteemed company?'

'No, that is not what I am saying.' Was the woman trying to put words into his mouth? 'But I do believe that travelling with just a lone knight, however esteemed his company, may be not so desirable for someone of your standing.'

'I see.' She tilted her head to the side. 'It would not do for a proper lady, *like me*. Is that what you mean?'

How had it come to this? Will had only wanted to

make her understand their delicate situation, travelling together just the two of them. He had not meant to be the cause of her indignation, yet he felt compelled to explain more.

'Precisely. I'm certain it would be what your family expects.'

She stiffened immediately. This was going from bad to worse.

'The fact that I am returning to England should be good enough, really, Sir William.' She bristled with barely concealed annoyance. 'Please, let this be the end and talk no more of it. I have no need nor do I require a handmaid. I assure you I can manage on my own.'

'As you wish, Lady Isabel.'

Will rubbed his brow and groaned inwardly. Had the woman no sense whatsoever? It was evident that she had not truly appreciated what he had tried to convey without stating it outright—that, since they were travelling closely together, it was not desirable for a young, impressionable, unworldly woman like Isabel de Clancey to have just his company for the long duration of their journey. He hadn't fully appreciated the realities of this himself until the moment they had left St Jean de Cole when he was suddenly aware that he was with Isabel…alone.

Not that he had wanted this imposed closeness with the lady in question for such a journey. But what were the alternatives other than what he had already suggested and had been emphatically refused in return? At least *he* could perceive the complications and obstacles that might come their way. It would mean having to navigate through these unsolicited feelings of concern for Isabel, not to mention protecting her and a whole host of other things, as was his duty. And entertaining her, which was not.

If only Will had retained his faithful squire or, better still, could have successfully convinced Lady Isabel that she needed a damned handmaid, but there was no hope there.

God above, anything could happen!

Well, he would just make sure that nothing did and they'd have the most uneventful and tedious journey possible.

The woodland teemed with a diverse range of wildlife, trees, shrubbery and late-blooming clusters of deciduous wildflowers.

He led the way on his black destrier towards a stream he had passed on his way to St Jean de Cole, knowing it was a good place to stop for a moment and cool off.

'We shall rest shortly and stretch our legs.'

'Very well, Sir William, whatever you think is best.'

Will coughed, covering his mild amusement. *That* was not strictly true, since it was wholly dependent on the lady's views on any given matter. He dismounted, tethering his horse to a nearby tree before striding towards Isabel to help her down.

'I hope you are no longer angry with me, my lady?'

She turned around to face him as the confusion on her face slowly gave way to a sigh. 'No, not with you, Sir William. That lies elsewhere.'

'I am glad, otherwise I'd have to apologise profusely for some unknown reason, despite your acknowledgement of my knowing best.'

'Are you teasing me?' she said, shaking her head.

'Absolutely, although I must admit it has been a long time since I have teased anyone,' he said, biting back a grin. 'But frankly, I'd rather that than your wrath. It would make our travail unnecessarily difficult, don't you think?'

'Yes, it would, but I have to let you know that, despite appearances, I'm not a wrathful person.'

'I'm sure you're not,' he said as he fetched a blanket from one of the saddlebags, while Isabel laid out the carefully wrapped parcels of sliced meat, small rounds of cheese and a large bunch of black grapes that she had prepared earlier.

'Exactly. I save *that* for particularly belligerent sorts of knight,' she said with a small smile.

'Well, I am glad that I'm not one of those either,' he said, popping a grape into his mouth.

'Of course not. You're the sort who knows best.' Her smile deepened as she turned her head and met his eyes.

'Naturally.' He had forgotten this. Forgotten how he could harness and use humour to break through someone's defences, and make them briefly leave their woes behind. 'It's good to see you smile, my lady.'

'Thank you,' she said, softly. 'I have had little to smile about of late.'

Will tore one of the rolls and offered her half. 'I know, Lady Isabel, I know.'

His fingertips grazed hers as he passed her the bread and the shock of touching, however transient, sent a regrettable frisson through him. He ignored it and continued eating before lifting his head and forcing a smile he knew didn't reach his eyes.

'Tell me something, Sir William, if you don't mind me asking,' she said, taking bite out of the roll topped with a wedge of cheese. 'Why did you imply just now that you are not a knight?'

Ah...

This was precisely what he had been worried about...

this. Unwelcome questions and intrusion into his life—his very private and solitary life—the moment his guard was down. Yes, he minded very much being asked questions he had no wish to answer. And this was what would inevitably happen since he was Lady Isabel's only companion. Questions, answers, revelations and judgement.

God, but the judgement…and all under the guise of getting to know one another. Well, he didn't want it, even if he had been glad that he could still make a woman smile. Look what that had earned him—her curiosity.

Isabel touched the sleeve of his tunic gently. 'I'm sorry, I didn't mean to pry.'

His eyes fell to her fingers still on his sleeve, which quickly fell away. She then pushed a golden honeyed tendril of hair behind her ear and smoothed her sheer veil.

He swallowed. 'You didn't, Lady Isabel.'

And even more unsettling was the growing awareness of her, which was damned inconvenient at best and altogether embarrassing at worst. He was supposed to escort the lady back to England. Not notice her or the colour of her hair in a wholly inappropriate way. What the hell was wrong with him?

He would do well not to notice Lady Isabel de Clancey in any way. Will had to remind himself that Lady Isabel was not for the likes of him—a bastard and a reprobate knight. He might now be pardoned, with his honour restored, because of the information he had gathered for the Crown, but he could never forgive himself for what had happened at the siege at Portchester Castle. The fault for which had been entirely his and the result was self-loathing and guilt. Yes, Will was destined to live alone in self-imposed exile for the remainder of his worthless life—and even that was far more than his due.

He got up abruptly and shrugged, hoping he looked composed when in fact he felt the opposite. 'I said what I did because I'm no longer a knight, my lady. Now if you're ready, we should leave.'

They had continued on their journey for many long hours, again in silence, and this time Isabel was far more aware of the awkwardness between them. All because of the strange exchange when they'd stopped for a short repast. Isabel had been lost in her own musings ever since they had left home, reflecting once again on the circumstance in which she had found herself. Apart from the rather constant suggestion that she would require a handmaiden—someone to monitor her every move—it had been a perfectly uneventful, humdrum morning's journey.

The welcome relief of light banter with a companion who was affable, not to mention very easy on the eye, had been unexpectantly pleasant. Yet the moment Isabel had innocuously asked about his past, the man clammed up completely, making it very clear that he did not invite any questions about it, not in any capacity. Which was a shame as she had hoped to get to know Sir William more and learn a little about his life.

But it was more than that. The moment she had touched the sleeve of his tunic, he seemed altered and had gazed at her as though…as though he was aware of her in a manner very different than before. But that could not be. Isabel must have imagined it.

'Lady Isabel, about my reaction earlier…' Will

looked over in her direction. 'I apologise. The truth is that I find it difficult looking back at my old life.'

'I understand.'

'Yes, I can imagine. And to answer your question—I was indeed once a knight of the realm, much like your friend Ralph, if my assumption there is correct.'

Yes, she had been very happy for his assistance regarding Ralph. She gave herself a mental shake. 'You were *once*? Does that mean you're no longer a knight?'

'I no longer claim that role, no,' he said bitterly. 'Everything I once owned that put price to that title has now been sold or given away.'

'Except for your sword.'

He looked surprised that she had noticed. 'Except for my sword,' he repeated.

'I see.'

'You do?'

'I hadn't expected that your life had been any easier than mine, Ralph's or anyone else's for that matter, Sir William. These have been and still are difficult times, but may I say something?'

'By all means.'

She pulled the reins, bringing her young horse to a stop and turned her head. 'Do not allow the past to define your future. I speak from experience.'

He brought his horse to a halt and watched her for a moment without saying anything, which emboldened her to say more. 'Since I now have to accept this imposed destiny, or whatever you may call it, Sir William, I must also accept that the past has finally caught up with me...and it will for you, too. Not today and not necessarily tomorrow, but some day. Even if you have sold off remnants of your past, there's no getting away from it.'

He frowned, as though he were absorbing her words, before he continued riding on. After some time, he finally spoke. 'May I ask something of you? Could you call me "William," or, better still, just "Will"? I could never abide *Sir William*, even when I was a fully-fledged knight.'

'By the same token, I insist you call me Isabel. Much like you, I really cannot get used to being a lady.'

He raised a brow. 'But you will have to, won't you, my lady?'

She chuckled. 'Yes, soon, but until then I'm just plain Isabel, which is also difficult to get used to, since I have been "Adela" for so—' She stopped, frowning. 'Is anything the matter... Will?' She noticed his shaking hand as he drew it through his hair. 'You're not ill?'

'Not at all. Shall we continue?'

Her brows furrowed, wondering what on earth was wrong with him.

'Yes,' she said absently as they resumed riding further along the undulating path through the woodland in companionable silence, broken now and again by small observations.

Eventually they emerged into a clearing overlooking a valley. Twilight had settled by now, with the last vestiges of sunshine blending with the dusky night sky.

Isabel blinked several times before her eyes widened in surprise as she watched in wonder at the scene in the basin valley below. There was a cacophony of colour and noise. Merriment and revelry.

Her eyes scanned the spectacle. 'What do you think that is?' She couldn't keep the excitement from her voice.

'Something that we should probably avoid, I imagine.'

She turned to meet his eyes, almost pleading. 'And what is that?'

'A particular brand of jollity.'

Well, that sounded incredibly tempting, didn't it? After the strain of the last few days, with the changes Will's reappearance in her life had brought and the even bigger challenges still to come, this particular brand of jollity was mayhap exactly what was needed. Just once, just for tonight.

He had been watching her, shaking his head. 'Oh, God, I can see what you're thinking and it's a definite no.'

'Please,' she implored. 'Couldn't we go?'

He rubbed his forehead as she continued to make her case.

'It might be just the sort of thing we could both do with.'

She waited, chewing the inside of her cheek, as Will deliberated the best course of action.

'Since you must know best, I'll to listen to your counsel...but what do you think?'

He exhaled slowly. 'In all honesty, I think it best we keep away from large crowds, especially one that is as bawdy as I expect that one to be.' He inclined his head in the direction below. 'I'm afraid it won't be appropriate, my lady.'

Her shoulders slumped. 'You're right, it probably won't be.'

She pulled the reins of the horse to move it away in the opposite direction.

'But then again,' he said from somewhere behind, 'I don't see why we shouldn't partake a little in the festivities.'

She turned the horse back round. 'A little could go a long way.'

He grinned and she smiled back. He was so ridiculously attractive when he did that, his eyes twinkling with mischief and amusement.

'So, *Plain Isabel*, shall we?'

'I think so, *Just Will*.'

He held her gaze and for the first time in a long while she felt a sense of carefree excitement bubbling up inside her.

Chapter Five

Oh, the joys of this particular brand of jollity were immense indeed! Especially for someone like Isabel. It was an inspired idea to forget everything for just one night—a reprieve from who she was and would soon become with all that expectancy. Besides, this was the sort of experience that seldom came her way and, even though this would be of a short duration, Isabel was going to enjoy it. She would enjoy tonight.

There were so many things to see, so much to sample and enjoy, that she didn't know where to look or what she should do first. Isabel had never really been exposed to anything like these festivities before—a wonderfully vibrant cacophony, a delight for the senses. There were long lines of trestle tables with meats, cheeses, plump berries, sweet breads and pastry from local villages, as well as kegs of ale and crisp cider from the north and sweet, fruity Aquitaine wine from the south.

Music blared, revellers danced in one area while troupes of troubadours with *jongleurs* and even death-defying fire-eaters were staged in another. The atmosphere of this colourful festival marked it as so different from anything she had ever seen before. Certainly different from anything in St Jean de Cole. The rowdy crowd was so congenial, welcoming and friendly that Isabel flitted from one place to another with a huge grin on her face as Will tried to keep up with her.

'Isn't this marvellous?'

'It is certainly something,' Will said wryly, crossing his arms over his broad chest as she bit her lip, choosing to ignore his lack of enthusiasm.

Jollity indeed!

'Ah, *mademoiselle*, sample this here wine from the most superior vineyard in all the Kingdom of Aquitaine.' A man pressed a cup into her hand of the ruby-coloured nectar with a wonderfully delicious scent. She took a big gulp and wiped her mouth with the back of her hand. Oh, and it was! It tasted of a deep, rich platter of summer berries and grapes.

'Mmm, *messere*, this is indeed very fine.'

'Well then have some more, *cherie*, have some more.' The man sloshed more of the vintage into her cup.

Will stepped forward and muttered in her ear, 'Don't you think you've had enough?'

She waved her hand, as if she were swatting an annoying fly. 'Nonsense, Will. Where is your sense of fun?'

'I left it back in England.' He paid the vendor and started to guide Isabel away by her elbow. 'Now come along.'

'Don't be such a miser.' She twisted around as someone else shoved slivers of more delicious delicacies of local saucisson and ale in front of her.

'Oh, Will, have some of this…oh, my goodness, the ale is divine.'

'Thank you, but, no. I need my wits about me.'

Isabel tilted her head and studied him. 'Oh, but who

would need their wits at a time like this and in such a place as this?'

She continued to sample the fine food and delicious wine, hoping that it would somehow fill the emptiness she felt even *in a place such as this*. An emptiness that was far from being satisfied. The truth was that she hoped this diversion would somehow dull the ache that she still felt regarding the mother whom she longed to see, her father and brothers' deaths, and her return to England and all that entailed. This was a much-needed balm for all of her troubles, or rather, she hoped it was.

Ah, but enough. She wanted to shake these thoughts out of her head.

She slipped her hand through Will's bent arm and leant towards him. 'Come, let's drink and be merry, for we may not get another chance.'

He raised a brow. 'That sounds ominous.'

'You may hold on to those wits of yours, but I for one, intend to enjoy myself.' She raised a finger and wagged it in the air. 'And I must say that it would be far more gratifying if I were not doing it on my own.'

She turned to face Will, saw that he was struggling not to smile and her breath caught. The man's face and jaw were such sharp planes that she itched to run her raised finger across the smooth angular surface to see if she would cut herself. And now he was looking at her so peculiarly, with those deep, deep blue eyes that she felt strangely warm.

Oh…oh, dear. Isabel had a sudden urge to lean up and press a kiss on those gorgeous lips of his.

She exhaled, moving away, and grabbed another cup of wine. What was the matter with her? She swallowed a big gulp. What was she thinking? She looked down at the cup and swirled the red liquid around. Could it be that she had drunk too much wine? Possibly, she thought, as she drained the rest too quickly, making her cough.

Will smiled softened as he gently patted her back 'You see. This is why I need my wits about me.'

'Of course, to play escort and nursemaid,' she said between coughing. 'To an unruly woman, like me? I pity you.'

'I don't need your pity, my lady.'

'Well, then, you should pity me, *Just Will*. I'm a hopeless case.'

'No, you're a little inebriated, that's all.'

'That's all?' She raised a brow and looked at him. 'Not a good thing for a supposed lady like me?'

'You not a *lady* tonight, remember?' he whispered beside her.

She shrugged, taking another sip.

Oh, she remembered, and that was why she was having such inappropriate thoughts about kissing William Geraint. Living as *Adela*, the miller's daughter, she had never had any notions of kissing anyone before, except for the few times when a few young men had dared to steal kisses off her. It had never been this way around, but then again, she had never drunk this much ale and wine before, had she? Oh, God, but her head hurt just thinking about all of this.

'You're right, I'm just *Plain Isabel* tonight after all.'

'Precisely, and there's nothing wrong with it as long as you're prepared for a hell of an ache in your head tomorrow.'

She threw him a sideways glance and saw he was enjoying this. 'We weren't going to talk about tomorrow, remember?'

'A thousand pardons.' He chuckled softly, shaking his head as they walked along. 'And, Isabel?'

'Yes?'

He smiled in that knowing way of his that made her stomach flutter. 'There's nothing plain about you.'

Isabel swallowed uncomfortably, feeling a little off kilter as if the very air she breathed had stilled altogether. Lifting her head, she gazed wistfully into the fathomless blue of his eyes, before Will gave himself a little shake and looked away. Oh, God, how mortifying. Here he was being nice and all she could do was notice him in a totally unseemly way.

She had hoped that this night might provide a respite from constantly reassessing her situation, but now she had this unbecoming awareness of her very tall, very attractive escort with eyes she wanted to drown in.

She shouldn't be noticing Will in this way. She shouldn't notice how the taut muscles of his arms and chest filled the linen tunic and the way the dark brown braes shaped the bulging muscles on his legs and she definitely shouldn't notice how large and looming he was, or the warmth where he touched her lightly on her elbow.

Oh, God, there must be something wrong with her. She glanced into the cup she was clutching, knowing she must have drunk too much and then looked back up again, swaying slightly as she met his quizzical eyes, pondering how she should diffuse this situation.

But really there was no need, not when she could embarrass herself further with a sudden onslaught of uncontrollable hiccups. Oh, but if the earth could just swallow her up at this very moment.

The woman was drunk!

Isabel de Clancey was Will's responsibility and it was his fault that she had consumed as much wine as she had. Of course, her uncertainty about her changed circumstances explained her rather erratic mood swings, as well as the necessity for the imposed enjoyment of this night—the chance of which Isabel believed she'd not have again.

There was something sad about that belief—there was something sad about Isabel de Clancey's outlook on life altogether. He might have a feeling of uneasiness about a woman of Isabel's standing being in such a crowded, raucous and, not to mention, visible place, but Will didn't have the heart to deny her this night. He could understand this need for release—he could understand it far too well...

It was more than that, though. Will could not help but be drawn to her—she was warm and endearing, possessing a quiet, determined strength which was as admirable as it was attractive. He had to admit that he liked her company, her quick wit, her open manner and lack of artifice. She had no idea of her appeal or of her allure, which for a world-weary man, used to the contrivances at court, was both surprising and beguiling.

But when he looked into those wistful and expressive eyes of hers, he saw something else there. An awareness of him and even a little desire, judging by the way her gaze kept dropping to his lips.

God! That would not be the sort of release that would help her situation.

It was certainly the wine that had put those amorous notions into her head. It was just as well that he had chosen to have his wits about him because it really wouldn't do to court *that* kind of trouble, however appealing Isabel might be. He really didn't need to add more complications to his already complicated life.

Will watched her from the corner of his eye as she

tried to cover her mouth with her hand while continuing to hiccup and something inside him shifted. A smile tugged at the corners of his lips and he shook his head absently. It really was difficult trying to be detached yet deferential, with their boundaries clearly defined. In fact, it was damned impossible.

The hiccupping became louder the more Isabel tried to stop. Her face was now infused with a particularly interesting shade of pink.

'Can I be of service, Isabel? Would you like me to fetch something that could help remedy your…ah, problem?'

'No, thank you,' she retorted between another fit of hiccups, as though nothing was wrong. 'I'm…*hic*… absolutely…*hic*…fine.'

'Try holding your breath while pinching your nose,' he said from the side of his mouth. 'That was always my mother's advice.'

She looked as though she were torn between attempting his suggestion or pretending that everything was well, but eventually she relented and stood there doing as he advised.

'It's not working,' she said as she held on to her nose while sucking in a gulp of air a few times.

He grinned. 'Try again.'

She looked sceptical, but attempted it again. 'This isn't your…*hic*…idea of fun, perchance?'

He swallowed down the laughter bubbling inside and held out his hands, open palmed. 'On my honour, it is not.'

'I'm glad to hear it.' She hiccupped. 'Because I'd hate to…*hic*…look even more ridiculous…*hic*…than I already do.'

His eyes fell on jugs of local spring water on a trestle table they were passing. He poured some into a cup and pressed it into her hand.

Isabel nodded her thanks and took a couple of sips as they continued to amble along aimlessly.

They had by now drifted towards the outer edge of the area—the liveliest by far, with a different type of energy emanating from the dancing couples and rowdy music. On one side it petered out into the darkness of the woods, where the couples could stray if they were bent on more lascivious pursuits.

Isabel turned abruptly to face him. 'Dance…*hic*… with me, Will?'

'What? No, this is not the same as anything you're used to.'

The jig was as unsuitably unrefined as it was frenetic.

'Good, now come.' She grabbed his hand. 'This jumping around and flinging your partner about may be just what is…*hic*…required to get rid these horrid hiccups. And that's what *my* mother would have advised.'

'Isabel, this really is not a good idea.'

But it was too late. She had already pulled him into the middle, trying to drag him along to the jig while clutching his hand.

Well, now he had two choices. He could either keep pace with her or let go of her hand and watch another man claim her. Will chose the former, but knew instantly that this was a bad idea. He could feel it in his bones.

They skipped together around the circle of people, alternating and criss-crossing between each dancer until they came back around to face each other, clapping and twirling. Will placed his hands either side of Isabel's small waist and lifted her in the air before setting her back down in front of him, trying to disregard the soft curves he could feel through the layers of clothing. God, he must not allow his mind to wander into dangerous waters like this.

He gave her a friendly smile, instead 'Any better?'

'I think so,' she said, relieved, but then proceeded to hiccup again. 'Oh, dear...*hic*... I spoke too soon.'

The dance repeated again and they were separated once more. Will would wager that it had become even more crowded than moments before and it was now more difficult keeping an eye on the woman. He caught glimpses of Isabel, but his vision was constantly blocked by groups of the dancers who had splintered off from the main circle.

Damn. He darted his gaze in every direction, but couldn't see her. This was very strange.

The hairs on the back of his arm rose as he sensed that there was something not right here. He could feel it in his marrow. Will turned his head in every direction, hoping he could locate Isabel. But, no, she was no longer part of the dance. In fact, Will couldn't see her at all.

Hell's teeth!

He marched towards the outer edge of the area, near the woods, and nodded at a man standing by watching and cheering the dancing, his heart hammering in his chest.

'Did you see a young woman, this height—' he motioned with his hand '—with a cream-coloured veil, green woollen dress and carrying a leather satchel across her front?'

'Possibly, friend, and possibly not.' The man shrugged as Will clenched his teeth.

He held out a silver coin. 'You better make sure you do know, *friend*, so which is it?'

The man shrugged, grabbing the coin. 'She left with two men.'

'Where did they go?' he hissed through his teeth.

'Through the woods, there.' The man indicated to one side. 'Mind your woman better next time. There are many wolves in these here parts.'

That, he knew…

Will broke out into a run, his senses heightened with the possibility of imminent danger. God, but he should have trusted his senses about being in a place like this. Hadn't he, himself, been followed several times during his search for the lady? But why now, when he had found her? Probably so the obsequious rat, Rolleston, didn't have to pay his due.

Will would have to think further about that later. All that mattered was finding Isabel and making sure she was unharmed. Anger coursed through him as he drew his sword from its scabbard. This would not have happened had he been more vigilant, more careful. This was his fault.

He prowled through the woods stealthily, looking in every direction, when he suddenly heard a high-pitched scream.

Isabel!

Will raced towards the direction the scream came from before coming to a halt and crouching low, spying three figures in the darkness. One of the men was tying Isabel's hands together while the other was trying to gag her. Will assessed the area quickly, making sure the assailants had no other accomplices, before pouncing on one of them, catching the man off guard.

Almost casually he delivered a swift punch, knocking him to the ground.

He flicked a quick glance at Isabel. 'Are you unharmed?'

'Yes, and I'm so happy to see you.' She winced. 'Watch out, Will!' she cried as the man he had brought down was back on his feet and was about attack him with a knife from behind. The other one was still holding tightly on to Isabel.

With just a few deft moves, Will had unarmed and rendered his opponent unconscious with a sharp jab and devastating blow, while Isabel and the other attacker gawped at his skills. The man's hold must have slackened momentarily, as Isabel swung her elbows back to hit him directly in the stomach to aid her escape. But that just emboldened the bastard to yank her back by her hair.

Will turned his attention, his gaze fixed only on the man holding on to Isabel.

'Let her go now and I might allow you to hold on to your life.'

The man snarled. 'See, this is what we're going to do—you're going turn around and go, while I take this wench to people who want her more than you.'

'I don't think so,' Will said, pointing his sword at the man, the tip close to his face. 'I am going to count to ten and you will let her go.'

The man grunted from behind Isabel, pulling her closer.

'Five, then... One, two...' Will moved forward, pushing the assailant back slowly, while assessing the uneven surface of the ground '...three, four...you're running out of time.'

'Wait.' The man blustered, but it was too late. Will had astutely manoeuvred the man to where the path suddenly dipped low. Before the assailant knew what had happened, Will had spun around and was just there, by his side, the tip of the blade pressed against his neck.

'Five,' Will's voice rumbled in his ear. 'I told you to let her go. Now!'

The man complied, dropping his dagger to the ground and holding his arms up, but just as Will turned his head towards Isabel, the man lunged. This time, Isabel stumbled forward and swung her satchel, hitting him hard across the head. He toppled over with a thud as Isabel took a few steps back and sank to the ground.

'My thanks,' Will panted as he dropped to his knee, looking at her with concern. So much for an uneventful and tedious journey.

'And mine,' she whispered lifting her head. 'You'll be happy to know that I no longer have the hiccups.'

'Well, that's a mercy.' The corners of his lips twitched. 'Are you hurt, my lady?'

'I'm fine, but allow me one moment before I get to my feet.'

'No need,' he said, gently, as he lifted her in his arms.

'I'm glad you came for me, Will.'

'Always… I hope you'll now readily believe that I won't let anything happen to you.'

'I do and I also admire your bold promise, *Sir William*…for you are a gallant knight, you know, whatever you may believe,' she mumbled, so softly he could barely hear her. Will flushed at her unexpected compliment.

'I'm honour-bound to protect you, Isabel.'

'I know, but I'm grateful all the same. As I don't know the way...*home*...' Her voice faded away.

Will looked down as her eyes fluttered shut and pressed his lips softly to her forehead. 'Neither do I, sweetheart. Neither do I.'

Chapter Six

Isabel awoke from a restless night's sleep the following day, irascible and with what Will had predicted—an almighty headache. God, but it hurt just opening one of her eyes. She screwed them shut again and felt splinters of shooting pain. She rubbed her forehead and eyes gently, trying to coax them to open.

'Good morning,' the pleasant voice that could only belong to William Geraint rumbled nearby.

The back of her throat felt parched and scratchy, so when she opened her mouth to return his greeting, she croaked, instead. Well, it wasn't as though she could embarrass herself any more than she already had.

Isabel sat up gingerly as Will passed her his flagon.

'Drink this. It may help,' he said with a little amusement in his voice.

She nodded her thanks, refusing to meet his gaze, before taking small sips, feeling the restorative cool water slip down her throat.

'If you feel up to it, Lady Isabel, there is a stream, yonder, where you can wash.'

That made her turn her head, wincing as she faced him. But, of course, she was back to being Lady Isabel de Clancey, wasn't she? And of course it was this very moment that the events from the previous evening were slowly tumbling back into her very sore head.

'How are you feeling?' Will's blue eyes glittered as he stood watching her, leaning against the bark of a tree.

Mortified, disconcerted, unsettled.

Isabel felt a twinge of guilt at putting both of them in danger the previous evening, but she hadn't anticipated that it would happen so soon after leaving St Jean de Cole. She should have known better, though. And she should also have known better than to have such humiliating notions in her head about the man standing opposite her. Thank goodness she hadn't acted upon her impulses last night as it would have turned out to be even more embarrassing than it had.

'I feel as though someone has taken a hammer to my head, but otherwise I'll live—' she grimaced '—thanks to you. I'm incredibly grateful to you and I am also, once again, in your debt.'

He shook his head, his lips pressed into a thin line. 'You don't owe me anything, my lady.'

'Apart from my life,' she said, meeting his eyes. 'I need to know what those men wanted with me.'

'I strongly suspect that they were Rolleston's men—the man who hired me to find you—hoping to take you back to your people themselves.'

Yet Isabel did not share the same belief. Those men weren't just trying to undercut any agreement this Rolleston had made with Will. There was much more to this and she would have to give it proper attention, but not now. Her head hurt just thinking about it.

She looked around, rubbing her eyes and drinking in the serenity of the area. They were surrounded by a couple of towering trees with long branches, populated with a mass of fluttering leaves, and the sound of the nearby stream could be heard. Her satchel lay beside her and the horses were grazing, tethered to a nearby tree. All very peaceful, all very unremarkable given the events of the previous evening.

'Goodness me, how did you manage to bring us here?' she asked in confusion. 'I was…incapacitated.'

'There are many things I have done on my own, Isabel, ever since I've lived in France.'

'I see.' Isabel wanted to ask why, but knew that it was wiser to hold her tongue. Her curiosity about William Geraint stretched to a time before his move to France, when he, possibly, wasn't as alone as he'd alluded to. Either way, she hoped that he would one day confide in her about his past. 'I, too, have learnt to be self-reliant, having no one but myself to depend on, even with the relative security of my adopted family.'

Isabel squirmed uncomfortably where she sat, wondering why she had disclosed such a thing to him. She had never said that to anyone before. Yet Will nodded at her as if he understood.

She sighed. 'Although I'm glad that I'm not alone in this,' she muttered awkwardly.

'I'm glad, too, Isabel.'

His perceptive gaze pierced through her, making her bite her lip as she looked away.

There was a blanket that had thoughtfully been put over her and another underneath, which begged the question of where William Geraint had rested.

'What about you?' She snapped her head back, wanting a change of conversation from anything too personal. 'Did you sleep well?'

'No, but I rarely do.'

'Do you mean to tell me you have stayed awake all night?'

He shrugged.

Oh, God! The poor man had stayed awake to keep watch by her side, hadn't he? That was why he looked pale this morning. Well, this would not do. She could not allow her escort to compromise himself on her account, otherwise where would they be?

She stood up and tilted her head. 'I will take your suggestion by going to the stream, but on my return, I want you take mine and rest while I keep watch.'

'That is not such a good idea. What if others like the men last night happen upon on us while I am fast asleep? I cannot allow for anything to happen to you again.'

'I'm not that useless, Will, and nothing is going to happen while you sleep. I'll keep guard with a dagger in each hand. I promise.'

'Isabel, I can't allow anything—'

'I am more worried about the prospect of you falling from your horse with sheer exhaustion, Will, than anything else.' She grabbed her satchel and moved away from the makeshift pallet. 'And there's no use arguing with me on this, my knight. I can be just as belligerent as you when I want to be.'

His lips quirked. 'Yes, my lady.'

Isabel marvelled at the slumbering man, who looked so much younger, so much like the boy she remembered, in his sleep, with his thick eyelashes fanned across his cheeks. A mop of brown hair had fallen over one closed eye, making her itch to drag her fingers through it, pulling it back and touching the outline of his chiselled face. She watched his breathing, shallow and deep, and sighed, not realising that she had slowly moved over him.

A hand sneaked out and grabbed her wrist as a slow smile spread across Will's face, his eyes still closed.

'Are you staring at me while I sleep, my lady?'

Her brows shot up. 'How could you tell?' She leant back, her legs tucked underneath her.

Will opened his eyes and yawned. 'A lifetime of experience being a soldier.' He stretched his arms out. 'And not withstanding that, my two older sisters were always bent on making mischief while I slept, so I learnt from a young age to be ready.'

'For any eventuality?' She smirked.

'Precisely.'

'My brothers, too, loved nothing more than to torment me with spiders in my skirts and worms in my bedding. I was always trying to keep up with them.' A surprising ache caught in her chest, making her smile feel forced. 'But I was always too slow.'

Isabel caught her lip between her teeth, unable to understand why she had revealed more than she had intended. The reality was that it all still felt far too raw. This pain of losing her brothers—shadows from another life.

Will covered her hand with his and squeezed it reassuringly, pinning his gaze to hers. 'I'm sure they would have been proud of you, Isabel, especially how you stealthily came to my rescue last night when you whacked your attacker with your sturdy satchel.'

She looked down at her hand, still covered by his much bigger and stronger one, and flushed. She wasn't used to anyone giving her this kind of compliment, but she appreciated it all the same.

'Thank you.' She nodded. 'And, yes, I'd like to think that they would have.'

They were both lost in their own contemplations for a moment, before Isabel got to her feet and turned to face Will. 'I've been thinking while you were sleeping about everything that has happened and I'll admit to being worried.'

'What about, my lady?'

'Many things,' she retorted. 'Do you think they will come back again?'

'No, I very much doubt that.'

Her eyes widened. 'You killed them?'

'I probably should have, but I didn't want any more stains on my soul than I already have.' He looked at her, registering the shock on her face. 'No, I tied them up and left them unconscious.'

'That was very resourceful of you.'

'I'd like to think so.'

She nodded absently. 'But I do think that there may be others as we make our way back.'

'Is that what is worrying you?' He pushed himself to stand. 'As I said earlier, I shall not allow anything to happen again. On my honour, my lady.'

'Of that I am in no doubt, however—'

'However?'

'I believe I should know how to defend myself, just in case we find ourselves again in a situation where it would be prudent that I did.'

Will crossed his arms across his chest, watching her for a moment. 'My good friend Hugh de Villiers was once given a similar request by his wife, Eleanor, but that particular lady was actually exceptionally skilled in combat.' His eyes glossed over with a faraway look, as though he were recalling a moment from his past. 'Not that Hugh had any notion of it at the time,' he chuckled softly, shaking his head at the memory.

But his smile vanished just as quickly, as if it was too painful to think of his friends. They were clearly people that Will cared for.

He nodded once and met her eyes. 'I hope that we do not encounter anyone else, Isabel, but you're quite right. You should know how to defend yourself.'

'You'll show me?'

'If you wish. First lesson is after we break our fast.'

Will knew that the decision to teach Isabel a few rudimentary defensive moves was sound, but it didn't mean that he should have readily accepted her request. Nor should he have betrayed anything about his past, especially disclosing anything about Hugh de Villiers and his wife, Eleanor of Tallany. That was all far too painful and a reminder of a life he had left behind when he went willingly into exile in France.

The truth was that he no longer deserved friends like Hugh De Villiers. Will was now a different man to the one he had once been. But that didn't mean that it wasn't painful when Will thought about them. He missed them—he missed Hugh, Eleanor, and his family. Will shook his head to rid himself of these unwanted recollections and took a step towards Isabel.

'Now, for today we will think about the different ways to get away from an assailant, who would more than often attack you from behind.' His hands on her were on shoulders, turning her slowly. 'So, imagine I am approaching you without you seeing me.'

Isabel turned fully as he pressed against her back and drew his arm around her neck and inhaled deeply, trying not to notice the enticing scent that wrapped around him with its warm summer floral notes and the essence that was simply *her*.

What was wrong with him this morn?

'Good, so this is the position that the man had you in last night, if you remember.'

'Not a wonderful memory, but one I am hardly able to forget.'

'Indeed… Now, always remember that any assailant will want to grab you from the back as it's the most expedient way to capture you, so at all times be vigilant. Don't allow the rear to be exposed. Failing that, you shall find yourself in a position like this.'

Will certainly did not need to hold on to Isabel for this length of time or to press this closely to her, but he couldn't help being enveloped by her soft curves, or the silkiness of the exposed skin at her neck. His breathing became a little constricted as he noticed a few smatterings of freckles on her skin and the loose, honey-coloured tendril of hair that had escaped from under the sheer veil brushing against the curve of her neck. It was all he could do to prevent himself from pushing it away and touching her skin to satisfy his curiosity.

'Yes? What next? Will?'

He cleared his throat, giving his head a little shake. 'I am going to tighten my hold while you try to break it. What should you do first?'

'Since you're holding me this tight, it's difficult to know how I can pull away.'

'Exactly, you should not try to pull away from me, Isabel,' he whispered in her ear, feeling her faint shudder. 'You must do the very thing that would be unexpected by your assailant.'

'Which is?'

'If you are ever held as closely as this, with your

captor overpowering you from behind, there really is only one course of action. You lean to the left, only slightly, yes…like that. This allows you to manoeuvre your hands below to be able to grab his…his, er… well, his unmentionables and you squeeze as hard as you can. Imagine that it's fruit, such as ripened plums.' This conversation was getting more uncomfortable by the moment. 'Trust me when I say you'll surprise him enough to release you.'

Isabel turned her head around slightly, her face and neck flushed. 'I… I see. Well, I am grateful that you have not concealed such a defensive move from me on account of my being a woman.'

'God, no. If you are ever in such a position, then you must use any means to escape effectively. I hope it would never come to it, but as I said, it would be a wholly unexpected way to defend yourself so it is useful to have in your arsenal.'

Isabel smiled. 'I shall. Anything else?'

Will chuckled, his mouth still close to the curve of her neck. 'Are you telling me that the thought of having to employ such a move does not deter you?'

'Not if it means I can get away.'

'Very good. You are thinking in a pragmatic way.' He hesitated before continuing. 'Now, there is another similar move, just as devastating and just as unexpected. Make a fist with your hand, like this.' He covered her hand, curling her fingers under, with his free hand. 'You'll need to punch like the devil and in the same area as before.'

'Shall I refrain from employing that on you?'

He released Isabel and turned, walking away from her. 'I'll be grateful if you didn't, my lady,' he said with a spark of amusement.

What was he thinking?

These rather unconventional defensive moves that he'd once shown his mother and his sisters were a good idea, an astute idea but really... Did he have to start with such a move? The mere mention of *that* part of a man's body was making all the blood in his body swoop there, making him feel exceedingly uncomfortable.

Hell! He should not be thinking about the soft curves of her glorious body, the freckles on her neck or her delicious scent. It was all highly unseemly.

'I'll try to remember that,' she muttered. 'Is that it?'

He cleared his throat, turning to walk towards the stream. 'No, I shall give you further instruction every day if you wish, my lady, but I really do believe that we should continue moving now.'

'Yes, of course...are you well?'

'Perfectly, we'll pack up and leave after I drag myself to the stream and fill up the flagons. Now, if you'll excuse me, Lady Isabel.' He ambled along, conscious that he also needed the water to douse all of these pent-up feelings about Isabel de Clancey. It damn well would not do!

After many hours of riding had passed, Will acknowledged that despite his attempts to keep their exchanges light and friendly, he couldn't simply ignore the lady he was travelling with, just because he was reckless and misguided enough to feel the stirrings of attraction for her. He would just have to suppress and ignore these unwarranted feelings.

Will had a job to do and it would be best to put all his efforts into accomplishing that, especially since Rolleston was bent on dishonouring their agreement. But then, men like him seldom had any honour.

'Do you wish to rest soon, my lady?'

'I'm not fatigued, if that is your concern. We could continue for a while longer in the hope that there won't be any more disruptions along the way.'

'And if there are, Isabel, we will overcome them.'

'Having witnessed what you are capable of, Will, I am in no doubt, of that. And…now that I know I would only need to crush a man's…private area as though they were mere plums, I hope to rise to that challenge.'

'Oh, God, Isabel, what have I done!' He snapped his head around to meet her amused gaze. 'Promise me you'll forget everything I've taught you once you're back home?'

'Once I am the lady I am expected to be?'

'Precisely.' He rubbed his brow, not knowing how to put this into words.

She looked ahead. 'I'm just happy you have consented to teach me how to protect myself properly. I value and appreciate that immensely.'

'As long as it gives you some peace of mind. But remember, Rolleston won't want to harm you as the reason he is trying to capture you is merely so that he can renege on our agreement.'

'I see,' she said stiffly.

'You don't believe me?'

She didn't respond. Will noticed the way she sat on the horse, the way her jaw was set and how she clenched the reins of her young palfrey so tightly, that her knuckles were white. It seemed to Will that she was grappling with something that preoccupied her, or possibly scared her…

He pulled on the reins, bringing his horse to a gradual halt, making Isabel do the same.

'What is it, my lady? What is this all about?'

She met his curious gaze and bit her lip. 'I don't think that you'll understand.'

His brows shot up. 'Whatever it is, I hope you know that you can tell me anything.'

'I do—however, this is not something that can be so readily accepted.'

'Just tell me, Isabel.'

She sighed deeply. 'Very well. You once asked me what I was afraid of.'

'Yes…' he said slowly, his eyes never leaving hers.

'Well, the truth is that I don't believe that those men from last night were trying to renege on whatever deal you struck with Rolleston.'

'Then what?'

'I don't think any of this is a coincidence, Will—the ambush when I was child, my father and my brothers' deaths. Even last night, with those assailants.'

'Are you trying to say that you believe the incidents are all somehow related?' He shook his head. 'You're mistaken, Isabel.'

'I told you that you wouldn't accept what I had to say.' She exhaled.

'I'm sorry, but how do you know this and what makes you say it?'

'I don't know,' she said in a whisper. 'There are things that I vaguely recall in the haze of my memory. Things that I have tried to forget.' She took in a deep breath before continuing. 'I was a child whom no one noticed much, but I was naturally inquisitive, especially when I was told I was being sent to France to live with my betrothed and his family—the second son of the Count d'Albret. I knew I wasn't to marry him until I came of age, but can you imagine my concern and shock at being told that I would one day be wed to a man who

was close to my father's age. I needed to know why.'
She sighed before continuing.

'I knew my father was out of favour with King John and needed to strengthen our family alliance, but I needed to know what would become of *me*. I needed reassurance. Instead, I heard other things. Voices in the dark spilling secrets and promissory oaths made that could not be unmade.'

'Can you recall who and what that could be?'

'No, I can't remember that—not yet, anyway. And until you appeared in St Jean de Cole, I hoped I never would need to remember my old life…but now, everything has changed.' She gulped, looking down at her hands before lifting her head. 'All I know is what I have told you and the fact that somehow, in some way, it is all related to that pendant you have around your neck, Will.'

He stared at her in disbelief and clutched his hand around the pendant unwittingly, drawing it out from under his tunic and looking at it several times. 'Is that why you gave it to me? For safekeeping?'

'No—' she shook her head '—I wanted you to have it for saving my life, but also with the knowledge that I had found an identical pendant in my satchel, before we were ambushed.'

'An identical pendant?'

She nodded. 'That was what rendered that man unconscious, last night, I believe. It's at the bottom of my satchel, as I never wear it, and must have caught him on the head when I whacked him.'

Will hissed an oath under his breath. There couldn't be anything to what Isabel said, could there?

She tilted her head and smiled wryly. 'I can see that you have a problem believing in what I am saying.'

'To be clear, all you have said, my lady, is that there are two silver and ruby pendants, one of which you gave me all those years ago, and a handful of disturbing memories, which you can't recall very easily.' He paused and dragged his fingers through his hair and softened his tone. 'I'm sorry, Isabel, but there doesn't seem to be anything in this except your unsubstantiated fears of the unknown. Which I do understand, by the way.'

She dropped her head and made a single nod. Her whole demeanour tugged at Will's chest and he almost jumped down from his horse to comfort her. 'I'm sorry.'

'Don't be. I didn't think you'd believe me, but then you did ask.' She sighed, pressing ahead with her horse, edging forward down the path, surrounded by shrubs and coppices. 'Although there is one thing I forgot to mention,' she said from over her shoulder.

'Oh, and what is that?'

'The pendants should never, ever be kept together and must always be kept apart.' She turned her head slightly, affording him a view of her profile against the shadows. 'That, I *have* remembered.'

Chapter Seven

Dusk had settled. They had ridden for many long hours avoiding towns, villages and small hamlets where people might be encouraged to remember a man and woman travelling together on horseback.

Eventually, they had set up a small camp in another sheltered area of yet another part of a secluded woodland, close to a fast-flowing river.

It had been Isabel's insistence that they pushed ahead without stopping for respite. The more they stopped, the more time she would have to think. The more time she would have for lengthy conversations with a man who was starting to invade far too much of her inner sanctum.

Will was a frustration that intrigued Isabel even though he shouldn't. He was confounding and, with everything in her life as precarious and uncertain as it was, this was something that should not be worth her time. Yet, she couldn't help it.

Isabel splashed in the river, glad of the opportunity to wash away the day's dirt and travelling grime. She poured the river water over her head and applied a cleansing oil and soap that she had prepared and brought with her from St Jean de Cole, inhaling the calming scent.

The journey already felt much longer than the two days since she had left home. She missed and mourned that life once again, but knew there was no use thinking of it. That life was no more, but what the new one waiting for her in England would entail, she could only wonder.

Isabel finished bathing and paddled out of the river, ringing the water out of her long hair and using lengths of linen to dry herself. She removed the wet tunic that she'd bathed in, putting on a clean, dry one, and finished dressing. After taking a big glug of chilly air into her lungs, she wandered back along the leafy path to where they had set up for the night.

She shivered, moving towards the fire that Will had kindled, watching the flames lick the lengths of wood. It seemed that the first cold bite had finally arrived as one season was giving way into another.

'You're cold, my lady.' Will strode towards her and draped a blanket over her shoulders. 'Here, take this.'

'Thank you.' Isabel glanced up and noticed his swift intake of air, his eyes fixed to her unbound and unveiled hair. 'It's still wet,' she said and flushed instantly, knowing it was plainly obvious. Needing to do something instead of standing there feeling self-conscious, Isabel drew the long length of her hair over one shoulder, allowing it to fall to her front, her fingers prising through the wet strands, untangling it.

For some unknown reason Will was still watching her, as if beguiled under an enchantment. She raised her brows in question and, as though he was pulled back to his senses, he gave his head a firm shake and offered her a place to sit by the fire before perching on the other side, leaning against a tree.

They descended into an uncomfortable silence, with Isabel unable to think of anything to say. She huddled close to the fire, allowing the warmth into her weary bones, listening to it crackle and spit as she rested her chin on her raised knees.

It was different now they were sated from the last parcels of food that she had brought, had washed, cleaned and were now ready for...sleep.

This time, it was very different to the way she had passed out last night. This time, she was very aware that she was alone in the middle of the woods at night with a handsome warrior. A man whose very presence made her stomach plummet to her toes. Isabel trusted Will implicitly, but not her own reaction to him, which made her feel quite ridiculous. She knew nothing of men, but did understand that her feelings were muddled up at a time when she was in need of a friend. Yes, that's all this was. Nothing more than needing someone to converse with.

Will picked up a small object and Isabel watched in fascination as his big, strong hands moved carefully, carving intricate shapes into a piece of what looked like a bit of slate with a small knife.

'What are you making?' she muttered, after a while.

'Nothing in particular.' He shrugged. 'This is something I always do when I need to think.'

'What have you to think about that would necessitate for you to be this assiduous?'

A faint smile played at the corners of his lips. 'Am I being assiduous?'

'Oh, I believe so and I believe it is what I said earlier today that has you in such a quandary.'

He lifted his head and dragged his fingers through his hair. 'It is all so…'

'Fanciful?'

He shook his head. 'Your fears are natural, Isabel, and they stem from what happened to you when you were a young maid. However, that doesn't mean that there is some conspiracy against your family involving a couple of silver pendants.'

'I thank you for your summary, but you will, I hope, understand if I don't share your opinion. Whatever you may believe, there's far more to the pendants than meets the eye.'

'Do you not think it possible that the ordeal you suffered as a child was so monstrous that in time your mind began to contrive a different narrative?'

'You're all but saying that I must have made all of it up in my head.'

'No, I am just trying to consider why you might believe that everything that has befallen you and your family was not merely coincidence.'

'I do not need your consideration, Will. You don't have to share my beliefs,' she said, pulling the blanket tightly over her shoulders. 'All I want is your understanding.'

'You have it, my lady.' He met her eyes and made a curt nod before resuming his carving.

'Thank you.' They descended once again into silence, which Isabel was keen to break. 'You seem highly skilled. Did you learn this at a guild in England?'

Will shook his head and continued shaping the small bit of slate, exchanging the knife for a chisel. 'My father was a stonemason…that is, my stepfather was.' The words that he spoke seemed forced and tainted with bitterness. 'He was the one who was truly skilled—commissioned to make gargoyles and ornamental mouldings on the underside of arches, along columns and buttresses of many a holy church and its outer buildings.'

'It must have been inspiring to be around someone who could produce such…such beauty.'

Will tilted his head, keeping his eyes pinned to what he was creating. 'When he favoured me with his time, which wasn't often, it felt…special. He would sit and teach me how to hold whatever it was I intended to carve as well as how to hold the knife, the pressure I'd need to apply to get the desired effect. It was intricate, time-consuming work and an effective way to spend a little time with the man. At least it stopped us from incessantly arguing.' He sighed deeply, looking away.

This was one of a very few times that Will had freely revealed something significant about himself—about his past. Even if he was still reticent. It was preferable to Isabel—she would much rather talk about his past than her own.

'It must have been…difficult.'

He shook his head. 'I have always enjoyed cutting, carving and moulding—creating something with hopefully a little beauty out of nothing.'

'I understand the need to elicit a little beauty from this sometimes unforgiving and unkind world.' Isabel hugged her knees tighter. 'That's why I extract parts of flowers, herbs and plants to prepare tisanes, poultices and salves that may heal and soothe. Or if I'm feeling particularly indulgent then I'd create scented oils and soaps.' She looked up then and caught his steady gaze, a faint smile playing on his lips.

'And that is why your own scent is like an enchanting floral garden.' He smiled as Isabel felt her cheeks getting warm.

She looked away for a moment before turning her attention back to Will. 'Has it been long since you have seen your family, your father?'

He frowned before answering her. 'Not since…well, for the past few years. My father—stepfather—died around that time.'

'I'm so sorry.'

He shrugged. 'Despite this,' he said, nodding at the slate and chisel in his hands, 'we were never close. I wasn't his natural-born son.'

Isabel warmed her hands, holding them out near to the fire, watching the flames flare, her gaze distant, recalling a faraway memory. She blinked and lifted her head. 'My father never favoured me either and I *was* his natural-born daughter.' She grimaced, shaking her head. 'I was an inconvenience who held no interest for him, except when he was arranging my betrothal. Even then I cannot recall he ever spoke to me much about it other than make demands.'

'Is that why you didn't tell anyone—me, the priest, the nuns who took you and even your adopted family—who you really were?'

'Not exactly. My father commanded me not to and I was only a child at the time so I obeyed his edict without question.' She shrugged. 'He told me that our family's position was precarious because of his downfall with King John. And after what happened at the ambush, I was scared, Will. I even thought at one time that it had been the King's agents who were responsible for what had happened. I believed that I was in danger, so I kept my vow and told no one who I was.' She sighed.

'Besides, I trusted my father would come looking for me once my family realised what had happened. But no one came for me, no one cared…so I decided to forget

everything that had happened and forged a new life—
one of my own choosing.' Isabel might have longed for
her mother desperately, but she had feared her father's
wrath more, believing that somehow the ambush would
be perceived as her fault. But how could it? She had
only been a child—a terrified child. Isabel's throat suddenly felt tight as she lifted her head and met his eyes.

'You should have been treated with more care, Isabel.'

Yes…yes, she should have been. Not that Isabel
blamed her gentle mother, who'd never had a say in
anything. But she certainly blamed her indifferent, con-
trolling father. His blood might run through her veins,
but it had offered her no protection from heartache.
And in time she'd realised that she could only ever depend on herself.

Isabel's need to guard herself from further hurt
stemmed from that very moment in her life when everything shifted. When she journeyed down a path very
different to the one she was meant to.

'My father used to say to my mother that I must be
cursed because of my strangely coloured eyes.'

'You are not,' Will growled, as if he were annoyed
on her behalf. 'And they're not strange, but beautiful.
I remembered you after all this time because of your
remarkable eyes.'

Heavens above…

Isabel's cheeks felt as though they were on fire. She
swallowed, unable to think of what to say, her words
drying on her lips. Yet she couldn't break away from
Will's intense scrutiny daring her to believe him.

She stood up suddenly. 'I think it must be time for
me to get some sleep. Shall we take it in turns to keep
watch?'

It was not quite the best way to diffuse whatever had just passed between them, but she couldn't think of anything else.

'Apologies, my lady,' he said stiffly. 'I did not mean to embarrass you.'

'You didn't, Will,' she said, biting her bottom lip.

'I'm glad.' He rose as well and passed her his blanket. 'Here, just in case you get colder later.'

She frowned. 'What about you?'

'I'll be fine. Now try to get some sleep.' He held out his hand. 'Before you do, may I possibly take a look at the other pendant—the identical one—to satisfy my curiosity?'

Isabel woke up at the break of dawn. She had meant to rouse earlier to afford Will the opportunity to rest and sleep as well, but she must have been far more tired than she had anticipated. The moment Isabel's head had touched the blanket, she had fallen into a deep slumber.

She sat up, yawning and stretching her arms, her eyes darting around until they settled on Will, finding him frowning over the two pendants.

'I'm so sorry, I meant to wake much earlier than this.'

'Not necessary, my lady.' He waved his hand absently, without looking up. 'But there is something you should know about these pendants,' he said, holding them up.

Her brows creased. 'What is it?'

Will looked up then. 'They are *not* identical.'

'That's not possible,' she said slowly.

'Nevertheless, it's the truth, Isabel.'

She slid over beside Will for a closer inspection, blinking several times at the two pendants, held in the palm of his hands. 'I don't know what you mean. They still look exactly the same to me.'

'That's what has been baffling me.' He shook his head. 'Why go to such lengths to make these pieces of jewellery look as though they're one and the same, when they're not.'

Isabel looked closer and noticed that actually the ruby inset in the centre of each pendant, although exactly the same in size, was differently set.

'Can you see it now? Notice how the gem, the silver filigree work around the edges and all the beautiful metal work are all perfectly the same in design.'

'But on one pendant, the design is raised…' she said slowly.

'While on the other, it is set back to an exacting precision,' he finished her sentence.

'I don't understand.' She met his eyes, shaking her head. 'Why?'

'I cannot say, my lady but I do think that whoever commissioned these intended for them to *look* identical.'

'There must be a reason. Why go to all this effort to make them appear the same?'

They sat side by side for a moment staring at the two pendants before Isabel shook her head and turned to Will. 'We're not going to get any answers now, so why don't you try to get some sleep, while I keep watch.' Before he could object, she added, 'Please, I insist.'

'Very well, but only for a short duration. We must leave soon.'

Chapter Eight

$$\sim\!\!\mathcal{O}\!\!\sim\!\!\infty\!\!\sim\!\!\mathcal{O}\!\!\sim$$

They reached the small bustling town of La Roche-foucauld before noon. Here, they could replenish their supplies and allow their horses a much-needed rest at a nearby farmhouse. But it had been a mistake to have come into a place so open, exposed and very conspic-uous. Isabel couldn't explain why or how, but a deep sense of foreboding gripped her the moment they ar-rived.

She pushed the feelings away, knowing they were irrational and based on fears she had manifested and embellished in her head. Will was no doubt right in his estimation that everything she had always supposed to mean more, was purely coincidental. Even the pendants weren't identical, as she had always believed. None of it seemed to mean anything or make much sense.

So, why did she still feel so apprehensive?

Isabel sighed, realising that it was the first time since the night of the attack that she had been in a place that was so busy.

The two of them strolled alongside one another in the market square, which was filled with an array of different vendors and farmers selling an abundance of produce. They ambled past master bakers selling honey bread topped with sprigs of lavender, milk cakes, pastries and delicate meat and cheese pies. Elsewhere, there were flowers and herbs being sold as well as harvested vegetables and fruits.

Isabel selected the juiciest plums, turned to Will and gave them a gentle squeeze, her eyebrows arched playfully. He shook his head at her and covered a grin with his hand. Isabel was surprised by her shocking behaviour and yet it was certainly one way to stop her from focusing on her anxious musings.

After purchasing essentials, including the delicious plums, they meandered away from the market square and towards the farmhouse through a few cobbled pathways. As they turned into a narrow road with tall dwellings on either side, the fine hairs on Isabel's arm rose. Something felt very, very wrong. The path was deserted except for a man at the far end, who was leaning against stone wall, whistling.

Will grabbed her by the elbow, making her stop. 'Turn and walk back the way we came,' he muttered urgently, from the side of his mouth. 'Easy now.'

She did as he bid, noting that he had obviously had similar suspicions. They both walked a little quicker, but came to halt when two men entered the path, walking towards them.

'They don't look particularly friendly.'

'No, I don't believe they are.'

She snapped her head round to him, her breathing laboured, 'What now?'

'I'll create a diversion and then I want you to run as fast as you can. Can you do that?'

'Absolutely not, do you think I'm going to leave you the mercy of these men?'

Will took his dagger out its sheath, held it in one hand and took out his sword from its scabbard. 'Isabel, we do not have time to argue about this.'

'I'm staying with you,' she said defiantly. 'Hand me a spare weapon.'

'What?' He frowned. 'No. You need to know how to use it, otherwise there is hardly any point.' He looked in both directions at the men prowling towards them as he pushed her behind him, his body shielding her from whatever the men were about to inflict.

Good grief, she was not wholly incapable of helping, even in this terrifying situation. Or mayhap it was the proximity of this big, strong warrior that was making her a little braver than she would have otherwise felt.

'Pass me a weapon, please.'

This time Will complied and handed her a small, slim knife which had been strapped to his ankle, all the while shielding her behind his larger, taller and broader body. He made a few, determined steps back and to the side, making her shuffle along until she was positioned inside a wide doorway.

'When the time comes, I want you to do exactly as I say, do you understand?' he said, scanning the buildings on both sides. 'Isabel?' he hissed.

'Yes,' she said. 'I can see that you're formulating some sort of plan.'

He made a quick nod. 'We'll see.'

The men from either side sneaked closer, trapping them.

'There's no need for any violence here, if you do as we ask,' one of men said, holding out the palms of his hands, showing that he carried no weapons. He was wiry, of small stature, and his face was severely pockmarked. 'All we want is the woman and the pendant you have dangling around your neck.'

Will shrugged as though he was discussing something inconsequential. 'I don't think so.'

'What exactly do you hope to achieve except ending your life here and now?' the man retorted before throwing down a small coin purse filled, presumably, with silver. 'Here. For your troubles.'

Will ignored the leather purse that lay on the ground and smiled nonchalantly. 'I think I'll take my chances.'

'There are five of us and only one of you.'

Will's smile turned rueful. 'Not a problem for me. I've taken on more than half a dozen men on my own.' He held his sword arm out, ready for battle. 'So, it is I who should advise you all to turn back now and return from whence you came.'

'And it's not five against one, anyway. I'm here, too.' Isabel muttered from behind him, gaining a low groan from Will, as the five men descending on them stopped momentarily to laugh.

Trust Isabel to come out with such brave yet unwise words, undermining his own. Yet Will couldn't help but appreciate her spirit.

Ah well, now, mayhap they could use this to their advantage. He flicked his eyes to the buildings again, taking in the different heights and angles of the roof. Yes, it could work. He waited for the men to edge closer just a little bit more before he could undertake his hare-brained plan.

Two of the men sprang forward at the same time. Will fended off the attack from the right with a few expedient swipes of his sword, bringing the man down, then spun quickly at the exact moment the other assail-

ant attacked. Will blocked him and lunged forward unexpectedly, bringing him down as well. But there were
still three men left and they seemed to have purposely
held back since they were smirking as though expecting this outcome.

They were trying to tire him out, but these men had
no idea of his stamina. They would need a whole garrison of soldiers if they wanted to achieve *that*.

'Watch out!' Isabel cried from somewhere behind
him as another, much larger, man attacked from the
side. He caught Will somewhere on his body, but he
had little time to dwell on any minor gash.

The man to the other side moved forward, relishing
the chance, it seemed, to clash swords with him. But
he was certainly better than the others, who had been
no match for Will. No, the man was better than that—
he was skilled enough to draw Will slightly away from
Isabel. It was then that he realised that while he was
doing that the others were trying to grab her.

'Take cover, Isabel. Remember the unexpected and
be ready for any eventuality!'

'I'm trying!'

Will continued with the swordplay and with a few
decisive swipes and lunges he successfully made the
man drop his weapon, bringing him to the ground. But
when he turned swiftly, he found one of the men holding Isabel from behind, with the knife Will had given
her against her throat.

'Now, as you were.' The man smirked. 'We want
that fine pendant, see. So, take it off and pass it here.'
He pressed against Isabel with the blade a little closer
against her throat.

The man was a thug, panting heavily and looking
unnerved and agitated, which made him far more dan-

'Are you well?'

'Yes,' she whispered between breaths as he rested his chin on the top of her head. 'Oh, my God…but you're not! Will…' Isabel lifted her head, her eyes wide, staring at her outstretched palms that had been resting on his chest. They were covered with his blood.

He shrugged, making a face. 'This is not nothing to be concerned about, Isabel.'

'I disagree, this is very much something to be concerned about.'

He chuckled softly, shaking his head. 'Let us get out here. Then I'll welcome your ministrations, my lady.' He grinned. 'I'll promise to be brave.'

They had managed to get to the farmhouse without attracting any more unwanted attention, thank the lord. After paying coin to the farmer, they'd mounted their horses without their provisions—having lost them in the skirmish—and left the blasted town.

By sundown they had managed to ride through to a thick forest, their intent one of concealment since it was now plainly evident that they were being pursued. Eventually, after halting their progress for the day, Will made a fire and saw to the horses before finally being able to see to his injury from earlier. He went for a wash in the nearby stream, cleaning away the grime from the day's riding and all the dried blood down his chest from the wound on his pectoral muscle. It stung like hell and the wound was bigger than he had anticipated. He submerged his head in the freezing water, welcoming the icy coldness as it sluiced down his aching body.

Will had difficulty containing his anger as well as concern for their situation, knowing it had all been

gerous than any skilled soldier. One false move and he could kill Isabel.

'Do as he instructs, Sir William,' the pock-faced man who had spoken from the outset said. 'And drop your weapons…now!'

Damn, they should never have ventured into this town. They had walked straight into a trap.

Slowly, very slowly, Will crouched low, placing his sword and dagger on the ground.

'Boot them towards me, if you would be so obliging,' the man said, his stony eyes fixed on Will.

He did as he was bid, but noticed from the corner of his eye that the man who was holding Isabel had eased the knife he was holding from against her neck.

'Isabel…*plums*!'

Will snapped his head around as Isabel delivered the devastating blow he had taught her, causing the man holding her to widen his eyes in shocked pain, releasing her just as Will elbowed him in the face, making contact with his nose and hearing it crack, broken.

Isabel rushed behind Will once again as the pock-faced man bellowed. As he suspected, more men, who had been waiting at either end of the openings of the pathway, ran in.

Will pulled himself up on the door plinth and kicked the pock-faced man before grabbing his weapons and climbing upwards, gaining purchase on the flat base.

'Here, give me your hand, Isabel,' he said, holding out his hand. 'Quickly.'

She placed her hand in his and he hauled her up to crouch beside him.

'My thanks,' she said as he nodded. 'What now?'

He looked above and back to the trusting woman beside him. 'Now we climb, my lady.'

Thank heavens she didn't argue, although he could see her visibly gulp. Will clambered up the stone roofs and held out his hand, grabbing hers and pulling her up. Repeating this, they continued upwards, gaining footing to balance their weight until they landed on the flat roof at the top that he had observed earlier. They dashed to the end of the building, catching their breaths and scanning the area for the best way to continue to their destination. They both turned as they heard another person climbing up the building in pursuit of them.

The distance between this building and the next one was too far.

'What are we to do?' she said, panting and out of breath.

'Isabel, do you still have the rope you used to climb down from your room in St Jean de Cole?'

'Yes, but…'

'Hand it to me, please…now.' He watched as she fished for the rope in her satchel, her hand shaking as she passed it to him.

'Will, he's on the roof…he's on the roof!'

'No need for panic, my lady.' He looked around and settled on a stone stump post the original builders had obviously forgotten to break down, tying a couple of knots around it, and pulling it several times to test that it could take their weight. 'Come, let's go, Isabel.'

He held out his hand and grabbed hold of her just as the pock-faced man staggered towards them. Isabel put her arm around Will, holding on to him for dear life, wrapping her body around him as he swung from one building to another. He slipped as they reached the other building, making them swing back.

Will pushed against the wall and this time when they swung over to the adjacent building, he managed to get

a foothold on the ledge of the roof. He held on to I͏ making sure that she was steady before he grabb͏ knife and started cutting the rope.

'I'll get you another one,' he said, noticing I͏ dismay and nodded at the pock-faced man with before guiding her away.

This roof was not flat, but pitched instead, ͏ it incredibly difficult to manoeuvre their way ͏

'Careful now…easy,' He muttered. 'Use yo͏ and feet to grip for dear life. Imagine you're a c͏ bering on a roof.'

'I'm trying to.'

'And doing wonderfully well, my lady.' ͏ keep her calm, as one false move and she ͏ down—and this time no one would be the͏ her. 'By the way, you were magnificent bac͏ anything, I hope all of this has shown you t͏ indeed very courageous.'

'I would never think of myself as such, ͏ for you.'

'We make a good team.'

They continued round until they came ͏ slope gave way to a flat base, which they s͏ gerly. The wooden planks were not too ͏ were missing and some altogether broke͏

Holding hands, they felt their way ac͏ their feet down on each length of woode͏ whether it was secure enough to hold ͏ slowly they got across and jumped ac͏ gap to another building. They made t͏ towards ground level gradually, Will c͏ rections to make sure it was safe befor͏ and lowering Isabel. He held her for ͏ than necessary.

far too perilous. Far too bloody close. One thing was certain—that bastard Rolleston was not going to stop trying to renege on their agreement. He couldn't help the nagging feeling that Isabel might be right.

Could it be that the pendants were significant somehow?

He trudged back to Isabel, who had been busy laying out blankets and her herbs, salves and other supplies, ready for his return.

She lifted her head and beamed at him, making him stop momentarily. God, she really had been remarkably fearless earlier. She was far more resilient and determined than she believed and the fact that she had put all of her trust in him to get them out of that difficulty humbled him.

Will returned her smile as he continued to walk towards her.

'Sit here, please, and I shall take a look at your wound.'

He crouched on the blanket in front of her and winked. 'I'm all yours.'

What the hell was the matter with him? Even Isabel, who had been concentrating on the wound, froze, flicked her eyes to his and blinked several times before attending to his small slash.

Her small hand squeezed over his skin. 'Does it hurt?'

He pressed his lips shut in case he made any more half-witted, improper remarks and nodded instead.

When had Will become like this? When had his easiness around women—something that he was known for—become so difficult? Not that Isabel de Clancey was just any woman...

'I'm afraid this is going to need stitching,' she muttered, the tops of her fingers grazing his chest. 'First, though, I will clean it with a salve made to Sibylla's recipe.'

'Whatever you think is best, my lady.'

'I'll try not to hurt you.'

He grinned. 'I know—' he leaned forward slightly, ignoring her alluring fragrance '—but I must tell you that I have been stitched up more times than I care to remember.'

'Ah, then I have much to live up to.' She raised her brow. 'I hope I exceed your expectations.'

Isabel just had to say those words just as she brushed past him, making him inhale sharply. God, but his reaction to her was wholly inappropriate. He should not be admiring her in any capacity. His destiny lay in a lifetime of solitary existence, doing his duty for the Crown and atoning for his sins. Sins that had cost him dearly.

'I'm sorry, Will, I shouldn't jest. It must hurt after such a long time in the saddle without any due care. We should have stopped much earlier than this.'

She had noticed his reaction, but misconstrued it to mean something quite different. Thank God!

'Possibly, but we had to put distance between us and Rolleston's men.'

'Even so, I cannot help but think that your wound is worse because of it.'

'I'm fine. All I need is to drink a good measure of ale, so if you'd be good enough to pass my flagon.'

Will took big gulps of the glorious drink, hoping it would help numb the pain that would surely come.

'Shall we begin?'

He nodded, taking another big swig. 'Do it, my lady.'

Chapter Nine

Isabel cleaned the area of the flesh wound with a swab drenched in the same ale that Will had consumed. She then continued cleaning the deep gash with an unguent made from honey she had brought from St Jean de Cole. Threading a sharp needle with a fine catgut suture made using the intestines of sheep, she coated the thread with the unguent. She then plunged the metal of the needle into the flames of the fire, as she had watched Sibylla do countless times before.

Taking a deep breath, Isabel started on her task, her fingertips resting on the hard muscles of Will's chest. She had to forget whom she was tending to, forget the strong, rippling muscles of his hardened warrior's body, forget his skin glistening with moisture after bathing. Heavens above, but he smelt…delicious. She had to forget that too!

Isabel gave herself a brisk shake of her head, furious with the direction of her musings. The poor man was probably hiding his agony from the pain induced by such a wound and here she was pondering his manly scent. What on earth was wrong with her? Just because Will gave her the confidence to be able to do all those amazing things she had done earlier—things that she would have thought highly improbable only days ago—did not mean she had to lose sight of what she was doing here. Not just the sewing of his wound, but the fact that she would soon become the eponymous Lady de Clancey. And these unwelcome feelings for her escort were not only distracting, but imprudent and unwise. She had to remind herself that he could be nothing more than a friend.

Isabel fixed her concentrated gaze on making the first few stitches with precision instead. He inhaled sharply through his teeth.

'I am sorry, Will.'

'Whatever for? It was not you who struck me, now was it?' His face contorted with a sting of pain making Isabel work a little quicker, with small, deft stitches.

'No,' she said, shaking her head. 'Do you still maintain that those men are only interested in breaking whatever agreement you made with Rolleston?'

'Possibly.' He looked at her strangely before giving in to a sigh. 'And do you still believe that all past and recent events have been as a result of a conspiracy against your family?'

'Yes. Mayhap even more so.'

'Why even more so, my lady?' He was looking so intently at her that she stopped for a moment before answering him.

'I have been pondering on a memory that struck me this very morning.'

'Which was?'

'On the eve of my departure to La Rochelle all those years ago I was… I was apprehensive and looking for assurance and for comfort. In truth, I was looking for my mother. Instead, I stumbled on my father in the bower of Castle de Clancey…and someone else.'

'Go on…'

'The man my father was conferring with had his back to me so I cannot remember who it was, but it was what they were talking about that I now recall—that is, where I heard my father explain that the two pendants could never be kept together.'

She finished the last stitch and made a secure knot. 'There, I'm all done here, but do not move as I've yet to apply a special comfrey and hyssop salve to help heal and soothe the wound.'

'I'm much obliged.' He smiled faintly.

She rubbed the salve liberally over the wound, her fingers lingering over the smooth, taut skin. 'But that wasn't the only thing I remembered,' she continued, flicking her eyes up to meet his.

'Oh, what else was there?'

'Something about giving one of the pendants to me—as part of my dowry. Of course, I've always known about that, but, you see, the second one must have been placed in my satchel quite by accident.'

'By accident?'

'It all happened a long time ago, Will, and the words are all such a muddle. However, I do remember that when my father referred to the pendants, he also mentioned the words *well matched* and *corresponding*.' She sighed. 'Although, the more I think about it, he could frankly have been referring to my betrothed and I.'

She fetched lengths of clean, dry linen and wrapped it a few times around his broad chest, which of course brought her tantalisingly close to him.

'Quite,' he whispered, his lips only a fingerbreadth

apart from hers. His eyes dropped to her lips and naturally she licked them without intending to.

Oh, dear… Her stomach flipped on itself and her breath hitched, stuck in her throat. They both stared at each other for a moment, neither of them moving. There was a question in Will's gaze, a question that she was only just beginning to understand. He wanted to kiss her and, to her shame, she wanted him to…very much.

He edged near, his lips hovering just above hers, his breathing coming in shallow breaths.

'I shouldn't, Isabel,' he muttered, his voice a low rumble.

Her heart was pounding her chest. 'I shouldn't allow you to.'

Will cradled her cheek with one hand, running his thumb across her bottom lip. 'No…you mustn't,' he whispered, as he dipped his head, pressing his lips to hers lightly.

Just as she felt something pulling her tantalisingly closer to him, they suddenly both heard an animal's shrill sound.

Will jerked away, getting to his feet and expelling a breath as he dragged a shaky hand through his hair.

She blinked, feeling a little awkward, knowing that the promise of a kiss had ended. 'What…what was that noise?'

'I believe that may be a wild boar.' He frowned, tying his sword belt around his waist. 'I had hoped to avoid this forest, since it's famed for having an abundant supply of them, but we were left with little choice. Go and mount your horse, Isabel.'

Isabel watched as Will retreated and absently touched her lips with shaking fingertips.

'Where…where are you going?'

He didn't meet her eyes. 'Hunting.'

It never came to that. The forest was riddled with wild boar and Will deemed it too dangerous for them to stay there overnight. They had no choice but to pack up and start back on their journey again, riding animals that were too tired. In truth, Isabel was far too tired as well. It had been a very, very long day yet they needed to keep moving—needed to push ahead.

But, oh, God, Isabel felt as though she might actually fall off her young palfrey. Though, at this moment, she would gladly receive a knock on the head for her foolhardy behaviour towards Will and her bewildering reaction to him. She must try to contain her ridiculous and unwarranted attraction to the man and ponder on something else instead. Something surely of greater importance and significance. She could not afford to get close to him. Will was her escort back to England and nothing more.

As her horse pounded the dry ground, trotting to a monotonous beat, her mind turned to her father's words, spinning them over in her head, again and again.

Eventually they came upon a dwelling belonging to the local forester. After waking the man and paying him silver, they secured a draughty chamber which had dirty rushes strewn on the floor. But it was a chamber, nevertheless, with a bed, which, thank the lord, was clean. Will bid her goodnight, insisting that he would sleep outside the door, sparing her blushes. Not that Isabel was surprised after what had happened—after they had kissed—even if it had been fleeting.

Lucky for her, Isabel was far too tired to consider

that disconcerting episode and soon fell into a deep yet troubled slumber.

She was running through dark woods. Shapes and shadows, whispers and murmurs. Scarred, faceless men chased her until the storm clouds gathered. Until she was suddenly on the roof of a tall, dark building and she couldn't get off. She was alone and she felt trapped, but she had to get away, had to keep on running as the faceless men followed her, getting closer and closer. But then she fell, hurtling down into darkness, with no one to catch her...

'Isabel?' a voice muttered. 'Isabel, wake up.'

She stirred before opening her eyes abruptly, her breathing laboured.

'I think you must have been dreaming,' Will's voice calmly coaxed her back into consciousness.

Isabel blinked at Will who was sat on the bed, rubbing her arm. She jerked back, feeling a little embarrassed at exposing herself in such a way.

'I...yes.' She rubbed her forehead, feeling the dampness. 'I'm well. It was just a dream.'

'Yes, but sometimes even a dream can be surprisingly distressing.' Will sighed and drew her into his arms as she nodded. 'There's no shame in admitting that, my lady.'

'Thank you,' she muttered, not knowing what else to say. She felt surprisingly at peace cocooned and protected in his big, strong arms.

'What was it about?' he murmured, stroking her hair.

'The usual thing of being chased, but this time I was on top of a roof, running for dear life.'

'That is understandable after what happened yesterday.'

After a moment of the tranquil stillness, she pulled away slowly. 'Is it time to leave yet?'

'Rest a little while longer.' He stood up to go. 'And remember, I'm only outside this room.'

She didn't say a word, knowing that if she opened her mouth to speak, she would urge him to stay with her and hold her all night...which really would not be a wise thing to do. A shiver went through her. No, it would not be wise at all.

The following morning, Will acquired strips of cured wild boar, cheese, dried fruit and warm rolls of bread from the forester and his wife, who also took the offer of coin for their silence in case Rolleston's men came looking for them here. It was vital that his men did not know the route they were taking, especially as it had been extremely close yesterday, with everything that had happened at La Rochefoucauld. Next time they might not be so lucky.

Will sighed, rubbing the tension from the back of his neck after an uncomfortable night's rest. He reminded himself of the necessity in being prudent when it came to Lady Isabel as well. He must think of her only as the noble woman she was rather than the woman he desired and was beginning to care for. God, but it had been a very close thing yesterday with *that* as well, when he had tasted her lips. That innocent kiss could have led to all sorts of trouble. He had to be strong and resist her, even though it was becoming increasingly difficult to keep some sort of distance between them—how exactly was he supposed to resist when he was not only drawn to her, but in close proximity of her every moment of the day? If only she had consented to having a hand-maiden to travel with them and act as her companion.

He flicked his eyes to the heavy curtains that formed a partition, leading to the sleeping area of the chamber. As they were pulled back, Lady Isabel walked through.

'Good morrow, my lady.' He stood and inclined his head slightly. 'I hope you slept well and are ready to break your fast?'

'I did eventually, thank you, and, yes, I'm famished,' she said as she perched beside him.

'Come, I have procured food and Madame Forester is bringing up a small pot of hearty wild boar stew as well.'

'Thank you, that sounds delicious.' She took the plate from him and helped herself to the food.

They sat side by side eating quietly, the atmosphere a little strained. Will threw her brief sideways glances as he pushed the food around his plate. He was glad when the forester's wife knocked, bringing with her a hot steaming pot of stew and a couple of clean bowls and utensils.

'Our thanks, *madame*,' he muttered to the woman who dipped a curtsy before leaving the room.

'Here, allow me.' Isabel's fingers brushed against his as she grasped the pot and began spooning the stew into two bowls, handing one to him.

'This is delicious.'

'Yes.'

'Very warming.'

'Quite.'

They continued to eat until Isabel turned her head round. 'Will, is anything wrong?'

'Should there be, Lady Isabel?'

'No.' Her brows creased. 'And I thought we agreed to drop the formalities until we resumed our roles in England. Don't you remember, *Just Will*?'

He swallowed uncomfortably, feeling uneasy with the direction of this conversation. 'Yes, but you are not, nor shall you ever be, *Plain Isabel*, my lady.'

'Why ever not, for goodness sake?' she said on an exhale of barely suppressed annoyance. 'Is this because we kissed?'

Will almost choked back the contents in his mug.

How damned typical of the woman to get straight to the heart of their predicament.

'Isabel… Lady Isabel, I can only apologise for that, as it should not have happened. I'm honour bound to protect you and take you back to England. Anything beyond that crosses a boundary, which is why I had originally advised the need for a handmaiden to accompany us.'

She squirmed before putting her plate down and standing up. 'I believe you're thinking too much about it, Will. It was quite an extraordinary situation that we found ourselves in yesterday and the fact that we managed to get away so effectively from Rolleston's men made us feel huge relief and, well…that chaste kiss was possibly due to the euphoria we felt for getting away, do you not think?'

'Yes, but—'

'And as for your advice of a handmaiden, I thought we had agreed to that as well. I really do not want someone following my every move while we travel to England. There will be time enough for having many handmaidens and I'll be ready for it, but not…not just yet.'

He expelled the air he had been holding. 'Very well. As you wish.'

'In the meantime, I suggest we continue our progress as companionable friends.'

His lips twitched as he watched Isabel, her head tilted upwards, her hands clasped together, her back straight as she waited patiently for his response. She was showing glimmers of the woman she was destined to become—Lady Isabel de Clancey. His chest clenched as he reflected on this. Oh, yes, Isabel would fulfil that role wonderfully.

He stood and stretched out his hand. 'Very well, we shall go on as amiable friends.'

Her lips curled upwards as she placed her small hand in his, heat spreading from their joined hands throughout his body.

'And as an act of friendship, I think it my duty to inform you that you have got a little bit of stew on your chin.' She motioned with her finger. 'No, not there. Oh, allow me.' She licked her thumb and used it to wipe his chin as he stood there, unable to move, his eyes wide with disbelief and bemusement.

Friends, indeed... God help him!

Chapter Ten

They had left the Foresters' dwelling soon after they had finished their repast and purchased some much-needed provisions from the couple for their day's journey. The long day yawned on and the riding stretched as they travelled through woods and farmlands, until eventually they stopped for a quick respite alongside a brook, allowing the horses a drink and Will and Isabel to stretch their legs.

Will had been glad that the journey that day had not continued in the same vein as the conversation had that morning. That whole episode was a source of damned embarrassment, especially since he was still having entirely unacceptable thoughts about his *friend*. He had to apply discipline and cease thinking of Isabel as anyone other than who she was—a noble woman whom he was escorting back to England. But it was not easy. He snapped his head up and sighed deeply, watching Isabel splashing in the stream as she led her young palfrey to drink. She had taken off her boots and short hose, so Will was able to snatch glimpses of the pearly smooth skin of her ankles and feet.

'Are you quite sure that you do not want to join me, Will? The coolness of the water is very gratifying.'

Why was this woman insisting on driving him to distraction?

'Thank you, but, no. I will use my time to work industriously on my carving.'

He needed to do something other than to allow himself to ponder on her small ankles or the insteps of her slender feet.

God's breath, he needed to contain himself and these redundant feelings.

She splashed back towards the grassy verge and sat drying her feet on a strip of linen.

'I'll take your horse,' he said gruffly as he tethered the animal near his.

'Thank you, I have been wondering about Rolleston. Do you suppose we may encounter him again?'

'Not if I can help it, Isabel. But remember that if we do, we shall deal with his men as we did yesterday.'

'With the element of surprise.'

'Precisely.' He shook his head with a ghost of a smile. 'Again, I marvel at how you implemented that surprise. Without it we would never have got away.'

She smiled slowly. 'Oh, we both know that we got away due to your ingenuity, Will, but I shall accept your compliment all the same.'

'As I shall yours.' He grinned, returning her smile.

'In that case you must be right.' She shrugged. 'We do work well together.'

'Yes, we do,' he whispered. His eyes locked with hers momentarily and incredibly he could sense the warmth in them, but also veiled beneath there was sadness and uncertainty.

Damn!

He could drop a boulder on his head for his insensitivity in the way he had handled the delicate situation that morning, despite her nonchalant response. He had not only offended Isabel, but had also hurt her feelings.

Yet, he had to remain resolute. He had to protect her, even from himself. This morning's clarity between them was necessary for the remainder of their journey. However much he desired and longed for Isabel, she was not for him—a bastard son of a noble, a disgrace and a man responsible for the deaths of so many. He tore his eyes away in disgust at himself.

'That is why I need your help, Will,' Isabel said quietly.

He flicked his head up. 'I'm at your service, my lady…as always. What would you have me do?'

'Help me uncover the riddle of the unidentical pendants.'

'Ah, yes,' he said, welcoming the change of their discourse. 'In truth, I have been thinking about them.'

She tapped her fingertips absently against her lips. 'I must admit that this has been puzzling me all night, apart from that childish nightmare.'

'Nightmares are not childish, Isabel. They reveal underlying fears.' He grabbed the leather flagons from the mat, and strode to the stream, filling them up.

'It may, however, help me sleep better at night if I could only figure out the mystery behind the pendants—' she shook her head '—and unlock their secrets.'

'You do realise that they may not have any secrets to discover.' Will filled the last flagon with the crystal-clear water and stilled. He snapped his head in her direction, suddenly alert. '*What* did you just say?'

Her eyes widened, excitedly, as they met his. '*Unlock*…unlock…oh, my goodness, Will!'

'Exactly.' He nodded. 'The reason why they are almost identical, but the design is indented in exactly the same places…' He closed the gap back to her.

She smiled brilliantly. 'Is because they lock together.'

Will quickly took off his pendant from around his neck and Isabel fetched the other one from her satchel.

They each held a pendant in the palm of their hands, studying both intently.

Will rubbed his chin and stared in wonder. 'They are the perfect opposite to each other. Here, take this and try putting them together.' He dropped his pendant in her other hand.

Isabel slid the two pendants together, placing them on top of one another with the decorative design and gem locked together, making a single solid diamond-shaped jewel.

The thickness of the sides was that of a nail now, with a continued etched pattern, revealing some form of written characters.

'They fit together, just as we thought…but what now?' she asked.

'Try twisting it, so that they lock together.'

Isabel did as Will suggested, but the solid pendants didn't move, let alone twist in any direction that she tried. 'Mayhap they only fit together and that is all.'

'But that makes just as little sense as having them look identical, only to slot them together for no apparent reason.'

She ran her fingertips along the solid silver edge. 'Could it have something to do what is scribed on these sides?'

'Possibly.' He held out his hand. 'May I?'

Isabel moved to pass the pendants to him, but as his hand brushed hers, she accidentally dropped them. Will instinctively caught them mid-air and in doing so pressed the middle of the adjoined pendants. His eyes widened in surprise. 'Did you hear that, Isabel? They clicked in together when I pressed the centre.'

She beamed at him excitedly. 'Look at the side of the pendants. It's released an opening.'

Will ran his fingers across the silver edge of the locked pendants, as Isabel had only moments ago, but this time caught his fingers over the opening. 'There's something inside, but my fingers are too big to get it out.'

'Let me try.' Isabel pushed back the silver compartment that had jutted out a fraction and slid her finger inside, dragging out something soft. 'What on earth is this?'

Will picked it from her open hand and rolled and spread it out. 'It's a roll of velum,' he said, studying the contents. 'With strange marking and symbols on it.'

'I don't understand any of this.' She lifted her head. 'Do you have any notion of what these markings signify?'

'No, I'm afraid I don't.'

'So how are we to understand what they mean?'

Will's brows rose. 'Should we find out what they mean?'

'Yes!'

'If we go on some quest to find out what these markings signify, then we have more of a chance of running into Rolleston's men and, more importantly, we would delay in getting you back to England and back to your mother.'

'True, but think about it, Will. I believe that these

pendants are what motivates Rolleston and whomever he might work for in their pursuit of us. If we uncover its secrets, then we are closer to understanding the reasons for that and possibly the reasons for a lot more.'

'And what about your mother?'

'From what I remember of Mama, I believe she'll understand. Or rather, I hope she shall.'

He grimaced. 'We might be inviting unnecessary peril on a journey that is already far from running smoothly.'

She touched his sleeve. 'Please, Will...let me try to unravel this and understand what it might mean in relation to the past... To *my* past.'

'But you do realise that this is all supposition. It could end up meaning nothing.'

'Yes, but unless we try, we shall never know.'

'God, I know I'm going to regret this, but very well. If it is so important to you to uncover the truth about all of this, then we shall. But I want your word that you must accept whatever we find.'

'You have my agreement.'

'Come what may?'

'Yes.' She nodded. 'Come what may.'

'In that case, there is only one person I know who may be able to help us with this and, if not, may know someone who does.' He expelled a deep sigh. 'We shall divert the course of our journey to St Savinien.'

'Thank you, Will! You really are a true friend.'

He inclined his head a little, his eyes never leaving Isabel's. 'I'm happy to oblige.'

Chapter Eleven

They had made their way to St Savinien by sundown and wandered through the back streets, before reaching a single-storey grey stone dwelling—a presbyter on the outskirts of the village close. They had crossed the River Charente and arrived at a time when there was not a soul around. Even so, both Will and Isabel had donned dark cloaks with hoods to conceal their identities.

Will knocked on the arched wooden door, looking around in every direction before an old, balding man opened it tentatively.

'Yes, may I help you?'

Will pulled his hood down and smiled. 'I hope so, Father Gregor.'

'Saints above, if it's not William Geraint. What are you doing here? No, don't answer that! Come in, come in, my boy,' the old man said, as he ushered them inside.

'And who is your lady friend? Your wife, I assume. Blessings to you both.'

Isabel flushed as Will shook his head. 'No, Gregor, you know that I'm not a marrying man… Let me introduce you to Lady Isabel de Clancey, whom I am escorting back to England.'

'Ah, excuse the folly of an old man. I'm honoured, my lady. Please come within my humble abode. Come, come. You are more than welcome. I'll get the serving boy to take your horses to the stable round the side.'

After they relinquished their animals, Isabel and Will followed the old priest through a narrow hall and into a small, sparsely decorated parlour with a fire in the hearth and a few candle wicks lit and dotted around, giving the chamber a hazy glow.

'We're sorry to disturb your evening, Gregor.'

He waved his hand dismissively. 'Come, sit by the fire and rest. You must both be hungry. Here, it's not much fare, but you're welcome to share my evening meal.'

'Thank you, Father, but we have already eaten,' Isabel said.

'Well, in that case, let me fetch you some wine?'

'That we shall readily accept.'

They watched as the priest poured the dark red drink into three separate mugs, passing one to each of them.

'Our thanks, Gregor. Salute!'

'So—' the older man took a sip, and glanced from Will to Isabel '—to what do I owe this pleasure?'

'The truth is, Gregor, that we hoped you'd help us with something.'

'Happily, my boy. How can I be of service?'

'Well, Father Gregor,' Isabel said, 'recently we acquired something that neither Will nor I can decipher. It uses symbols that we cannot unravel.'

'And you thought to come to me?'

'I cannot think of any other scholar, philosopher or alchemist with the knowledge that you have, Gregor.'

'You put me to the blush, William. Allow me to see your manuscript.'

Isabel handed the vellum to the older man. 'Please do take a look.'

Father Gregor studied the vellum and the inscriptions on it, his eyes widening in shock. He snapped his head up. 'Where did the two of you come by this?'

'Never mind that, Gregor. Do you know what any of it means? From my limited knowledge I can see that there is more than one dialect inscribed here, plus these strange symbols.'

'Three to be exact—Aramaic, Hebrew and Greek—and the symbols are ancient Christian iconography.'

Isabel and Will exchanged a look of surprise.

'And do you understand what it says?' Will took a sip of wine.

'No, I'm afraid I don't. Although I can understand some of this, the rest…well, it is far too faint to fathom. I need a little more time to translate it and carefully decrypt it.'

Will grimaced and shook his head. 'Sadly, we don't have time, Gregor.'

'Then I'm not sure if I can help, William.'

Isabel gave Will a speaking look before turning to the priest. 'We're sorry to have troubled you, Father Gregor, but is there anything you can tell us about it? Anything at all?'

The old man glanced between them and sighed deeply, nodding his head.

'Very well, follow me.'

He hobbled to the far wall with floor-to-ceiling wooden shelving, containing a few items. He pushed the second shelf, making the whole length of the false shelf click and slide open. It was actually a door that revealed a secret passage, which Father Gregor motioned for them to walk through. He led them down the dark, narrow passage which twisted around a corner, eventually opening out to the most mesmerising chamber that Isabel had ever seen.

Her jaw dropped as she spun on her heel, taking in the square-shaped room filled with an astonishing array of curiosities. There were fascinating items pickled in various-sized jars, many scrolls of papyrus tumbled on top of each other, big tomes and strange-looking apparatuses and tools that were probably used for alchemy. Isabel walked around the chamber, her fingers grazing the surfaces, her eyes drinking it in, trying to commit this wonderful place to memory.

At least coming here, meeting the scholarly priest and seeing his marvellous chamber was a welcome relief from the tumultuous feelings she had about William Geraint.

Good grief!

The more time Isabel spent in his company, the more she felt the pull of attraction. She had told herself time and again that he was just an escort, a friend, but it was apparent that Will was more than that. When had that happened? When had all of these feelings begun? Was it when she caught sight of him on the back of his horse that her heart leapt, or when he smiled at her in that teasing way of his? When had the ground started shifting beneath her feet as he fixed his gaze at her?

Isabel must come to terms with these confusing emotions and concentrate on the other more pressing matters—like unravelling the mystery surrounding the two pendants and the vellum they had found hidden inside.

Father Gregor searched among the many scrolls on the coffer before fetching what he had been looking for, as well a huge tome. He summoned them to his side and turned to face them.

'Ah, here it is. Come, there are few things I want to show you.'

Will and Isabel flanked the older man as he spread out the scroll.

'Now, do you see this?' he said, pointing at a faint oval shape on its side with small tails at the end. 'Have either of you seen this before and know what it could possibly mean?'

'No but it looks a little like a fish.'

'Very good, my lady.' The older man nodded in approval. 'That is precisely what it is, five interconnecting Greek letters used by our brothers and sisters of the early church to symbolise Christ. That's what you have on your vellum, here and also here...do you see?'

'Yes, I do. What about these four—no, five...flowers grouped together?'

He nodded. 'They are roses, to symbolise the five wounds of Christ.'

'And what about this symbol?' Will asked, pointing at symbol in the shape of the letter 'X' with what looked like the letter 'P' in the centre, accompanied with the alpha and omega signs.

'This is mayhap the most interesting part, because these, too, are early symbols—used from the time of Emperor Constantine to mean the Cross.'

'And these tallies here?' There were five marks— one at the top, another at the bottom, one in the middle and one on the left and right side. 'If it wasn't for this mark in the middle, it would also look like the cross.'

'That's true, but sadly I do not know what it is in reference to.'

'What about this? Is this also a sign for the cross?' Isabel said, pointing at the larger round motifs at the top and bottom of the vellum.

Will exchanged a look with Father Gregor before giving a single decisive nod and turning to Isabel. 'That, my lady, is the Croix Celeste, the insignia of the Order of the Knights Templar.'

'Oh… I see,' Isabel said, digesting the information.

'And this, here, is the emblem of Acre.'

'Acre? In the Holy Lands?'

'Yes.' The old man sighed. 'When the Holy City of Jerusalem was lost a century ago, many important relics and artefacts were moved to Acre, with the Knights Templar as their custodians. However, what this has to do with your vellum, I do not know.'

'What would you suggest, Father?'

'You must go the Cour de la Commanderie—the Templars' base in La Rochelle,' Father Gregor said, holding up the vellum. 'They will, mayhap, assist with the translations quicker than I could and, more importantly, will be able to explain why their insignia is on this as well as the emblem of Acre.'

'Thank you, we must go there anyway.'

'Take heed, my lady. I cannot help feeling that what is written on the vellum could lead you to mortal danger.'

She covered his hands with hers and smiled solemnly. 'We shall and thank you again for everything, Father.'

They had set off at dawn. Even though Isabel had once more slept on a pallet and not on the lumpy ground, she'd had a fretful night's sleep, yet again. There was an ominous feeling the closer they got to La Rochelle, but she told herself it was nothing more than her imaginings. Father Gregor's revelations about the symbols were both unsettling and exciting, giving her hope that they were close to finding out the truth about the pendants, the message in the vellum and her past.

Yet she could not shake this uneasiness away.

On top of her feelings of restlessness, there was also the lingering awkwardness with Will. It made her all the more annoyed with herself when her gaze would constantly wander to him. Isabel must stop these silly, reckless and frankly ill-advised feelings for the man. It was futile.

'Is everything well, my lady?'

'Yes, of course,' she said, not able to meet his eyes.

'I am glad.' Will compressed his lips together. 'But you have barely said a word since we left St Savinien and that was a long while ago now.'

She didn't say anything.

'I hope nothing untoward is troubling you, Lady Isabel.'

'Thank you for your concern, but, no.' She smiled faintly. 'I have a lot on my mind, that's all.'

That was not all.

The growing tension between them as they made their way to La Rochelle made it difficult to continue as they had before. For all her assertions that they were only companionable friends travelling to England, Isabel could no longer pretend that it was not actually more. Yet it was better to deny and conceal her feelings. It was prudent to protect herself from getting too attached to anyone—least of all a complicated man like Will. After all, she'd relied on no one but herself for so long as everyone she had ever cared for always ended up letting her down. No, she couldn't allow anyone to get too close to her. Isabel should, instead, turn her thoughts to what they might find out in La Rochelle.

They rode along the River Charente, since Will believed it to be the best way to remain inconspicuous. The closer they got to the mouth of the sea, the wilder and more expansive the river became, with a rampant, tumbling noise as it gushed past. Strangely though, it was comforting, even though it was decidedly cooler beside the river. At least it filled the discomfiting silence.

'Are you ready to take a short respite, my lady?' Will asked quietly.

She sighed. 'Whatever you think is best, but I do hope we'll get to La Rochelle by eventide.'

'We'll get there earlier than that. I'm hoping to be there by twilight.'

Will brought his horse to a gradual stop and came around to help Isabel dismount. His hands wrapped around her waist as he brought her down easily and remained there, sparking a warmth throughout her body from where his fingers spread around her.

He realised that he was still holding her, removing his hands abruptly as though he had been burnt. Will moved away, tethering the horses to a nearby tree.

'And when do you believe we can see someone at the Templars' base?'

'If we get to La Rochelle early, then I don't see why we can't go there tonight, but otherwise in the morn.' He frowned slightly. 'The only thing I should say, Isabel, is that they will not allow a woman, even one of the nobility, to enter the Cour de la Commanderie, but we'll see once we get there what we can do.'

'You seem to know much about the Knights Templar?'

Will took a sip of water from his flagon and nodded. 'The Order certainly held a lot of appeal for a young, impressionable knight,' he said with a faraway look. 'My friend Hugh and I had always envisaged that it would be our calling one day. But it was not for him—not now that he is a married man with a family of his own.'

'Does it still hold an appeal for you?'

He leant back against a tree, his eyes pinned to the surging waters of the river as he answered. 'Yes—' he shrugged '—as long as they can overlook my past.'

Isabel's curiously got the better of her. 'What would they need to overlook?'

He said nothing, then, just when she was convinced that he was not going to respond, he spoke. 'Many things, Isabel…many things that I must atone for before I could even hope to be accepted.'

'That's what you'll do once you take me back to England, isn't it?'

'Yes.'

'Will?' She walked towards him. 'What would you need to atone for?'

She watched as his throat worked, his eyes not meeting hers.

'I'm afraid I am not the man you take me for. There are things that I have done, that I'm responsible for… things that I must seek penance for.'

'Is this what you were sent into exile for?'

'Sent into exile?' He laughed bitterly. 'I haven't been banished by the Crown, Isabel. Not any longer.'

'But I thought that—'

'You believed wrong. My exile in France for the last two years has been self-imposed.'

'But why would you do that?' She searched his eyes. 'What is it, Will?'

He pushed away from the tree, walking to the riverbank, his back to her as he picked up a pebble and flicked it across the surface of the river. 'The truth is that I should have known what would happen. I should have anticipated it.'

Isabel waited patiently for him to continue, knowing somehow that what he was relaying was incredibly painful. It made her aching heart go out to him, knowing he was confiding in her about his past.

'I was made the Sergeant and Commander of the garrison at Portchester Castle by King John...which was a great honour,' he said eventually. 'After the Rebel Barons, who had by then invited Louis of France not only to join their cause but also to lead them, captured Winchester Castle, I knew it would not be long before they turned their attention to us.' He picked up another pebble and swung it sideways, watching it dart across several times before it was swallowed up by the water.

'Portchester is a strategic castle used to defend the Solent and the sea that separates us from France. We were ready and waiting. What we weren't prepared for was trickery and dishonesty.' He spat, shaking his head in dismay.

'What happened?'

'I was invited for a parley in the nearby Forest of Bere. With my suspicions heightened, I should have known better, but I assumed I was dealing with honourable men.' He grimaced. 'It was the oldest trick, Isabel, and I, with all my experience as a damned soldier, fell for it.'

She moved slowly to stand beside him, watching the river run past, as he continued. 'By the time we made our way back, it was too late. The castle had been taken, but not before a huge amount of blood had been spilt unnecessarily.'

'I'm so sorry, Will.' She took his hand in hers.

'One could almost admire it—the whole thing being

so efficiently executed—if it wasn't for the fact that it was all so unconscionable and wholly dishonourable,' he said, clenching his jaw. 'You know, I had always been sympathetic to the Rebels' cause, but not after that blood-sodden summer's eve. Not after what I witnessed.'

'I can understand.'

'Can you?' he asked softly. 'Because I never could. Not with the damn conflict tearing the kingdom apart—tearing families and friends apart.'

'And that is when you went into self-exile?'

'No, initially King John served the banishment himself, but after his death, after I…well, let us just say that the work I did gaining information led to the Crown's victory at the Battle of Lincoln. I was given a full pardon by William Marshal.'

'And yet you decided to remain in exile.'

'Yes,' he whispered.

'Because you blamed yourself for what happened?'

'How could I not, Isabel?' he said indignantly. 'I lost control of the castle, lost control of the keep. All those knights, villagers—they were all under my protection, were my responsibility, and I failed. Yes, the blame lies with me and me alone.'

'But if you've received a full pardon, by the Lord Protector himself, then why would you continue to repudiate that decision?'

'Because I could never forget what happened. I could never absolve myself from my failings on that day, Isabel.' He turned, facing her. 'I deserve to be in exile. Frankly I deserve far more than just banishment.'

'I see. And you believe that punishing yourself with this self-flagellation might somehow lessen the pain?'

Will stared down at their joined hands as if he had

only just noticed them entwined that instant. He lifted her hand and turned it round slowly, fanning open her fingers one by one and gently brushing his callused fingers along the open palm, up the length of each finger and back down again, reaching her wrist before caressing the sensitive skin there.

'Nothing would lessen that, Isabel,' he whispered as he met her stunned gaze, letting go of her hand. 'Nothing ever could.'

'But…'

'If you're ready, my lady, we should continue to La Rochelle.'

Chapter Twelve

They reached the bustling port town of La Rochelle by nightfall as Will had predicted they would and entered the walled citadel with caution. Concealed under their woollen hooded cloaks, they wandered through narrow cobbled streets with rows of white sandstone dwellings packed on either side, shielding them from the brisk breeze. A smell of the sea, mixed with the sweat and toil of ship workers, sailors and merchants as well as the musty smell of the port, wafted through. The chipped, weather-beaten shutters of the dwellings were closed despite the few stray revellers from the quayside. Will grabbed Isabel's hand as she stumbled and nearly fell, placing his arm around her waist, guiding her forward. 'You need to rest and take some sustenance, otherwise where will we be?' His voice was muffled under his cloak.

'Closer to where we need to be.' She tilted her head up to peer at him from under her hood. 'Please let's not halt our progress on my account, I'm perfectly well.'

'We have enough time, Isabel, and anyway I'm famished, even if you're not. Come, let's find somewhere discreet where we can have some repast and confer about what we need to do next.'

They entered a small tavern on the corner, set slightly apart from the harbour which was bursting with carousers.

Isabel threw him a sideways glance. 'I thought you wanted to go somewhere discreet.'

'We might be more inconspicuous and well hidden somewhere as busy as this.'

They secured a small table in the furthest corner out of view of the door. Will made sure that Isabel was sat on a stool with her back to the busy tavern, hiding her in a place crowded with mainly only men.

He sighed, dragging his hand through his hair and wondering why he had suggested Isabel dress in a few items of his clothing. It was a good notion to pass her off as his young squire so that they could blend in and avoid being noticed, but when Will looked her up and down properly for the first time since she had changed her clothing, he felt his loins tighten uncomfortably. The thought of those long lean limbs encased in *his* braes and hose caused another wave of frustrated longing in him.

Damn!

The reason for her to dissemble was a good one, but the effect it had on him was not.

Not only that, but for some unknown reason Will had unburdened his shame to Isabel and earned her pity. No…not quite *that,* but certainly gained her understanding. What he had told her about his past should have earned him her censure, not her empathy, but then Isabel was like no other woman he had ever met before.

'Wait here while I get a jug of wine and whatever food this place might serve,' he said quietly. 'Don't make eye contact with anyone and try behaving and sitting a little more like a man.'

'What…what do you mean?'

'Slouch a bit more, look stoutly…that's it.' Will took in her appearance, knowing that her hair was tightly bound and hidden underneath the hood. He leaned in and tugged it forward more. 'And sit with your legs apart, rather than that dainty, feminine way you're sitting.'

'Dainty?' Confusion etched on her forehead.

His lips twitched at the corners. 'Try for a masculine stance, Isabel, otherwise you shall not fool anyone.'

She widened her legs, making him swallow with difficulty, his mouth suddenly dry, annoyed that he couldn't seem to tear his eyes away from her.

'Better?'

'Yes,' he said, gruffly. 'Don't go anywhere.'

Will ordered food, glad that he was doing something rather than think about Isabel's long legs. Returning with a jug of wine, he sloshed a measure into one mug and then another, pressing one into her hand. 'The Rochelais certainly know how to make excellent wine… but easy, Isabel. Sip slowly.'

'Are you afraid that I might become as inebriated as I did that first night?'

Will couldn't see her expression concealed under the hood, but her voice was laced with amusement.

He shrugged. 'Or worse still, succumb to another uncontrollable bout of hiccups.'

Her shoulders rose up and down as she shook her head, chuckling softly. It made his own lips curve upwards in response.

'I would be careful, Sir William, since you know

that I'm masterful in the art of punching a man in his unmentionables and crushing plums.'

'Duly noted,' he said, finding it hard to contain his laughter. 'I could never contradict that, my lady, especially after your valiant display in La Rochefoucauld.'

Their shared laughter was a welcome respite in more ways than one since the last few days had been mired with the difficult tension growing between them.

A tavern maid set down a pot of steaming hot fish stew, bowls, utensils and a plate of bread and local butter. Isabel dished some into each bowl and passed one to him. They were silent for a moment as they both tucked into the food.

'Do you still suppose that there is danger here?' Isabel asked.

'Absolutely.' Will nodded grimly. 'Rolleston and his men know that it would be from La Rochelle that we would depart for England. They will be everywhere, especially near the port.' His eyes darted around the busy tavern. 'And that's why we need to be extremely careful while we're here. The longer we stay here, the more the chances of danger.'

'It's a good job that I pass so easily as a young boy, then.'

He almost choked on his food. 'Finish up, Isabel. We can't linger here for too long.'

They made their way along the cramped lanes, taking the shortest, yet quietest, route to the Cour de la Commanderie. Will slid her a sideways glance.

'What are you doing, Isabel?'

'Shouldn't you call me Alain or something?' she hissed from the side of her mouth. 'Anyway, I'm doing precisely as you advised. I'm trying for a masculine stance, remember. I'm trying for bluster and a little swagger.'

'Is that what that is?' Will's eyes gleamed with amusement. 'Your swagger is certainly different to anything I have ever seen.'

'Yes, but I am only a squire, sir.' She glanced up and bit her bottom lip. 'I'm still perfecting my blustering and swaggering to the standard required from a squire.'

'And doing an admirable job.'

'My thanks, but I do have the most patient knight to direct me.' Isabel looked up and saw the smile vanish from Will's lips as he uttered an oath under his breath. 'What is it?' she asked, instantly alert.

'I cannot be sure, but I believe that I saw the pock-faced man turn into this road.'

She halted. 'Shall we turn back?'

'No,' he muttered from under his hood. 'Keep walking and keep your head downcast. Remember you're a squire and doing rather well, especially with your swagger.'

Isabel knew that he was trying to put her at ease, but the situation was suddenly more precarious than it was just moments ago. The air was charged with an uncertain, menacing quality evoking darkness and danger. And it enveloped her. She clenched her clammy hands as she strode along beside Will, her heart hammering in her chest as they walked past the pock-faced man. Everything seemed to slow at that precise moment when they passed him. The man turned his head slightly and took note of the two of them, a small scowl mapped on his face.

'Keep moving quickly, but do not run. Not unless we're forced to,' Will's calm, low voice rumbled beside her after they had passed the man.

They turned a corner and went into another smaller lane, but again there was a lone man walking, looking scrupulously at everything and everyone. Before they could pass him by, Will guided her down the next road, bringing them to a junction. He dragged her left, down a wider, busier path and milled their way through before taking another left-hand turn.

'Do you know where we are going?' she panted.

'All that matters for now is to rid ourselves of the clutches of Rolleston's damned men,' he said through gritted teeth. 'Don't look now, Isabel, but we're being followed.'

'What are we to do?' She couldn't seem to hide the panic in her voice.

'Steady now,' he said evenly. 'We carry on as before… but with a little more urgency.'

They turned the corner down the next cobbled road, backtracked and went straight ahead, hidden among a group of boisterous sailors. Will crouched low as he was the tallest man among them, but just as they passed a doorway Will hurled her sideways into the dark recess.

'Apologies, my lady,' he whispered.

'What is this fascination of yours with arched doorways?'

Will nudged her gently, until she was backed against the door. 'Hush, Isabel.' He placed a finger to her lips, as she looked up, blinking in the darkness. Oh, dear… how close he was to her. They shared the same small space, even the same air. He jostled his big, hard, protective body close until there was no room left, until he was pressed against her, circling his free arm around her, holding on to her.

She watched in fascination as his chest rose and fell and a sense of momentary calm prevailed as she stood ever so still in Will's arms. Even though, in truth, there was little to feel safe about.

'Do you think they'll find us?' she asked quietly against his finger still on her lips, but his only answer was a slight frown and a quick shake of his head.

She snapped her head up. 'Did you hear that, Will?
'Hush.'

'Yes, but I think it may be footsteps, I think that it could—'

Isabel didn't get to finish what she was saying as Will let out an irritable breath before bending his head and catching her lips with his. Her eyes widened in surprise at being kissed at such a moment and in such a place as this. Isabel knew instantly that this was one way to shut off her nervous chatter. And yet, and yet...

William Geraint was kissing her! And although it was meant only to silence her, it gradually changed and softened with an altogether different fervour.

His lips slanted across hers, shaping them, in feather-light kisses before pressing with a little more pressure. He slid one hand up her back, tugging down her hood and cradling her head round the back, his fingers sinking into her hair while the other hand moved up and down the column of her neck, his fingers and thumb grazing her skin. His lips probed a little more, making her gasp against his mouth. A spark of potent heat was rising in her body and running through her veins...an unstoppable, heady desire.

Will's lips touched the corner of hers, as he tilted her head to press hot kisses along her jawline and down the curve of her neck, his breath so warm against her skin that it made her quiver in his arms, hopelessly clinging on to him. He returned to her mouth, coaxing her lips apart as she felt the surprising touch of his tongue.

He explored her mouth gently, as if he was tasting her, with tender, probing strokes. And then once again with deep, lush caresses. Nothing seemed to exist except this kiss, except them.

It was a good thing that Will had his strong arms clasped around her, as Isabel could quite easily have melted into a boneless puddle at his feet. A needy moan caught in her throat and just when she felt brave enough to copy him tentatively, Will tore his lips from hers, finishing the kiss with a few light brushes on her lips.

He pulled back, staring at her almost in shock, his breathing ragged, their faces still so close. Even in the dark recess of the doorway, Isabel could see his eyes blazing brightly. She touched her inflamed lips with a trembling finger, already missing his touch, and shuddered. He silently urged her to remain quiet, not that she could speak, or move.

She turned her head then, suddenly alert to noises nearby. Her heart was pounding so fast and so loudly, that she wondered whether anyone could hear it.

'I think someone is coming.' Isabel was shaking in his arms, but wasn't certain whether it was from Will's heart-stopping kiss or the fact that Rolleston's men might be close by.

His hand went up and down her back, soothing her gently, and his lips rested against her forehead. 'Hush, Isabel.'

Was it her imagination that she felt something move against her on the ground? Isabel pulled away slightly. 'What was that?' she murmured quietly. 'There's something at my feet…oh, God Will, is it a rat?'

'No,' he said hoarsely against her forehead. 'It's a small dog, sniffing around for food. Easy now.'

'Oh…' she said with the faintest of whispers.

There were soft footsteps treading back along the pathway that came to a halt, somewhere nearby, it seemed, to where they were hidden in the wide doorway. Isabel covered her mouth with her own hand to stop from making even the slightest noise. Her eyes widened as she looked up at Will in silent question, wondering what on earth they would do if they were discovered. Whatever it was, though, Isabel had total faith in this man who held her, protected her, against any adversary who wished them harm.

But it never came to pass, as the little dog scampering about their feet started to bark, relentlessly making whoever had been there to walk away. After a long moment, Isabel exhaled in relief. She crouched down and fetched a few scraps of dried meat from her satchel, holding them out in her hands.

'Thank you for your help, little one,' she said, patting the small dog. It wolfed down the food eagerly and tilted its head as if studying her, panting with its tongue hanging out, wagging its tail.

'I believe you've made a friend there.' Will poked his head out of the doorway and looked in both directions.

'It would seem so,' she said, blinking as she walked out of the dark doorway, her heart still pounding after everything that had just happened.

'Come.' Will grabbed her hand, rushing in long strides down the path. 'Time to go.'

It had grown dark. Thankfully, Will and Isabel had not encountered Rolleston's men, but they were still vigilant as they made their way through the cobbled maze of La Rochelle with the small black and white dog in tow. They skirted around the gleaming white Vauclair Castle and down one street and then another, eventually walking down a quiet road that led to a large, yet inconspicuous grey building. It seemed incredible to believe that this was the main headquarters of the Templars.

The ordinary exterior looking out on the road was a far cry from the inner sanctity of the Cour de la Commanderie that somehow seemed to emanate great power and wealth despite being shrouded under a hidden façade. Isabel couldn't help but gasp as they were admitted from a dark hall that opened out on to a courtyard with the emblem of the Templars Cross emblazoned in the centre using muted coloured mosaics. They walked through a cloistered walkway that edged the courtyard and were taken into a small chamber to wait for the Templar Knight Father Gregor had recommended that they meet.

Will paced the room restlessly with his hands behind his back, unable to meet her gaze. She watched him with growing impatience. 'Is anything the matter?'

'Nothing, my lady.' He stopped and flicked his brooding gaze at her for the first time since they had left the dark doorway—since the kiss.

Ah… She closed her eyes momentarily realising that it was the was kiss itself that troubled him. '

'That is to say, Lady Isabel, that…well, I must offer my apolog—'

'Don't you dare apologise for the kiss, Will. I shall not allow, or accept, it!'

He baulked, running his hands through his hair. 'But I took advantage of the situation we were in and—'

She tilted her head high and straightened her spine. 'You did no such thing! I'd say that it was a very fine, very acceptable kiss, but when all is said and done, it was just a kiss.'

He spun on his heel to face her. 'What do you mean just a kiss?'

She shrugged. 'I admit that I'm not a great connoisseur of such things, but let's not make too much of it, shall we?'

Will regarded her with an incredulous look, as if he were insulted by her nonchalance. But she would rather die a thousand deaths than admit how his earth-shattering kiss had affected her to the core.

'In truth, it was rather a delightful diversion, while we threw Rolleston's men off our scent,' she embellished.

She felt a twinge of pain, uttering such ridiculous lies. But Isabel knew that it was better to utter such falsehoods than admit her growing feelings for Will when nothing could ever come of it. Some lies were necessary, especially when it safeguarded her heart.

'Is that so?' Will stared at her with the ghost of a smile on his lips.

'Yes…well done for thinking of it.'

Will arched a brow. 'I'm glad to be of service.'

'Oh, the pleasure was all mine.'

Just then the door creaked open, admitting an elderly man wearing a plain tunic with a long white surcoat over it. He looked reserved as he nodded at Will and then widened his eyes when he turned to Isabel, realising that a woman had entered the hallowed domain of the Templars.

William pushed forward and inclined his head briefly. 'Sir Phillippe de Sens, we're happy to make your acquaintance. Please allow me to introduce Lady Isabel de Clancey.'

'My lady.' The old man bowed as he turned on his heel to face Will. 'This is most irregular, Sir William

Geraint. You must know that women are not permitted within these walls, even esteemed ladies, such as Lady de Clancey—posing, I see, as a young man.'

'We apologise for our shortcomings, Sir Phillippe, and we mean no offence by flouting your rules,' Will said. 'But we had to meet you as a matter of great urgency and, as explained to your man earlier, you were highly recommended by Father Gregor de Savinien.' Will held out the vellum. 'There is something that we need your aid with.'

The old man looked from one to the other, ready in his protest, but it seemed Will had piqued his interest. 'Oh, and what has Gregor requested from me this time?'

'This is our request, not his,' Will said. 'We need your help to decipher the meaning of this, if you would care to take a look.'

The older man regarded Will with indignance before taking the vellum reluctantly. But as his eyes scanned the contents, they became wary, if not agitated. 'Where did you get this, Sir William?'

'That's of no importance, Sir Phillipe. What we are seeking is the meaning behind it all. Can you help us?'

The old man flicked his gaze from Will to Isabel and rubbed his pointy chin, seemingly weighing up something. Isabel had the distinct feeling that the old man was holding back, wondering whether he should disclose whatever it was that he knew.

'Please, Sir Phillippe, this is of great importance to me and my family,' she murmured. 'We would recompense you for your troubles.'

'If what I believe this vellum alludes to is true,' the old man whispered more to himself than either Will nor Isabel, 'it is not something that can be measured by anything of earthly value.'

'I don't understand, sir, what do you mean?' Isabel's brows furrowed in confusion. 'What can it be measured in, then?'

The old man opened his mouth to say something, when suddenly they heard a noise from outside the chamber, startling them.

Phillippe de Sens turned and faced Isabel, bridled with a new urgency. 'Not here, my lady,' he whispered. 'Leave the vellum with me for a closer look, then we can rendezvous elsewhere and discuss everything in due course.'

'Sir Phillipe,' Will said, shaking his head. 'That is not a good idea. Even now we compromise our safety being here.'

'As you compromise mine,' he retorted, before rubbing his forehead and closing his eyes. 'I'm sorry, it's all I can offer you.'

Isabel gave Will a pleading look as he acquiesced. 'Very well, where do you want to meet?'

'As well as my work here, I'm the Sergeant at the Tour de la Lanterne, by the port. Do you know it?'

'I do. When can we meet you?'

The old man lifted his head. 'The Compline prayers are the last of the day with the resounding ring of church bells as a reminder,' he said, tapping his fingers together in contemplation. 'I will unlock the Tower to let you in just after that.'

After a moment Will sighed and made a single nod. 'Very well, we shall see you there later tonight.'

'Until later, Sir William,' The old man inclined his head. 'My lady.'

He waited patiently as the two young people left the chamber and exhaled in relief. Slowly he approached the hearth and stood over it, staring at the fire before throwing the piece of vellum into it. He watched as the flames licked around the edges, making it twist and curl on itself, emitting a rancid black smoke. Once he was satisfied that the vellum was destroyed, he left the chamber.

Chapter Thirteen

Hell's teeth!

The whole damn evening was proving far more perilous then Will had first anticipated and now they had to
wait undetected until they could meet Phillippe de Sens
later. It was already difficult to navigate the town without alerting their presence to Rolleston's men, but he
had little choice in the matter. And while they waited, he
had time to reflect on the fact that he had finally given
into his baser instinct and kissed Isabel—thoroughly.

Initially, it had been a way to ease Isabel's anxious-
ness, but it hadn't taken long before it changed into
something very different entirely.

Damn!

His whole body had come alive with need and desperate longing, pressed against her glorious curves as
he tasted her lips, learning the softness of her mouth.
Even now, the after-effects hummed through his body.
He groaned inwardly at his foolishness.

He wanted Isabel with such intensity that it made
his head spin. Yet he shouldn't want her and certainly
couldn't have her. And although he had had a momen-

tary lapse earlier, he must take care not to succumb to his desires again.

It wouldn't be fair to Isabel or to himself.

He smiled absently at Isabel's aloofness and her detached tone earlier when he had wanted to apologise. She had tried to make nothing of it, even though they both knew differently. The truth was that, however unwise it had been kissing Isabel, he could not regret it. Yet Will had to make sure that it never happened again.

He sighed as he glanced at Isabel who was crouched low, feeding the scruffy little dog that had attached himself to her. 'If you keep feeding the little scamp, we're never going to get rid of him.'

'Ah but he's hungry and lost, Will,' she said, patting him. 'And after the way he helped us earlier I feel a sense of gratitude towards him.'

'For all you know it may be totally infested with fleas.'

'I've already checked and, no, he isn't.' She picked up the dog by its front paws. 'Yes, that's right…who's a good boy? Now, what are we going to call you?'

'Oh, good grief!' Will muttered, shaking his head. 'Come, we must keep moving.'

'What about *Rochelais,* since you came upon us here? But, no, I think not.' She tapped her fingertips together. 'Like me, little one, you could have come from somewhere entirely different, belonging nowhere and to no one in particular.'

Will's throat constricted tightly at Isabel's pensive words, revealing much about how she still felt.

'What about *Perdu*?' she said and the dog barked, wagging its tail enthusiastically. 'Very well, Perdu it is and I'm very pleased to make your acquaintance.' She gave dog another scrap of food before standing up

and meeting Will's bemused gaze at calling the dog…
'Lost'. She no doubt hoped the little mite might some-
day be found.

They continued walking side by side in silence, with
the little dog following behind.

Will flicked her a quick glance. 'Isabel, about what
we were discussing—I just want to say that, although
I was going to apologise earlier, I'm not sorry I kissed
you.' He could see a flush rise on her neck and cheeks.

'And as I said before, it was a good ruse,' she said
shrugging, as though she were describing something
inconsequential.

'It may have been initially, but it certainly didn't
end that way.'

'If you're trying to say that you enjoyed it, Will, then
let's say that I did as well and leave it at that.'

He stopped in his tracks abruptly. 'You're right. I
did.' He dragged his fingers through his hair before
continuing. 'But nothing could ever come of it, Isabel.'

'I didn't say anything would.' She straightened her
spine and continued to walk away. Will watched her as
a dull ache spread in his chest. He shook his head and
caught up with her.

They descended into a silence which Isabel broke,
eventually.

'Do you not think it strange that Rolleston's men
seem to have disappeared?'

He threw a glance behind them before turning
around. 'Yes, but then we never did actually see any
of them.'

'What of the men who were following us and the
pock-faced man you thought you saw?'

He nodded. 'I believe I did.'

'Good, because if you didn't, you kissed me under

false pretences, William Geraint,' she said in feigned outrage.

A slow smile spread on his lips. 'But you forget—I am a rogue knight after all.'

'And there I was, thinking that you had gallantry and valour coursing through your veins.'

'No, those epithets belong to another.' He chuckled softly. 'In all seriousness, though, I do believe it was his men, Isabel.'

'Yet they seemed to have disappeared—' she clicked her fingers '—just like that.'

'Yes,' he muttered, glad of the change of their discourse. 'But we be must be ready for any eventuality.'

'As always, Will. As always.'

He smiled despite himself. If anyone had courage and bravery *coursing through their veins* it was the beautiful woman by his side who was warm, witty and intelligent, as well.

Just then the church bells tolled, reminding them both of why they had been aimlessly ambling through the myriad of backstreets. Soon they'd meet with the old Templar Knight and find out whether he had the information they sought.

They made their way to the agreed meeting place, bringing them directly to the port side closest to the Tour de la Lanterne, a tall, grey, singular tower built only a handful of years before with crenulations around the edge topped with a steep conical spire.

The port was deserted by the time Will and Isabel grappled with the iron gate of the tower. It led to the heavy wooden door that had been left open, as Phillippe de Sens had promised. They slowly crept up the dank, spiral staircase, taking care not to misstep on the jagged, uneven stones as they made their way up. Streaks of moonlight poured through a few small square windows, providing the only source of light. An eerie, ominous undertone hung in the air. Catching his breath as they made their way to the top, Will pushed open the creaky wooden door with a foreboding sense of uneasiness. The hairs on the back of his arms rose. Something was very wrong here.

He entered the room slowly, with Isabel behind and the little dog pushing through to the front. Their four-legged friend began to sniff the wooden floor before beginning to bark and growl at something behind the door.

Everything happened quickly then. Will pushed Isabel behind him and stepped forward just as someone leapt from behind the door, ready to attack, jabbing a weapon in the air. His attack would have been devastating had it not been for the little dog, who had attached himself to the man's ankle as Will and Isabel darted out of the way. Shaking the animal off, the unknown assailant rushed forward to the doorway, which was now clear, and scrambled out of the chamber. Will was about to follow the man when Isabel called out to him.

His heart hammered in his chest, drowning out her voice. 'What did you say?'

'It's Sir Phillipe de Sens.' She crouched down beside a man sprawled flat on his back on the floor. 'He's been stabbed.'

Will rushed over to the other side of the circular chamber and crouched down beside the old man, taking note of the blood seeping on to the floor. Gasping for breath, the old man beckoned Will close and whispered his last words to him. They spoke for a short time before the older man pressed two coins into Will's hand, taking one last gulp of air. Isabel looked on in abject horror as the man went motionless, his eyes half closed.

'Oh, God…oh, God,' she cried, covering her mouth with a shaking hand. 'He's dead, isn't he? And it's all my fault.'

Will knew they had to act fast—they could not stay here. 'Come, Isabel, we have to go.'

He practically dragged her out, clambering down the spiral staircase they had climbed only moments ago.

Somehow, they made their way back through the backroads of La Rochelle until they reached Cour de la Commanderie and miraculously they managed to arrive expediently, without notice. Isabel had been glad that Will had taken charge when they were ushered into an antechamber to speak with one of Sir Phillippe's brethren. She stood still with her back straight, barely taking anything in as Will spoke quietly to the man, informing him of the old Templar's demise and his last words.

She vaguely noticed Will present the coins that Sir Phillippe had given him along with the murmur of the secret message to this man—this other Templar Knight—who responded with a single nod. Words and agreements passed between them and before Isabel knew what was happening, they were led through a dark hallway and then into a series of chambers, until they were once again outside, walking through the ornate cloister that led to the chapterhouse. With her hood lowered over her head she walked a little behind Will and the Templar Knight with the little dog, Perdu, beside her.

Here, they were shown into a small, inconspicuous chamber that held miscellaneous objects and scrolls. Once inside, the Templar Knight, with Will's help, moved a few bits of the furniture out of the way and rolled up the vibrantly coloured rug, uncovering a trap-door. Will opened this, revealing a spiral staircase leading to the shadowy darkness beneath.

Isabel blinked, as though roused from a deep sleep, realising that they were leaving the Templar headquarters differently to the way in which they had arrived.

'We need to go, Isabel.' Will exchanged a few more words with the Templar Knight and grabbed the flaming torch that he held out for them.

'I don't understand.' She frowned. 'Where are we going now?'

He held out his hands to her. 'Come, my lady, I'll explain on the way.'

Isabel clasped Will's hand as he guided them carefully down the slippery spiral staircase. She picked the little dog up and continued to descend further and further down until they reached the bottom. Setting Perdu on the ground, Isabel darted her gaze all around in surprise with what she saw—a large and well-constructed secret tunnel, complete with metal sconces holding unlit torches.

'Well, are you going to tell me why we are leaving this way?'

'It was the safest way to get out of the Templar headquarters without then being followed.' Will lit the torches as they went along. 'I believe that danger is too close and I just couldn't take that chance.'

For that old Templar, it had been fatally close. She shook her head sadly. 'I take it that Sir Phillippe was the one who advised us to come here. That's what he told you before he died?'

Will lit the torch in the metal sconce, made from

packed rushes, bound with hessian. 'Yes, I believe he wanted to help protect us.'

Dear God, that made Isabel feel even worse. The fact that Sir Phillippe would be thinking about their safety as he lay dying made her feel even more culpable for his death. It all made her feel even more disgusted with herself.

She suddenly realised another thing. 'On top of the poor man's death, the vellum is now lost—mayhap for ever.'

'I doubt that.'

'Do you think that Rolleston's men have it?' she muttered under her breath.

'No, Isabel. Phillippe de Sens was not as foolish as to bring it to the rendezvous.'

Confused, she grasped the edge of his sleeve, giving it a little tug. 'How do you know?'

'Because he told me.' Will stopped for a moment, turning to meet her eyes. 'He...destroyed the vellum.'

'What?' Isabel's jaw dropped. 'Why...why would he do that?'

'That he did not say, but before he died he made a bargain with me.'

Oh, Lord... Isabel did not like the sound of this. 'Go on.'

'He made me promise that if we do something for him than he would ensure our safe passage to England using the Templars' vast influence, not to mention their fleet of ships, anchored right here in La Rochelle.'

'What did you promise him, Will?' she said slowly.

'That if we ever were to find whatever the vellum alluded to—' he swallowed '—we would hand it over to the Templars.'

'What? You had no right to do that without asking me.'

'I didn't have the time to negotiate properly. The man was dying, Isabel…and needed some guarantee. I gave it to him by swearing on my sword.'

'But why would he—?'

'Whatever *this* is, means nothing, if I cannot ensure your safety.' He moved closer, resting his forehead against hers, making her feel close to tears. 'I'd make the same decision a thousand times again to ensure that. It's all that matters to me.'

'Oh…' she whispered, feeling as though something was stuck in her throat.

He nodded, seemingly unable to say anything as well. After a long moment, he exhaled and grabbed her hand. 'Come, we need to go.'

Isabel pulled his arm. 'Where are we going?'

'This should eventually lead to a safe haven. And tomorrow, God willing, we'll leave this blasted port for England.'

'You're right.' Isabel sighed deeply. 'In the end that's all that matters,'

'Exactly.'

'And in any case, I cannot imagine what this treasure could be, for it to be more valuable than silver and ruby pendants.'

'Something of far greater value to men like Rolleston and the Templars.'

'Well, whatever it is, it seems the secrets of the vellum have died with Sir Phillippe.'

'Possibly…' He slid her a glance. 'But we know more than you realise. The question, however, is whether we want to keep digging for it.'

'I don't know, right now,' she said with a frown, suddenly weary. 'But thank you…for everything.'

He gave her hand a squeeze. 'Come, we must go.'

Chapter Fourteen

They walked the remainder of the long passage in silence, both absorbed in their reflections on the night that had just passed.

It had been a turbulent night of extreme emotions, from the apprehensive excitement of their arrival, the chase through La Rochelle to that scorching kiss. But it had all given way to disaster and no matter how Isabel looked at it, she knew in the depth of her soul that the fault lay with her. If she hadn't insisted that they go on the quest to find out the mystery of what was inscribed on that vellum, the Templar Knight—Sir Phillippe de Sens—would still be alive.

The tunnel came to an abrupt end and once again they had to climb the lengthy, steep spiral staircase to reach another trapdoor. Will pushed it above his head and jumped up, reaching down to pull Isabel out and on to a cold stone surface.

They were inside an interior very different to the austere opulence they had left behind.

Blinking, Isabel adjusted to the dim light, looking round, taking in the small chamber. Will clasped her hand, just as a stout man, who had obviously been awaiting their arrival, opened the door and ushered them outside.

Will pressed a Templar coin into his palm. 'We received word, Sir William, that you and your companion would be arriving.'

'That was quick.' Will raised a brow. 'And who may you be?'

'You do not need to know who I am and, yes, we have our ways,' the man said. 'Now, if you'd follow me. We have made arrangements for you to stay somewhere no one can find you. Come along if you please.'

Isabel was ready to drop by the time they had reached the remote ramshackle wooden dwelling outside the town walls. They didn't have long—only a few hours to sleep—before the break of dawn and before their nameless guide would return to take them back to the port at La Rochelle.

Isabel looked around the small, well-appointed chamber. There were a few pallet beds arranged side by side, a hearth with a trestle table nearby with a few plates and mugs resting on top, as well as a few stools and a bench arranged around it. It certainly gave the impression of a room that had in previous times been used for surreptitious meetings by Templars and their associates.

It seemed incredible that they had gone to this much trouble, to give this much assistance to them. Yet Will had made an honour-bound oath with Sir Phillippe. A promissory pledge that would guarantee their safety in return for something that now seemed out of their reach.

Every time Isabel thought about the old Templar Knight, a knot would coil and tighten in her stomach. Her vain attempt at finding out about the secrets hinted

ated want to take away this burden of pain and replace it with pleasure.

She watched the powerful muscles of his chest rise and fall rapidly, his eyes glittering with unbridled emotion before he swept down, covering her mouth with his own. This time he kissed her with so much desperate need and intensity that Isabel felt her knees might buckle under her.

His large hands circled her waist, pulling her closer until she was pressed against the wall of his large body, her hands resting on his shoulders, feeling the tension beneath her fingers. His lips slanted over hers, his tongue pushing through her lips, inciting a moan from her mouth. Isabel followed his lead as their breaths merged together, their tongues tangling.

Dear God, what was happening to her?

Will lifted Isabel, kissing and devouring her mouth, before gently laying her down on the pallet. He nibbled the corners of her lips, his calloused fingers grazing up her neck, then diving into her hair before tilting her jaw upwards to gain better access to kiss, nip and taste the smooth tender skin there and down the column of her neck. He teased the opening of the linen tunic down using his teeth, his fingers touching and caressing her exposed skin. He moved back to her lips, pressing hot kisses a few more times before pulling away.

'Isabel… We have to stop.'

'No,' she mumbled, pulling him down, fastening her lips to his, kissing him deeply. 'We really don't.'

She loved the taste of him…

'You need sleep.' His voice was hoarse, ragged even.

'I don't…' She needed much more than sleep. She needed him, needed this closeness, needed the touch of

at on the vellum had led to Sir Phillippe's violent death and it was all her fault. Will had tried to warn her, but she hadn't listened…

'Why don't you rest for a while, Isabel?' Will's voice pierced through the bleakness of her mind.

'Not yet.' She lifted her head and swallowed, meeting his eyes. 'I've thought about what you said, Will, and you're right—it was always too dangerous.'

'Isabel…' He reached out for her.

'It's finished, it's over, I don't care about the vellum…but that poor man… I wish I had listened to you Will. We should never have gone down this perilous path.'

'You were not to know.'

The knot in the pit of her stomach was guilt and hopeless despair and it threatened to consume her. 'No, but you did warn me.'

'You mustn't blame yourself.'

'Who should I blame when it lies with me and me alone?' She gulped. 'The man would be alive if it weren't for me.'

Will pulled her into his arms as the tears Isabel had been holding on to with difficulty began streaming down her face.

'It's all…all—' she said between sobs '—my fault.'

'Hush, sweetheart, easy now,' Will ran his fingers up and down her spine. 'You can't blame yourself for something that was not in your control.'

'But if we hadn't gone to Sir Phillippe in the first place, if we hadn't gone down this pointless, futile path that was already dangerous, he might still be—'

'No, Isabel.' Will pulled away slightly, wiping her tears with the pad of his thumb. 'The men who are to blame for de Sen's death are the ones who perpetrated it. The man who ordered it and the other who stuck a dagger in his chest…not you.'

'I cannot help think that if we hadn't asked about the vellum than he'd still be alive.'

'Yes, but he knew what he was doing when he asked us to meet him later somewhere as deserted and isolated as that tower and outside the protection of Cour de la Commanderie. He knew the risks, yet he still made that decision.'

'But why there? That's what I cannot comprehend.'

'Who knows? In light of the fact that he burnt the vellum he may have wanted to throw us off the scent, as it were. Naturally, once he was attacked and facing his demise, he was forced to change tactic. But that is purely speculation.'

She stared at him blankly. 'And now he's dead because of his troubles.'

'Remember, you're talking about a hardened old warhorse who had seen many battles.' Will gave her a steady gaze. 'He died protecting what he had sworn on his sword to protect.'

'So, not us?'

He smiled faintly as he cupped her jaw. 'Not exactly, sweetheart. That was *my* bargain.'

'Oh, Will.' She tried returning his smile, but it felt brittle on her lips. 'I wish…oh, I wish that I never sought to find out about the vellum.'

'Yes, I know all about regret, Isabel,' he said quietly. 'But however much you wish things to be different, you cannot change what happened.'

'No…'

'You have to accept that it has happened. And you have to live with it,' he continued.

'It's not easy.'

'It won't be, but you can't allow this bitterness, this regret, to eat away at you because one day you'll come to realise that there's nothing left, just an empty shell of the person you used to be.'

Isabel tilted her head up as her fingers touched his jaw. 'Is that what happened to you after…after Portchester?'

She understood now much more than before—the pain, responsibility and regret that Will had felt and perpetually lived with. Understood how it must have almost ripped him apart.

'Yes,' he said softly, after a long moment.

But he was wrong about one thing.

He hadn't become a shell of a person, as he thought he was, devoid of any feeling. Isabel watched him in the moonlight, her fingers caressing the hard contours of his face. Without realising what she was about to do, Isabel went up on her tiptoes and pressed her lips gently to his. When she paused he sucked his breath through his teeth and watched her, motionless, as she repeated the gesture again and again. Dear God, but she wanted his kiss—wanted to be wrapped by his warmth.

She pulled away slightly. 'You are so much more than the shell you believe you've become.' Her words, a little breathless, needed to be said. For him, as well as for her. 'The man you were—' her fingers spread across his chest, tapping lightly '—is still *here*, Will.'

He opened his mouth to say something, but after giving his head a quick shake, closed it. Their eyes locked. Heat flooded her veins and stained her skin. Her pulse surged and quickened as she felt her stomach clench in eager anticipation of something—something she'd never known to exist before this night. An unadulter-

his hands and the feel of his kisses. She wanted to run her fingers all over him.

'Please, Will.' She pulled him to her, but he gently caught her hands and brought them to his mouth, kissing her fingers one by one.

'You don't know what you're saying, sweetheart.' His smile was faintly bemused. 'I don't want this to be another thing you regret.'

She sat up, her knees bent with her feet tucked underneath her, and closed her eyes. Leaning close, she kissed and touched him along his jaw, the sharp, angled cheekbones and his lips again and again before licking his bottom lip with the tip of her tongue. 'I…won't. I promise I won't.'

'Oh, God, Isabel. What are you doing?' Will growled, looking at her with so much intensity, so much suppressed longing, that it robbed her of breath. 'We mustn't get carried away like this.'

His words stopped mid-flow, seemingly caught in his throat, and his eyes dropped to her shaking fingers in disbelief as she found the edge of the tunic she wore and pulled it up and over her head. Isabel watched him with a bold stare, perplexed to understand where this unknown confidence had come from as she sat on the pallet baring the nakedness of her upper body.

'Don't,' she whispered softly. 'Don't you dare stop.'

Slowly her confidence with her brazen behaviour began to ebb away, her hands sliding up her body, to cover her naked breasts.

Oh, God, what foolishness…

Will didn't want her in the same way as she wanted him—either that or he had far more self-control than she had.

How mortifying…

Will's expression slowly changed then. His gaze under his hooded eyes smouldered and blazed. His smile was inscrutable. He sat opposite Isabel, slowly prising one finger, then another away, his eyes piercing through her. With each finger he took away, he brushed his fingers along hers, in a sensual stroke, up and down, before holding both of her hands in his, caressing the inside of her palm with slow circular motion, moving to the tender skin on her wrists. He pressed slow, wet kisses to the inside of her hands, where his fingers had been, tracing the tip of his tongue along the length of her fingers. She gasped at this unexpected pleasure, from the featherlight touch of his lips, tongue and mouth on her fingers, which bloomed and dispersed through her entire body.

It was only then that his eyes raked her up and down. He inhaled deeply before lifting the edge of his own tunic and echoed what she had done only moments ago, pulling it up and over his head. The corner of his lips lifted slightly, along with one arched brow, as he held it out before dropping it to the ground.

They knelt in front of each other on the pallet, watching and drinking in the sight of one another disrobed, exposed and breathless.

Isabel moved first, her fingers itching to touch the firm, taut skin of his magnificent chest dusted with a smattering of dark hair, up through to his powerful shoulders, taking note of the recent scar she had sewn up and past wounds—a reminder that this man was a seasoned warrior.

Her hands dragged round the bulging muscles of his arms to the hard planes of his back, feeling the smoothness as they made their way back around to his chest.

She pressed her hands flat against his beating heart, feeling his pulse surge.

He took in a sharp breath as he pushed her down gently, her head falling back to be nestled against the cushioned softness. He lay beside her, his elbow bent, one hand supporting the side of his head, while the other skimmed over the length of her body. She shivered under his touch as his fingers brushed from her shoulder around to the curve of her breast, down to her flat stomach and then back up again.

The pad of his thumb circled round her nipple agonisingly slowly. So slowly that she almost screamed. He dipped his head low and flicked his tongue over one nipple in exactly the same way as his fingers continued to caress the other. And this time she did cry out.

'Are you well, Isabel?' he said sheepishly, knowing perfectly the effect he was having on her.

Her whole body felt as though it was on fire and it was becoming difficult to think rationally. 'Oh, yes, thank you,' she ground out, her breathing ragged. 'How are you?'

'Never better.' He grinned as his fingers grazed the underside of her breast, moving down further and further before they circled her navel, his lips, tongue and teeth following the trail.

He moved back to her lips, catching her moan with his mouth. She felt his inquisitive tongue slip and slide along hers in a continuous dance, luscious and slow. His hand slipped down the side of her body, over the flare of her hips and around the curve of her back, drifting to her round bottom, giving it a squeeze, his fingers caressing and digging into her backside, learning the shape of her.

Dear God!

Her languid body didn't seem as though it belonged to her any more. A knot of uncontrollable need—something unknown and unfathomable—was building in her core, begging to be unravelled.

He caught her bottom lip between his teeth and sucked on it gently before pulling away, his fingers tracing her wet, swollen lips, over and over. He pushed himself up, supporting his weight with his arms. 'Isabel?' His whispered voice rumbled low, reverberating through her body. Her eyes flickered open in response, meeting his gaze.

She shuddered, as she felt Will's hand brush down the length of her body slowly, in a long sweeping motion, touching every dip, and curve, his mouth following the trail, reverently.

His fingers reached the fabric ties around her waist, holding up the braes—*his* braes—that she was wearing. He worked, expediently, tugging and pulling to open the knot, but then stopped abruptly, panting as his fingers hovered, curling over and under the fabric. He gave his head a swift shake and leant back.

'We must stop this now, before it goes any further,' he rasped.

She kept her eyes pinned to his, as her own breathing came in quick bursts.

How could she have known that her innocent kiss would ignite this feverish need? Nothing had ever felt like this—no sensation had ever matched this wonder.

But she wanted more.

She answered him by dragging her hand over to the knotted cord of *his* braes, undoing his ties and pulling them open, in just the same way he had done. She watched as he blinked several times and his throat worked, swallowing in apparent discomfort.

* * *

Will had not been expecting this response. All of his tantalising attentions had been a way to satisfy some raw need in her, in the hope that it would persuade her to stop this explosive connection between them. It had had the opposite effect on her instead.

Her hand slowly began to push his braes down his hips. His eyes widened in shock as his hand moved quickly to cover hers.

'Isabel?'

'Please…' Her other hand snaked around his neck, pulling his face close to hers. She lifted her head and kissed him open mouthed. 'Don't stop.'

Chapter Fifteen

Daylight broke through the cracks of the wooden walls, gleaming against the dark surfaces of the chamber, creating haphazard streaks of light in every direction.

Will opened his eyes and blinked, stifling a yawn. His hands searched the surface of the pallet, but found only a residual lingering warmth. Sitting up abruptly on the pallet, naked and alone, memories from the previous evening tumbled through his head, making him groan out loud.

Hell!

What had he done?

He shouldn't have done it—he shouldn't have allowed the spark of intimacy between them to become the scorching flame that it had. He was the one with the experience, after all, not Isabel, and he should have curtailed things before they had both lost all sense and reason...as they had. He should never have kissed her the way he had, tasting and touching her as he explored her body, eager to learn every secret part of her.

Isabel might not have been able to control her ardour, but Will should have shown far more resolve. He should have resisted her and not given in to weakness.

God, what a fool he had been!

Isabel had been hurt, confused and full of regret about the disturbing events of the previous evening. She needed his comfort, assurance, someone to lean on, yet she got a lot more for her troubles.

He had no right, damn it! He had no right to her at all! Yet, she had stirred feelings in him that he just didn't comprehend. They were new, unwelcome and utterly objectionable for a man who was half of what he used to be.

Isabel deserved better, much better than him.

He sighed as he jumped off the pallet, raking his fingers through his hair. His eyes darted around the room, taking in the neatness of the chamber. It had been cleared. Even his clothes had been folded on the table, along with his flagon and a small plate of food—the last remnants of their supplies. A few dry purple petals—from her medicinal stash, no doubt—had been placed beside it, decorating the table with a flash of colour.

He smiled to himself at her tender thoughtfulness as he began to get dressed.

Will dipped under and around branches of hardy trees that concealed the wooden hut, along the pathway littered with of long blades of grass that jutted out from the sand intermittently. He continued down the undulating sand dune that led directly to the long stretch of sandy beach and saw Isabel playing with the little dog, in the distance.

A flash of memory darted through his head as he recalled happier times as a young lad when they had moved close to the Norfolk coastline. His father—

rather, stepfather—had finally been accepted to join the Stonemasons' Guild and their family had moved to be near him as he assisted the Master Mason on a new church. For the children it had been wonderful, after living in the confines of London, to live in so much open space with the sense of freedom it brought them, even for a short time.

It wasn't long after that that Will moved away from his family to start his training as a squire with Sir Percival Halstead. He should have known, not then, but later, mayhap, that it was not the normal way of things for a young boy to be plucked from an ordinary family without any consequence to train with a celebrated knight. It was a rarity. Will always knew he was different from all of his siblings, who had their father's colouring. So, it came as no real surprise when his mother admitted that he was not Matthew Geraint's natural son, but the nobleman Guy, Lord de Manville. Yet the truth had still been bitter to swallow, even though it at least explained his stepfather's lack of interest and utter disdain for him, why nothing Will ever did could please the man.

Will gave himself a mental shake and returned his gaze to the scene before him. It struck him that he was taking Isabel back to what remained of a family which had all but given up on her, as he had freely forsaken his own. God, but he hoped that her transition into her new role would be smooth, that she was spared the pain of the loneliness and heartbreak that had become his constancy.

Which, of course, wasn't helped by the fact that he had bedded her when he should have kept her at a safe distance—for her sake and for his.

His eyes roamed over Isabel. She was wearing his

braes again, along with his favourite dark blue tunic, which was far too big for her. Grinning, she twisted, turned and skipped around as the little dog jumped at her feet, barking merrily and trying to get the wooden stick from her hand as waves lapped at her bare feet.

The light sea breeze played with her glorious gold-and-honey-coloured hair, which she had tried in vain to tie up. Stray tendrils fell and danced across her face as she ran and laughed with such free abandon, chased by her four-legged friend.

His chest clenched tightly…

God, but she was lovely. She was everything joyous and wondrous in the world.

He remembered how, only a short time ago, he was running his fingers through her hair, feeling its softness against his skin, taking in the heady floral scent. It had cascaded in soft waves over the curve of her shoulders, down her back to skim her waist as she had sat in front of him, baring her nakedness.

Isabel noticed him then and she lifted her head, meeting his eyes. Her small smile was shy as she held up her hand in greeting, her cheeks tinting a deeper blush colour that spread across and down her neck.

He returned her smile, keeping his eyes pinned to hers as he continued to amble towards her.

Will might have no right to her, but he'd be damned if he regretted his night with Isabel de Clancey. He shouldn't have done it. It would have been better if he hadn't, but regret their intimacies? That he could never do. Besides, hadn't he told her just hours ago not to hold on to regrets?

Yet, how to proceed?

'Well met, my lady.' He bent low to stroke the excitable dog dancing at his feet. 'I hope to find that you're well rested.'

'Good morrow and, no, not so much. How about you?'

'Aye.' He straightened his spine to stand to his full height, looking down at her. 'But not enough.'

She looked everywhere but at him. 'And have you broken your fast?'

'Yes, my thanks for what you left behind…and also for these…'

Will opened his hand to reveal the purple petals that she had decorated the table with and watched as her colour deepened.

She shrugged. 'Just a little fanciful whimsy.'

'Which was gratefully appreciated.'

She looked everywhere but at him again.

'You've got a little sand on your face there. No, not there…' He reached out and brushed it off.

They descended into an uncomfortable silence as they both pondered what to say next. The hypnotic sound of waves filled the quietness as it ebbed and flowed, dousing the sand. Thank God the sea was calm for their pending sea voyage today.

Eventually he broke the silence. 'Isabel… About last night?'

She turned to walk. 'Not now.'

He followed her as she strolled along the beach, kicking up the sand with the dog at her heel. 'Wait, my lady. This is something that I have to say,' he said, pushing a mop of hair out of his eyes. 'We still have many weeks ahead of us before we reach Castle Clancey.'

'Your point being?'

'The point is that I… I hope to avoid any awkwardness between us because of what happened last night.'

She huffed in apparent agitation. 'Shall we leave what happened last night in the past?'

He stilled her, catching her by the elbow. 'Isabel?'

She lifted her head and met his eyes, a crease on her forehead. 'As you said last night, what's done cannot be undone.'

She picked up a stick and threw it for the dog, who scampered after it.

'I don't want to deny what happened, nor do I regret anything,' he said softly. 'But you are a noble lady and I'm… I'm someone of no consequence. I should not have taken advantage of you.'

'Would you listen to yourself, Will? Can you not accept that we both…took advantage of one another in a moment of need?'

He rubbed his forehead, smoothing away a frown.

God, this was not going well at all. And once again he'd inadvertently insulted her.

Hell!

Yet it could not be helped. Isabel was not his. They had shared a fleeting moment—a brilliant burst of wonder and ephemeral joy shining brightly. Yet it had all but dimmed now.

They would eventually go their separate ways once he had safety escorted her back where she belonged. She would have her life and he would have his.

'Yes, well… I agree, my lady. We should be getting back. I believe we must ready ourselves for the journey today.'

No, Isabel de Clancey was not his and she never would be.

She hadn't known what to expect from Will after the night they had shared, but it wasn't this.

Saints above!

The man was positively infuriating, trying to take all the blame for what happened between them as though he hadn't given her the decision to make. Why did he have to be so honourable, so noble about it? Why did he have to constantly castigate himself?

Isabel sighed and threw a frustrated glare at Will as they walked back to the wooden dwelling together.

The truth was that she had wanted him—wanted those, oh, so delicious intimacies that they had shared. She might now suffer a dose of embarrassment, but she felt no shame about what she had done, even though the general belief was that she should for her wanton, sinful behaviour. But she didn't—she had no regrets.

At least Will felt the same about *that*. But to believe that he was somehow unworthy or had somehow taken advantage of her made Isabel want to scream. Her hands clenched into fists at her side when she pondered why men got such ridiculous notions into their heads. She was torn between kicking him in his unmentionables or wrapping him in a warm embrace.

The little dog barked beside her playfully and she felt a slight tug at the corners of her lips.

'Whatever am I supposed to do with you, Perdu?' she murmured absently. 'You know I can't take you back with me, boy.'

Will slid her a quick glance. 'I can always ask the man who brought us here if he can look after him, or knows of someone who possibly could?'

'That would be most appreciated.' The dog gave her a mournful look as though he understood that they were discussing him. 'You may be lost, Perdu, but you don't belong to me and, unfortunately, I don't belong to you.'

He barked several times, following them before

dashing out ahead, grabbing a stick between his teeth proudly and coming straight back to drop it at their feet while wagging his tail expectedly.

'No, we have to go,' she said quietly as she bent to stroke the little dog. She straightened her back and swallowed uncomfortably as she caught Will's eyes. There was a brief spark of emotion in the depths of his blue eyes, that somehow reflected every shade of the sea, before he masked over whatever had been there.

The truth was that Isabel was glad that her first time had been with Will—that she had chosen him. It had been unforgettable to finally see what lay beneath his mask, to find someone so passionate, warm and full of vitality. He had been so unbelievably tender, so incredibly caring. Yet she had no expectation of Will, knowing full well that once she'd claimed her birthright their worlds would be incompatible and wildly different.

But the thought that she would never see him again once their journey ended filled her with a terrible ache somewhere quite close to her heart.

This wouldn't do, she really must banish such thoughts, just as Will had done, and not allow her feelings for him to grow any further. She had to protect herself as she always had—it would only cause her pain otherwise.

They arrived back at the hut in silence and Isabel changed back into her dress and kirtle behind a flimsy wooden screen. She packed her meagre belongings and the Templar associate from the previous night came to accompany them back. Isabel took one last glance at the room and followed the men out.

Chapter Sixteen

Isabel had never seen a vessel as large and sturdy as the Templars' merchant ship, *La Fortuna*. The inclement weather of the past few days meant that it had been delayed in making its sea voyage, but it seemed that fortune was finally shining on them, as the ship was ready to set sail. Isabel looked up in awe at the sleek white sail with the red Templar cross emblazoned on it as it swayed slightly in the light breeze.

Huge barrels of cargo—wine, grains, and expensive spices that the Templars traded with, as well as many barrels of spring water, and food supplies—dried fish, meat and bread—had been loaded for the voyage.

Isabel sighed deeply as she realised that the last time that she had seen a vessel this imposing was the journey she had made, as a child, to this very port. And now, as a fully grown woman, she was returning back home.

Home?

Is that truly where she was going? Somewhere that she would finally belong?

She swallowed down her doubts, hoping and praying that she would.

Eventually it was their turn to board the ship and

Isabel bent low to pat the dog that had attached himself to her.

'Well, Perdu, I'm afraid it's time to say farewell.' Isabel stroked his black and white fur. She got up and straightened her spine, handing the little dog to someone who had been found to look after him. 'Be good, little one, I wish you well in your new home.'

Isabel and Will followed the skipper along the wooden plank to board the vessel as he explained the different parts of his newly built cog ship proudly.

In the end, however, Perdu made the decision that he did, in fact, belong to Isabel, despite all her protestations to the contrary, and before *La Fortuna* could embark on its long voyage to England, the little dog raced to the plank and fearlessly rushed across. It jumped down on to the deck, wagging its tail at Isabel in defiance.

'Oh, you are very badly behaved, Perdu,' she said, picking the dog up and snuggling it close as Will chuckled, shaking his head. 'But I'm glad you're coming with us.'

They were taken to the stern of the ship, underneath the huge raised platform of the aft castle, where a makeshift area for Isabel to stay had been accommodated. Here, a space had been created for her to dwell behind a hanging fabric screen, to provide further privacy. The space had been arranged with her comfort in mind, with a large threadbare rug on the floorboard, a small coffer set against the back and large bolsters and cushions scattered on the floor as well as a mattress with blankets made from hides and pelts to provide warmth.

Will pushed the fabric screen aside and ushered Isabel and Perdu inside. 'I hope this will suffice for the voyage, my lady?'

'Yes.' She nodded with a smile that seemed a little brittle on her lips. 'Thank you.'

'Good' he said, not meeting her eyes. 'And as agreed, please stay here for the duration of the journey, unless you need to stretch your legs. I can then accompany you for a brisk walk.'

'No need to worry about me, or whatever I may need. I'm sure I can think of something.'

'I'd rather you didn't, Isabel,' he ground out. 'We agreed with the Templars that you would keep away from the seamen and the rest of the crew. They're not used to women on board.'

'And you? Do I need to keep away from you as well?'

He exhaled, barely concealing his chagrin. 'I shall bid you good day until later, when I shall bring you some light repast,' he said, ignoring her question. 'Until then, I hope you find everything here to your comfort.' He bowed before leaving her alone with Perdu.

The dog barked a few times at her and she nodded. 'Yes, I know. So much for attempting to avoid any awkwardness.'

The following few days and nights blended into one as *La Fortuna* continued to sail across the choppy high seas. Isabel stayed in her appointed area and kept herself from the prying eyes of the seamen who had apparently never seen a woman on their ship before, which was frankly ridiculous. Not that she complained.

Isabel had to be mindful of these limited restrictions on her person, especially after her mistake a few days ago, when she had shared fruits that were brought from La Rochelle with the men.

It was on one of her few walks along the deck, so that Perdu could relieve himself, that she had thought to offer some portions of apples, juicy grapes and plums. Will had pulled her up on that and it still niggled when he had informed her that hardened seafaring men were used to meagre foods and not used to the luxuries of fresh fruits.

She had only wanted to be of some use, never having had to be idle before. Really, if Will felt disinclined to be in her company then she wouldn't insist on it. Being apart gave her time for reflection and everything that the future might bring. As the vessel sailed on, Isabel pondered about what her new life at Castle de Clancey would be like, but could think of nothing. She wished she could muster more enthusiasm for the changes everything would bring, but she just couldn't do it.

She felt more alone than before, particularly since Will was no longer by her side. They had barely spoken since boarding the ship. He afforded her the same courtesy as before, the same civility and care, but everything between them had changed. And once again he seemed to prefer to keep her at arm's length, rather than allowing any further closeness between them.

It was too late, however. Her feelings for Will were getting into deeper waters, to the point where it robbed her of the ability to think properly. It confused and frightened her as she tried in vain to ignore her feelings and push them aside.

The truth was that Isabel missed Will and the sense of comradery that they had shared along this journey thus far. She felt heartsick every time she glimpsed at him and it didn't help that she had lurid dreams about him every night, reliving their night of passion. She would wake in the morning in a state of confusion, hot and agitated, her body hankering for his touch.

But mayhap he had the right of it, mayhap the best

way for her to overcome these unsolicited feelings was to put as much distance between them as possible. She must do everything she could to protect herself from becoming any closer to Will. It would never do.

She stroked Perdu, who was curled beside her as the ship jostled them about. 'What do you think?' she asked, to which the dog replied with a bark. 'Yes, me, too. I wish things could be how they were before. But I'm happy to have you for company, little one.'

The vessel continued to jolt them about in every direction, making Isabel feel a little queasy. Goodness, what was going on?

As if in answer, she heard footsteps approaching and Will abruptly pulled the fabric screen aside.

'There are dark clouds ahead, Isabel—the skipper predicts a storm!' he said urgently. 'Grab the rigging ropes above you and tie them around your wrists. Tightly.'

'What are you going to do?'

'Assist the seamen where I can. It's going to get very bumpy.'

'W-Will?' she stammered. 'Be careful.'

He gave her a curt nod and rushed out.

Isabel sprang into action just as the ship swayed, dipped down and jerked to the side, throwing her off balance. She grabbed the little dog as well as the line of rigging that had been extended for this very purpose and did as Will had advised, winding it around her wrist a few times and tying it tightly. She said a silent prayer for Will and the seamen who were risking their lives to keep the ship watertight—and more importantly upright—so that they could pass through it safely.

The sea became progressively choppier and more turbulent as they tried to navigate around the eye of the storm. She could hear men shout over the gathering assault, as feet and hands pounded on the deck.

Just then the vessel tilted suddenly, hurling Perdu out of her arms. He slipped away from her, whining in distress.

Oh, God, no! Not the innocent little animal. She had to do something.

Untying the rope from her wrist, she dashed after him, pulling aside the hanging fabric, her eyes darting in every direction trying to see where he had gone. Her poor little dog tried in vain to scamper back to her, but kept losing its grip on the deck. Isabel clambered after him, as the wind whipped up and the rain thrashed down, impeding her progress.

'Come on boy, come back to me!' she shouted over the din, but it was useless. Just when she had given up all hope the dog managed to scurry and paw close enough for Isabel to make a grab for him.

'Oh, thank God. I've got you, boy,' she muttered as she nestled her face in his fur. It was then that she noticed how far she had managed to stagger away from the stern of the boat and it was also at that very moment that Will noticed her.

'What the hell are you doing here?' he shouted over the deafening noise, the worry palpable in his voice. Before she could give him an answer the ship jerked violently, tipping sideways and thrusting her with great force in the air. She saw the look of horror flash across Will's face before he sprang into action and dived to catch her. But the elements continued to pull her, hurling her further away.

This new cog ship was designed with higher wooden sides, as the skipper had been proud to point out, but the force of the storm was so strong that it pushed Isabel over. She hung on to the secondary rim of the vessel with one hand, the other clutching Perdu.

Suddenly Will was there above her, grabbing her hand. She was lucky that the ship had straightened and the seas were momentarily calmer, otherwise they would both have been swept away.

'Give me both your hands, Isabel,' he shouted.

'I can't.' She shook her head, knowing that she couldn't allow Perdu to perish, just so she could live.

'Isabel!' he bellowed. 'I can't hold on like this, for God's sake!'

She couldn't let go. It went against everything she believed in to sacrifice another living being. An innocent animal. Sensing that this was not the time to press his point, Will tried another tack. He yanked her up with every ounce of strength he had and pulled her back on to the deck.

'Thank God,' he muttered, just as she had moments ago, along with an oath that she hadn't. With one protective arm around her, Will used his body to shelter Isabel as they all staggered back to the stern of the boat, while the rest of the crew continued to battle with keeping the ship from careening off course.

Will yanked the fabric screen back and helped her inside, her body shivering uncontrollably.

'Hold on to the rigging rope,' he insisted. 'And you have to get out of those clothes.' She realised then that she was soaked through, as was everything that had been left on the floor around her.

'Go... I'll...do...it...mysel—' But she couldn't get the words out, her fingers stiff as they fumbled to remove her clothing.

'Allow me,' he said gruffly as she tried to swat away his hands. Taking no notice of her, he started to help peel the sodden clothes off as she trembled from the cold…as well as from his touch. But then, this was quite different from the last time his hands had touched her. Isabel grappled to cover herself and turned around as Will steadied her with a hand to the shoulder. He passed her satchel to her, which was thankfully dry.

'Now, if you don't mind telling me what the devil you thought you were doing there?'

She grabbed some clothes out of her bag and slipped on a long linen shift with her back still to him, feeling it whisper down her clammy body as she reached for her brown woollen kirtle. 'I couldn't let Perdu go, not if I… I could save him.'

'And so you put yourself in danger instead.'

She turned around to meet his furious gaze. 'As you did for me?'

'That,' he said curtly, 'is not the same thing. I have a duty to protect you. For pity's sake, Isabel, you could have been swept away!'

'I know, I know. I'm sorry, Will.'

He rubbed his forehead in obvious exasperation. 'Don't you realise how damn close that was?'

'I do, but I had to try to save him. I couldn't just let him wash away and drown. I just couldn't…'

He let out a shaky breath and pulled her against his chest, wrapping her in his embrace. 'That was the most reckless, frightening thing you have ever done, Isabel de Clancey, not that I'm really surprised. For a moment I thought…' He choked, unable, it seemed, to finish what he was going to say. 'Don't you ever do that to me again. Do you hear?'

'Utterly and completely.'

He hugged her closer. 'Ah, Christ, woman…what you do to me.'

'I'm sorry…and, Will?' she muttered into his chest, as he looked down at her. 'Thank you.'

He grunted in response as a sense of calm prevailed over her, wrapped in his warm embrace. They stayed like that for a long moment, his hands sliding up and down her spine before he reluctantly let her go.

'Listen, do you hear that?' Will's eyes widened as he looked up, his head careening round to hear something. 'It seems as though we've passed through the worst of the storm.'

'Oh, thank God!'

'I'm going to see if I'm needed. Stay here!'

She nodded and grabbed Perdu, tying the rigging around her wrist once more. 'See what a fix you got us both into…and it's no use looking at me like that. The whole incident was entirely your fault…but I am so glad that I have you now,' she said as he barked in response.

Chapter Seventeen

All hands were on deck, attending to the difficult task of ridding the swell of water from the vessel. Flouting his edict to stay away, Isabel mucked in as she threw bucket after bucket of water back into the sea. With the job eventually completed, it was time to take some rest and, judging by how Isabel looked—ashen and ready to drop on her feet—she needed it. It had been just like her to insist that she help instead of getting some warmth back into her body, but then Isabel could be incredibly belligerent, as she'd once pointed out.

Putting his arms around her so that he was able to support her weight, he guided her back to the stern and the small space beneath the aft castle.

The rug had been removed to dry off and, in its stead, dry blankets had been strewn on the floor for Isabel's comfort, not that she had been aware as her eyes fluttered closed and her head tipped back.

Will gently laid her down and watched as she curled to her side, already fast asleep. He settled beside her, pulling her close, with the blanket over them, his head too weary to remember the need for caution around her.

For both their sakes, he had purposefully kept away

from her during this sea voyage, giving her the deference that her rank deserved, especially in front of these seamen, mindful of giving them the wrong impression. But, in truth, Will just didn't trust himself around Isabel any longer. Every time he spent any length of time with her, he wanted more—nay, yearned for more. This moment now soothed away those concerns. Right now, lying beside her eased his mind and, as he held on to her, he knew he just didn't care. Not this night.

Not when he had almost lost her...

Will had never been so terrified, when Isabel had been flung to the side of the boat. They had been in perilous situations along this journey, but nothing... nothing had made him feel as helpless as when he'd watched her almost topple into the sea. Instinct had made him throw himself in the air for her...but, God's breath, it had been far too close for his peace of mind.

It was all part of his duty, he reminded himself. Isabel's well-being and safety came above everything. If that meant that he had to see to it personally, by holding her all night...then so be it. Besides, Will was too tired to resist her company any longer. The fight was not in him.

Will watched the hazy golden hues of the vivid sunrise burst through the opalescent horizon. The sea winked glimmers of light, forgiving now in its calm, temperate state, so vastly different from the angry, ferocious way it had almost devasted and swallowed them whole.

He turned, sensing Isabel move beside him, and gave her a small smile, followed by her little dog, which took to sniffing the area. They stood side by side on the raised aft castle looking out to sea and watching the dawn break together, immensely thankful they were able to.

She slipped her hand into his and gave it a squeeze. 'Are you still angry with me?' she asked quietly.

'Angry, mad and above all furious.'

'Oh, dear…'

'Indeed.'

'It was sheer instinct to save Perdu. I just didn't think.'

'That is admirable,' he said. 'But you compromised your own safety.'

'I realise that.'

'What you did was possibly one of the foolhardiest things that I've ever witnessed anyone do. It was more than even I would have done.'

'You?' She arched an eyebrow. 'Commit foolhardy acts?'

'That would be telling, Isabel.'

'I cannot imagine it. You are the most sensible of men.'

'Am I?' His lips twitched at each corner. 'One of us has to be, Isabel…and I've been called many things, but *sensible* has never been one them.'

'Ah, well, what about loyal, steadfast and resolute…?'

He inclined his head. 'Naturally, my lady.'

'As well as kind, caring and courteous.'

'Dear me—' he grinned '—you're putting me to the blush.'

'And above all, brave, valiant and honourable, as befits *my* knight.'

Well now, how to respond?

Much as he wanted to believe the picture Isabel had painted, the reality was far more distorted than that.

Far more complicated. He wished though, that for her, he was closer to that impression.

He raised their laced fingers and pressed a kiss to her hand. 'I highly esteem your opinion of me, Isabel, but I'm not what you believe me to be.'

'Much as I hate to contradict you, I think you are.' She gave his hand another little squeeze. 'You've just forgotten.'

'No.' He gave her a small shake of the head. 'But I thank you all the same,' he murmured.

'Does that mean that I'm forgiven?'

'I knew there was a catch for recounting my many virtues.' He chuckled softly. 'You, Isabel, are a confounding woman.'

'Don't forget belligerent.'

'That, too.'

They fell into a silence that was not altogether uncomfortable.

Will turned to face her. 'In truth, you are the most remarkable woman I have ever met with a kind heart, ready to care for everyone and everything around you.'

She shrugged. 'Now you're putting me to blush.'

'It's true, every word. Now promise me that you won't ever repeat yesterday's recklessness.'

'I give you my word, Will.' She smiled tentatively. 'It's just that I've never had a living thing attach themselves so completely to me as Perdu has.'

'I do know what that feels like,' he nodded, recalling a long-ago memory. 'I remember when I was a young lad, I had a little dog—the very best friend a boy could have—but I was forced to give him up when we moved to London. Like Perdu, we were always moving on.'

Isabel remained silent, encouraging him to continue.

'I remember the heartache when I had to leave him

behind. So, although your dog has not been with us for long, I do understand.'

The boy in him had found having to say farewell to his canine friend unbearable and painfully heart-wrenching. Will recalled his stepfather thrashing him for his display of unbecoming emotion, instilling in him the valuable lesson that he should always shroud his feelings—which he did with defiance, insouciance and later with a wry sense of humour.

'It must have been exciting moving around, seeing the different parts of the kingdom?'

He shrugged. 'We never settled anywhere that we could put down roots.'

'But at least you were not separated.'

Again, Will was reminded of the gut-wrenching pain that Isabel must have felt doing her duty by her family when they had sent her to live with her betrothed.

Their experiences as children had been shaped by the harsh realities of the world.

He gave her a tender smile, hoping it conveyed his compassion. 'True, that must have been extremely arduous when you were still so young.'

'It was initially, but the need to survive surpassed every other consideration. And as you know, my life in St Jean de Cole with the Meuniers was not altogether bad. It was actually quite pleasant.'

'Even so, it must have been difficult.'

She nodded. 'When I thought about what I had lost, it was. But after time, I forgot about who I had been and turned my attention on who I was becoming—of course your arrival changed the course of all that.' She looked a little wistful. 'Yet, lately I have recalled more about my brothers.'

'Good memories, I hope?'

'Yes.' Her eyes glazed over as though she was retrieving a small piece of her memory. 'I realised that I missed them, Will...or rather, the boys they once were. I wish I knew the men that they became.'

'I know it's not the same, but your mother could possibly tell you about them.'

She nodded. 'She could...she could fill in many of the missing gaps, I hope.'

Will sighed deeply. He, too, missed his family, friends and his old way of life. But sentiment and emotion were things he had tried to avoid, knowing they were a gateway to more misery and pain.

'Unlike you, I was most eager to leave home and get away from my stepfather. And soon enough, I began squiring for Sir Percival.'

'Did your stepfather not claim you as his son?'

'He did, though he never accepted me because the man was not my natural father,' Will said balefully.

'I'm so sorry.'

'So was I, especially since I only found out after he died.'

'I thought you had always known.'

He shook his head. 'It explained much. Why I didn't look like my siblings. Why Matthew Geraint resented me and why a son of a stonemason was permitted to become a knight.'

Will felt the perpetual bitterness about his past rise up from his gut. And yet expunging it, sharing this with Isabel, eased and shifted something inside him, as if something that he'd been holding on to was finally released.

'After Matthew Geraint died, following the siege at Portchester, my mother finally told me that my natural father was Guy, Lord de Manville, who had offered them money and helped Matthew become an apprentice, as long as he took on his bastard.' His lips twisted in disgust. 'When the time came, Lord de Manville assisted with obtaining a position for me as a squire.'

'Oh, Will…'

'Don't you see, Isabel? My whole life had been a damned lie.'

They stood there, looking out at the horizon, his throat suddenly tight. How had they got to discussing such private matters? Matters that even his friend Hugh de Villiers didn't know.

Isabel expelled a deep breath and turned to him. 'No, I see a man who is trying to make sense of his past, but condemning himself and everyone he loves in the process.'

'That is untrue.'

'Is it?' she asked gently. 'It seems possible that your mother, your natural father and even the man who raised you tried to do right by you.'

'Yes, but—'

She raised her hand before he could discount that untruth. 'No one is without fault, Will. No one is infallible. Even you, with your resounding virtues.'

'*That* I do know.'

'But that is what makes us mortal, is it not? We all make mistakes—you, me and all those who are supposed to love, nurture and protect us.'

'I appreciate what you are saying, but it's not quite as simple as that. My mother should have told me.'

'Yes, she should have, but have you ever considered…? Could it be possible that your mother may have made a promissory oath to your stepfather not to tell you about your natural father until after his death?'

Will was taken back by that statement. No, he had

never considered that. Yet it was possible that Matthew's pride would make him act in such a way.

'Do you believe that your mother purposely wished to hurt you, Will? I can see from your face that she would not...so don't allow this huge chasm to come between you. You don't need to redeem yourself; you need to forgive her and absolve yourself from all this unwanted blame and guilt you carry with you.'

'Isabel, I—'

'You once said to me that you are the shell of the man you used to be,' she continued. 'The man I see is so much better than that. Your standing in the world is not defined by what you believe others may think of you, rather, how you define yourself. Don't become something you're not.'

Will stared at her, trying to absorb everything she had said. He gave himself a mental shake. 'When—' he swallowed '—when did you become so wise?'

'I don't know, but I sometimes surprise myself.'

'Oh, you never fail to surprise me.' It was his turn to give her hand a squeeze. 'Thank you...' he muttered, unable to say any more.

She flushed. 'Glad to be of help. It's the least I can do after the many times you have saved my life.'

Sometimes it took another person's perspective to show a different way to view the world. Was it possible that Will had not fully appreciated the complicated arrangements that had been made to secure his future? He wished now that he hadn't acted so impulsively when he last saw his mother and had instead asked more about his natural father. But sentiment and emotion had woven their way into his head, casting aside sense and reason.

It had been at a time when he had been raw with grief and guilt from his failure after Portchester and the death of a man who had reared him as a son, yet cared little for him. One thing compounded the other until Will had forsaken his old life and replaced everything he had once known with darkness, anger and bitterness.

He turned and caught Isabel's worried gaze and smiled in gratitude, feeling as though something intangible had been lifted. His heart throbbed in his chest as her lips curved slowly, returning his smile. What also surprised him was the depth of his feelings for this woman standing beside him.

Isabel de Clancey was as kind as she was lovely. Indeed, the most remarkable woman he had ever known. A woman he cared about deeply.

They spent several more days at sea, before finally reaching the port of Southampton. Isabel stood out on deck, clasping Perdu as the vessel came to dock, her eyes fixed on her first view of England since she had been a child.

Home...

Try as she might, though, she could not muster any meaningful feeling regarding this significant moment in her life. In fact, she felt bereft and a little empty, but it was probably nothing more than a little trepidation. She would ostensibly find that flicker of emotion once she reached Castle de Clancey and saw her mother again.

Isabel felt a presence beside her and knew it would be Will. She smiled at him and felt the warmth of his response reflected in his eyes. Bewildered, she wondered how it was possible that every time he smiled at her in that way of his, she felt the same sensations. Her stomach would flip over itself and she would always feel the heat of his gaze, all the way down to her toes.

He turned his head to watch the same sweeping scenery as they arrived back home to England. It occurred to her that this was just as much a homecoming for Will as it was for her.

'So, here we are, my lady.'

'So here we are,' she repeated in a voice that even to her own ears sounded flat.

'And are you well?'

Isabel could feel the concern dripping from his words. She gave herself a mental shake. 'Indeed, and you? It must be strange coming back for you as well.'

He raised a brow. 'Yes, I suppose so. When I left England, I thought I would never see this kingdom again.'

She nodded. 'Neither did I.'

'And yet, here we are,' he muttered again as he turned to face her. 'Though this must be far more bewildering for you?'

'I suppose it must be.' She sighed. 'I thought I'd feel anger, bitterness or sorrow, possibly even a little excitement about being back, but I feel…nothing.'

He threaded his fingers through hers and brought her hand up to his lips. 'That's more than understandable, Isabel, after everything that has happened.'

'Do you truly believe so?'

'Of course, my lady. You left England when you did not know much about your future, leaving everyone you loved behind. Coming back now must seem a little unreal. Does it?'

'The truth is that I don't know what to expect now that we're back.'

'And that makes you uneasy?'

She nodded. 'It may sound nonsensical, but I somehow feel as though I'm walking into the unknown.'

He turned her hand round and soothed the palm with the pad of his thumb.

'I know. I feel the same,' he murmured, nodding. 'In life, we often take paths that are plagued with uncertainty, that force us to make decisions blindfolded.'

Her brows furrowed. 'A little like this journey.'

He chuckled softly. 'Yes, exactly. This whole journey has been a voyage into the unknown, as you put it.' He grazed her knuckles with his lips. 'The same as when I was a soldier, on the eve of a battle.'

She lifted her head. 'Do you miss it, being a soldier, that is—a knight of the realm?'

'I've been on my own for so long, Isabel, that I don't know any more,' he said, gazing into the distance. 'But I confess that I miss the sense of camaraderie—the friendship.'

'And now that you're back, you won't need to be on your own any longer.' She flushed, meeting his gaze.

'I hope not.' He shrugged. 'Although, I, too, don't know what to expect.'

'That's the problem with having an expectation. You hope that it doesn't all turn to dust.' She frowned. 'Like you, I have been on my own all these years—oh, I know I was luckier than most being adopted by a family, but I could never be me. But now, I'm not sure that I can be the noblewoman I'm expected to be either.'

'You don't need to be what others expect of you. Be the noblewoman you want to be, Isabel. You're incredible and your strength lies in your kind heart. Don't ever change for anyone.'

Isabel stared at him, speechless, unable to say anything, her colour deepening.

He thought her incredible and kind-hearted?

She was not used to such compliments, but knew that Will would never say them unless he meant them.

Good grief!

He was still ardently talking to her. 'I'm not the same man that I once was,' he said softly. 'Nothing in life stays the same.'

She remained silent for a while as they drew closer to the port, the outline of the dwellings, boats and people becoming clearer.

'When did you become so wise?' she said finally, repeating the same words Will had said as they had watched the sunrise together a few days ago.

He didn't reply, but gave her an eloquent look instead.

Isabel hadn't seen much of Will since that resplendent morn, after his poignant revelations. It had been cathartic for Will to be able to unburden himself to her. He seemed much lighter, happier even, without the weight he had been carrying for so long. And though it had made her ache for all that Will had suffered, it had made Isabel feel humble that he had entrusted her with his woes. It also meant that she understood him a lot better.

Since then, things had changed between them. The overwhelming tension seemed to have drifted away with the storm. In its stead was an unfettered connection between them that was stronger than before. A powerful attraction that simply took her breath away.

The truth was that Isabel cared deeply for the man standing beside her, but knew it was futile. It would cause her a different sort of heartache now that they were back in England, so close to the end of their journey.

She pushed away these musings. 'I just wish that I felt something now that I'm back in England.'

'Allow for more time to get used to it, Isabel…just as I shall have to.'

Time…

It was the one thing that she knew was slipping away from her. This precious time she had left with Will. Mayhap that was also the reason why she was also feeling apprehensive. The knowledge that it would all come to an end soon.

'I suppose I shall have to.'

Chapter Eighteen

Once they had disembarked, Will knew that, without the Templars' protection, there could once again be the possibility of danger from Rolleston and his men. He would take no chances now that they were back on English soil. He must be alert to any eventuality.

The lodgings Will had secured were with the local shipyard's carpenter and the furthest dwelling along the quay. Before doing anything, Will asked for parchment and ink so that he could write to Hugh de Villers, Lord Tallany, hoping that he was at Winchester Castle so that the messenger would not have to travel as far north as Tallany Castle. The matter of urgency in his missive could not be helped. He must get through to his old friend and hope that the strength of their friendship still carried favour.

Will also wrote to his mother, knowing that although she could not read, his message would be imparted to her by the local priest, who could.

They were given turned-out chambers with beds, clean bedding and, for extra silver, a hearty meal of mutton stew, freshly baked bread and warm ale for them and a huge bone with scraps for Isabel's dog. As well as that, they had the luxury of blissful hot baths in tall wooden tubs.

Will had sunk into the scented warmth in the private, secluded courtyard as Isabel had her bath in her chamber. He caught a shadowy glimpse of her as she looked out from her window, but she disappeared from view straight after.

Later, before retiring to bed, they sat side by side in front of the hearth in the small antechamber, the warmth of the fire penetrating their weary bones. It was distinctly cooler in England, particularly being so close to the sea with its brisk northerly wind, which rattled against the windowpane.

Will resumed his carving on the oval-shaped slate that he had now sanded and shaped. He wanted to complete it before…before the end of their journey. He slid a quick glance at Isabel and sighed. She seemed so pensive since their arrival, lost in her own musings.

'You look troubled, my lady.'

She reached down and stroked Perdu, who was happily snoozing by her feet.

He tried again. 'If you're still worried about your meeting your mother and—'

'No, it's not that,' she interrupted, looking straight ahead.

Damn.

Will knew what was troubling her. The moment he had told her of his plans for the following day, she had stiffened and withdrawn from him. It didn't sit well with him either, but it was the only way forward. Painful as it was, it had to be this way.

Their last night travelling alone…

He had secured a wagon for Isabel to be conveyed

back to Castle de Clancey, along with a widowed female companion. As well as this, new clothes had been bought from the local clothier, who was more than happy to have such a commission to work on through the night, for it meant a generous amount of coin for his troubles. Will would travel alongside them on a horse he had yet to procure, with a young stable boy who would act as a page as well as another man to help as guard. There were still a few details to resolve, but he hoped that they would leave for the final part of their journey on the morrow.

All of these plans were good, made with sound reason, and yet they meant that, from tomorrow, they would no longer share their journey as they had done... just the two of them.

From tomorrow, Isabel would officially become *Lady Isabel de Clancey.*

'Let's talk of different things,' she said abruptly. 'Would you show me instead how to carve the stone in that intricate way you're doing?'

Will's brows arched in the surprise. 'Very well.' He put down his tools and fetched a small stool, placing it in front of where he was sitting. 'If you would oblige me by sitting here, Isabel, facing the hearth.'

She sat where he suggested as he resumed his seat behind her. Will leant forward and heard Isabel gasp as he dragged his arms around her, closing his fingers around hers. This close, he could see the delicate dusting of freckles along her smooth neck. This close, the scent from her skin and damp hair engulfed his senses. This close, he was reminded of things he yearned for, but could not have.

He cleared his throat and grabbed his tools in one hand and the slate in the other. He passed them to Isabel and once again covered her hands, marvelling at how small they were and how well they fit into his.

'Shall we start with this chisel or would you like something smaller?'

'This will do well.'

'Good. You can see the designs that I have already carved and can either continue with what I've done, or come up with a different pattern.'

'Should it be something that complements what is here?'

Will watched, mesmerised, as she gathered the length of her hair and allowed it to tumble over one shoulder.

'It should be anything that you choose. Anything that pleases you.' He helped guide the angle of the chisel, tilting it to the side as he murmured from behind her, 'Hold it like so, sweeping down from this angle in one motion…now hold the slate around the edge firmly. You don't want it to slip away the moment you make contact.'

They continued to work silently. Carefully. Slowly.

He helped guide the tools, deftly showing her the correct way to carve intricate shapes. Her back rested his chest as he leant forward, his head over her shoulder, his breath close to her face.

'That's it…very good,' he whispered encouragingly. He slid her a quick glance, noticing the tip of her tongue sticking out with a look of concentration on her face. His chest tightened in pain as though he had been speared through his damned heart.

He swallowed uncomfortably, knowing that he would always remember this. He would always remember the way she looked this eventide, settled in his arms with her hair draped over one shoulder, working with quiet diligence while adding her marks on the stone. He would have to put it all to memory—everything about her.

Eventually, she leant back, relinquishing the tools to Will, and held the stone in her hand, her task evidently complete. 'What do you think?'

He studied the swirly patterns etched around his efforts, joining the sharp ends of his designs and extending them to form rounded shapes. The inexperience of her crude marks, somehow endearing.

'Infinitely better than before.' He grinned at her.

'We both know that's not true.' She moved to sit beside him again. 'Are you teasing me, Sir William?'

'I, your errant knight?' he said in mock outrage. 'Do you think that I could ever stoop so low as to give false praise to a fair lady?'

She raised a sardonic brow. 'Wouldn't you?'

'Absolutely not. Along with being a sensible sort of man, as I've often been called, I would never dream of being dishonest…especially as you still hold my chisel in your hand.'

She chucked. 'I'm glad to hear it. My errant knight would know better than to do that.'

'Indeed.' Will placed his hand underneath Isabel's so that he could take a better look at their joint endeavour. He tilted it around and examined it. 'It does have a certain charm, though.'

'In the flaws that I've added? Its imperfection?' Her shoulders slumped. 'I fear that I've spoiled your beautiful design.'

He lifted her chin with one finger so he could gaze into her eyes and memorise every shade of green, amber, ochre and the striking splash of brown.

'I would always rather the imperfections and flaws, Isabel.' His lips held a faint smile. 'And now there is a little bit of me and little bit of you imparted on this stone…for ever.'

He watched her blink several times, her eyes filling with tears. She handed him the stone and shot up abruptly, taking a few steps away and turning her back to him, her hands on her hips.

Hell.

He hadn't meant to upset her. He had wanted to… to…what exactly? Soothe her with such overblown sentimentality?

Yet…they were words that bared his soul. Words that reminded them both that while the patterns on the etching might last for all of time, they could not…even if they wanted to.

The truth was that he felt it, too. This overwhelming heaviness around his chest, making breathing unbearable. Knowing that tonight would be their last in the manner that they had become accustomed to on this journey. Tomorrow would bring a change and bring them closer to Castle de Clancey. The moment they would have to part.

He moved to stand behind Isabel, brushing his hands over her shoulders and down the length of her arms before threading his fingers through hers.

'I apologise, Isabel.'

'Why?' She spun around with a strained smile that didn't quite reach her eyes. 'There's nothing to apologise for.'

His hands flexed around her waist. 'Isn't there? I hadn't meant to distress you.'

'You haven't…' Her smiled slipped from her lips and

she sunk her teeth into them instead. 'It's just that this is all so...so difficult.'

'Yes.'

'Everything is going to change.'

'Yes,' he muttered again.

'What if we don't want it to?'

He shook his head. 'We don't have a choice, I'm afraid.'

She covered her face with her hands. 'I have always known it could come this. I have always known that it would be too dangerous for me to get close to you.'

'I am a dangerous man,' he said wryly.

Her hands dropped to her sides and her cheeks darkened. 'No, you're not, Will. You're the best man I know.'

He wished that was true. He wished for many things that were out of his reach, but mostly he wished that he had the power to change his past and be a better man for Isabel.

'Some changes can be a force for good.' He shrugged. 'After all, nothing ever stays the same, as you well know.

'I'm not sure I'm ready for these changes, Will.'

He closed his eyes and rested his forehead against hers. 'I know that in your own inimitable way, Isabel, you'll rise up to any challenge.'

'You have more faith in me than I have in myself.'

'Ah, but then you have more belief in me than I have in myself.'

He pulled away and they stood watching one another for a long moment. Every flicker of emotion passed through her eyes.

'Know this, William Geraint,' Isabel whispered as she brought up her hand to cup his jaw, caressing his face. 'You are worthy of more than just my belief in you. You are worthy of my love, my heart. In fact, I give them freely to you.'

Her hand shot out to cover his mouth as he opened it to speak. 'No. Please don't say anything.'

Will peeled her fingers away gently, never taking his eyes off her. 'Oh, but I must, sweetheart.' He bent down and swooped her up in his arms, carrying her into the larger bedchamber he'd given to her to use. 'How else would I tell you that I care for you?' He pressed his lips to hers and kissed her softly. 'How else would I tell you that I love you?'

He heard her gasp and saw her eyes widen, her lips opening in response, but it was his turn to drown out whatever she had wanted to say. The time for words was no more.

He caught her mouth again as he carried her to the bed, setting her down and lying beside her. He bent his arm and placed one hand under his head as the other caressed the soft contours of her body.

'You…you love me?' She sounded as though she had difficulty believing him.

'With all my heart.'

'Oh, Will…' Her arms came around his neck, pulling him close, so that they were sharing the same ragged breath. 'How can I ever let you go?'

'You must, Isabel,' he whispered against her lips. 'As I shall have to let you go.'

'I know. I have told myself that a thousand times, but it doesn't make this any easier.'

'No, it doesn't.' He ran his fingers down the velvety softness of her hair, now almost dry. 'But we have tonight.'

'Yes—' she shifted beneath him, so that his body, his hands, his mouth were closer still '—we do.'

* * *

Words were not enough to show the extent of what Isabel felt in her heart, which pounded a deafening tattoo in her chest.

Her overwhelming desire for Will was threatening to consume her, so much so that she began to tremble in his arms. They had hurriedly undressed one another and lay skin to skin, panting, craving with dizzying need. She wanted more of his kisses, his touches, his hands over her body, but it wasn't enough. Not nearly enough.

She wanted to be part of him in every way. She wanted to hold on to this moment for as long as possible before it slipped away for good.

We have tonight...

Very well, if that was all that she could have, then she would take it, everything he had to give, and in return she would show him what he meant to her, pledging her heart and soul to him.

She gasped as he entered her body, his midnight-blue eyes glittering above her with raw emotion, raw need. Hands touched, fingers explored, mouths tasted and they devoured. Tongues licked and tangled and, oh, heavens, wickedly sucked parts of her body that shocked her. Excited her. Teeth nuzzled as they nipped every curve, every crevice with maddening reverence.

Isabel felt emboldened to do the same. Her fingers, hands and lips grazed a path over his taut body, the taste of him making her weak with need. Her fingers traced the bulging arms that held her, the scars on his rippled chest and along the curve of his sinewy back. She covered a vein throbbing in his neck with her mouth and nipped it gently, feeling the pulse quiver. Her hands dipped down his lower back and then to his firm buttocks, hard under her touch. She could feel the smattering of hair on his chest rub against her breasts as they slid against each other. Her back arched as he drove himself into her with languid strokes, her ripened body stretched to take him. Again, and again, quickening in pace, until a certain uncontrollable wildness took over. Something beguiling and intangible.

Blood pumped through her veins. Her body was slick with heat, with a rush that pooled in her stomach and in her core. She felt boneless, ready to melt into nothing.

And then it came—a feeling that was still new, still unexpected, still heart-stopping. Her breath caught, her body thrashed and burst into a thousand little pieces.

'Always…' Will shuddered above her as she tried to make out the words he had whispered in her ear moments before. 'I'll always love you.'

She swallowed, unable to say anything as the beat of her heart slowed, her breathing shallow. The side of her face and neck were wet, her tears pooling into her hair.

Tears? Oh, God, how mortifying!

'Isabel?' he whispered. 'Is anything the matter?'

'No, nothing.' She twisted her head around as he stroked her face, wiping the last of her tears. 'But could you do something for me? Just one more time.'

'Anything.'

'Kiss me.'

Yes, Isabel would have this night to remember. She would have this night to believe that there could be wondrous possibilities that weren't governed by what was expected of her. Even if it meant that her heart would later shatter. She would endure it. Isabel had the rest of her life to think about what she was about to lose, but not tonight.

Tonight was for loving.

Chapter Nineteen

The morning *did* come, all too quickly, and it was an auspiciously grey and cold one at that. Will had remained with her all night, making love to Isabel once more until all that was left was sleep. She woke to find her limbs tangled with his, one arm draped over his flat stomach. She lifted herself a little to watch the slumbering man beside her. He looked so peaceful in sleep, without the worries he faced in the day, this man who made her heart soar.

His lips curved slowly into a smile that made him ridiculously handsome. 'You're doing it again, Isabel, you're staring at me while I sleep.'

'You're not asleep though, are you?' She caressed his jaw softly, feeling the brush of stubble beneath her fingers. 'And I don't know how you know what I'm doing, with your eyes shut?'

'It is a talent I have, among many.'

She gasped in mock outrage. 'We're brazenly impudent this morning, aren't we, my knight.'

She squeaked as Will grabbed her by the waist and rolled her over until he was on top. 'We are.'

He dipped his head, slanting his soft lips over hers

and kissed her opened mouthed with a restrained longing that took her breath away. He ended the kiss by pressing his lips to her cheeks, her forehead and her neck before lifting himself off to sit on the edge of the bed, his breathing coming in short bursts.

He dragged his fingers through his hair. 'I shouldn't have done that.'

'No?'

'No, Isabel, it leads to more of a damnable coil for both of us.'

His head bent forward, rubbing his forehead, 'You, Isabel de Clancey, are hard to resist.'

She wanted to reach out and touch him, but she sensed he was already withdrawing from her.

'Come,' he whispered softly. 'It's time to get up.' He got up, wrapping a piece of linen cloth around his torso before washing from a bowl of water left on the coffer. She stayed under the coverlet, watching him as he picked up his clothing and started to dress, one garment at a time, until he put the pendant she'd given him over his head. Just as soon as he had done so, he held it in his hand and looked at it before taking it off it again, as though he was suddenly struck by something.

He held it out. 'Here, take it, Isabel.'

She stood and closed his open hand over the pendant. 'No, it's yours.'

'But it's a family heirloom.'

'That I chose to gift to you.'

'Even so, you should keep it with the other one. Now that the vellum is destroyed, there is no reason why they should not be kept together.'

'And yet I want you to keep it, Will. Think of it as something to remember me by. Please, I insist.'

'Very well, you honour me with it, but know this—I

don't need a pendant or anything else to remember you by.' She felt the heat emanating from his eyes before he looked away and walked towards the doorway with her little dog following him. 'I'll see to getting food to break our fast and, yes, for you, too, Perdu.'

The dog jumped around his feet excitedly, following Will outside the chamber as Isabel laid down once more and stared up at the beamed ceiling with a deep sigh.

Will returned, bearing food that he had procured from the wife of the carpenter who had rented them the rooms, to find Isabel washed and dressed.

'Your new clothes shall arrive shortly, Isabel and I hope the cloak will be warm enough as the wind is exceptionally bracing.'

'You've been outside?'

'Perdu needed to go and I had to check on a few things before we have to depart.'

'Thank you—' she gave him a weak smile '—for organising everything.'

'It's a pleasure, my lady…as always.'

They sat together, eating in silence. Each passing moment brought the stark reality that this would be last time they'd be together alone. The carpenter's wife had already informed him that her friend, Mistress Mildert, was on her way to meet them shortly, with huge excitement for her new position as companion to a lady.

He realised Isabel was playing with her food after taking just a few bites of the roll of wheaten bread and knew that she was finding this as difficult as he was.

'You're not eating?'

'I find that I have lost my appetite.'

'Allow me to wrap it up, for when it may return.'

'That is not necessary,' she said, trying but failing to smile. 'I shall see to it myself.'

'Very well.' He sighed. 'As you wish.'

They would still see each other for the remainder of the journey. They would remain cordial, but the familiarity—this connection between them—had to cease. It must, for both their sakes.

'If there's nothing else, I shall settle with the carpenter and then we should leave to sort out supplies and other matters.'

Will moved to get up as her hand clasped his sleeve. 'Wait...please? What I wish for is for you to know something.' Her eyes were filled with unshed tears. 'The reason I stare at you, even when you are asleep, is because...because I want to remember everything about you.'

He screwed his eyes shut. 'Isabel...'

'You have my heart, Will. Surely that's enough?'

God, he hated this. The selfish part of him wanted to take her and make her his for good. But he couldn't do it.

'I'm afraid to say it's not, sweetheart. Not for either of us.'

'What if we want it be so?'

He reached out to cup her face, his thumb stroking over her tear-dampened skin. 'Look at me. I'm a bastard and I'll not taint you with that.'

'But—'

'You have no idea of the implications once it is known that I'm not the man I was thought to be—that I'm a bastard-born son. That my name is a lie. That everything about me is a lie. The rumours, gossips and disparaging remarks made behind our backs by courtiers would bring shame on you. I won't allow that to happen.'

'Then let's go back to Aquitaine. Run away from all of this.'

'We can't, sweetheart. We've come this far to get you back home. Besides, it's time we both stopped running away.'

'Then there's no hope for us?'

He got on his bended knees in front of her and shook his head. 'If there was a chance—a way that I could win you—do you not think I would take it?' He noticed every emotion swirling in her eyes before she finally gave a small nod of her head in resignation. He wanted to wrap her in an embrace, hold for a moment longer, but what would that achieve apart from prolonging all this? 'Come, we must be away. We have a long day ahead of us.'

They began the final part of their journey travelling west to Somersetshire. Isabel travelled on a sturdy wagon alongside an exceptionally chatty companion and a curmudgeonly old driver. Will rode beside them, with his appointed squire who was in fact the carpenter's younger son, and a guard he had contracted from goodness knew where.

Although they were a ramshackle group, it was arranged with much efficiency, as most things were when organised by William Geraint. He never lacked for anything, including silver. Will would be recompensed handsomely once he delivered her safely.

Isabel knew that was unfair, but they had barely had any contact and even less conversation since they had left Southampton. She knew the reason for this, but it wasn't easy and Isabel could feel the weight of his brooding whenever she caught Will's eyes. He remained protective of her, and courteous to a fault, seeing to her comfort along the journey, but it was clear that things were not the same between them. And it was clear that Will was pushing ahead, working tirelessly to get her back to Castle de Clancey, so that he could rid himself of this unbearable tension. A small voice inside her reminded her that he would finally rid himself of her as well.

Isabel gave herself an exasperated shake of the head to dispel these unnecessary musings. It simply would not do to dwell on the state of her relations with Will. They had settled everything before they'd left Southampton and she would do well to remember that. More pressing was Isabel's pending arrival at Clancey de Castle and the welcome she was likely to receive.

Indeed, she was apprehensive about it. After all, it had been a long time since she had last seen or heard from her mother. There was no way of knowing what to expect and so she could only remain hopeful. After all, Will had been commissioned specifically by her mother to find her and bring her back. Yes, she would focus on that sign of her mother's good judgement instead of worrying about the changes that would follow her return.

Oh, yes...so many changes.

With each day, she was becoming who she was supposed to be—the Lady de Clancey. It could be the heavier and more refined clothing, or the way in which she was greeted by their accommodating hosts along the way—be they farmer, blacksmith or merchant— but it was with an awed, deferential appreciation. This singular respect from people she had never met before was as odd as it was humbling and stifling. It would certainly need time to get used to.

Will was also gradually becoming the man he had once been. He had procured new clothing: a fine linen tunic, new hose and braes, padded leather gambeson and even a soft hauberk that reflected his position. Even though he wore no particular coat of arms on his surcoat or cape, there could be no doubt that Will was anything other than the man he was—a knight. And a powerfully strong one at that. Whether he truly felt this change, however, Isabel did not know, but hoped that he did.

After a few more days of travel they finally arrived at her childhood home—the splendid Castle de Clancey. Isabel had felt little more than numbness after they had docked at Southampton harbour, but this…this was different. Her response surprised her, catching her off guard as she tried and failed to swallow the lump that had suddenly lodged in her throat.

Dear God, but she felt close to tears.

Pieces of her memory were now brought together as one to form the idyll that she saw as they approached the castle. It was everything she remembered it to be. Castle de Clancey was perched on a hill hugged by its rugged curtain walls, four grey towers at each corner standing tall, a large keep at the centre of the inner bailey and the wide expanse of watery moat.

The village dwellings were studded around the outside of the castle walls with the demesne land and wooded forest beyond. Isabel noticed her family's banner with the colours of red, black and grey swaying in the breeze atop each tower and she swallowed hard. She turned and met Will's eyes as he gave her a single nod with a ghost of a smile, which she returned as they made their way down the hill.

Their small entourage made their way through the village to the entrance of the gatehouse. Isabel could hear the gasps as people stopped and stared at her, no doubt wondering whether she was whom they suspected her to be. Uncomfortable at being so conspicuous, Isabel sat with her spine straight, a benign smile pasted on her lips.

Her heart pounded in her chest as the drawbridge came down for them and, before long, they had trudged into the inner bailey. Her eyes darted around, taking in the familiar surroundings, from the garden and the separate building that housed the great hall to the woman who seemed to have rushed out from the castle keep.

Isabel recognised her immediately and jumped down from the wagon to stride towards her, stopping in front of her and sketching a formal curtsy. They stared at each other for a long moment as Isabel's eyes filled with tears.

'My lady mother.'

The smaller woman stepped forward and looked at her with a curious intensity before enveloping her in her arms. 'Oh, Daughter…oh, Isabel, it is really you!' she cried between tears. 'Thank the saints that you are finally home!'

Chapter Twenty

Will walked with the rest of their party behind Isabel as she was swept into the heart of the great hall, a large hammer-beamed chamber that was handsomely yet simply decorated with wide tapestries decorating every space of the stone walls, metal sconces around the edge of the room and a dais at the far end. Here, kitchen maids were busy laying out pewter jugs of ale and goblets as well as trenchers of cold meats, cheese, bread rolls and harvested apples.

'Allow your lady mother and me to welcome you, Lady Isabel.' A man whom Will had noticed in the courtyard when they arrived smiled as he spoke. He then proceeded to take Isabel's hand, bowing over it. 'Please make yourself comfortable, my dear, and partake in a small repast. You and your party must all be in need of sustenance.'

Will realised he must have been staring at the tall, thin man when he turned and met his eyes, handing him a goblet.

'You must be Sir William Geraint.'

'I am and who may you be, sir?'

'Sir Geoffrey Fitzwalter, at your service.' The man

inclined his head. 'You esteem us by finding Lady Isabel and accompanying her back here, where she belongs.'

Us? What the devil was this man talking about?

Will suddenly remembered a cousin by marriage whom Rolleston had mentioned. He had stayed on to help with matters after the death of Isabel's father and apparently continued to stay on, making himself indispensable to her mother, it seemed.

The man looked at least a decade older than Will, with receding hair, a long face and inscrutable eyes. His smile was slightly off kilter, especially when he addressed Isabel, making Will uneasy. Which brought him to another point. Where the hell was Rolleston? Had he fled or was he hiding somewhere within the castle walls?

Until this and other concerns were satisfactorily resolved, Will could not leave Isabel unprotected here. They had not travelled this far for Will to allow anything to happen to her now.

'I was honoured to bring my lady back to her mother and to protect her.' He flicked his gaze to Isabel, who was holding her mother's hands, and felt his chest tighten.

He had deliberately kept his distance ever since they had left Southampton, knowing it was the best way to eventually ease himself out of Isabel's life. His efforts had been a necessity to safeguard their bruised hearts and yet it had still been incredibly painful.

By God, she was lovely. She was dressed in a dark green woollen kirtle over a cream tunic with a scalloped-edged neckline. Her long hair was cascading in long, flowing waves to the small of her back, with intricate braids looped together at the back and pinned to a sheer veil, as was the fashion in Aquitaine.

'Sir William, I hope that your sojourn with us here will be a long duration?' Her mother tilted her head to speak to him, still holding her daughter's hands in her own. Will noted that despite the difference in height, the two were remarkably alike in appearance.

'You're too gracious, my lady. I shall stay for a short duration, if that meets with your approval?'

'We would have you stay longer, sir, for words cannot convey what you have done in…in bringing my daughter home.'

'My lady.' He sketched a bow.

He registered Isabel's brow rise, even though she didn't voice her surprise. She had not expected this sudden change of his plans, but then she had been so preoccupied with being reunited with her mother that mayhap she didn't feel as he did, the sense of foreboding he'd had since arriving in Somersetshire. Will could not dispense with the feeling that Isabel might not be safe here in her own ancestral home and he couldn't leave until he felt certain that she was.

Will didn't see much of Isabel again until the evening banquet in celebration of her return. In that time Will had familiarised himself with the castle's stronghold and asked its sergeant and others about Rolleston. No one, however, had seen the man for a sennight. He questioned Fitzwalter as well, who also denied knowing the man's whereabouts, but assured Will that he would get the silver promised to him. That was not the reason Will had asked, but the man did not need to know that. There was something untrustworthy about Fitzwalter, compounded by the fact that Will sensed he was lying about Rolleston. For now, though, all he could do was watch and wait.

One thing for certain was that the guards at the castle seemed to have cast their loyalty with Fitzwalter, unless they were his own personal guards to begin with. Either way, it was a precarious situation. The man had presumed the role of Lord in the absence of Isabel's father.

Will took a swig of ale as he watched Fitzwalter on the dais where he stood next to Isabel, fawning and being damned attentive. They were even sharing the same trencher of food, with the best cuts of choice meats selected by Fitzwalter himself. The man's ambition was clear, yet Will was not in a position to do anything about it except warn Isabel about his suspicions, such as they were.

He stabbed a small piece of mutton in herby mint sauce with a knife and proceeded to chew it without registering the taste. He seemed to be the only person in the hall who was not enjoying the convivial, festive atmosphere. Even Perdu was happily tucking into a bone.

Will sighed deeply and looked away from the revelry, peering around the hall instead. He noticed the tapestries that decorated every surface of the stone wall properly for the first time. The rich, opulent colours and stitchwork were magnificent by any measure, but it was the depiction of the ecclesiastical setting that was intriguing. What was strange wasn't that each tapestry told a different biblical story, but that each seemed to include a de Clancey family member. As though they had been there in the Holy Land at that very time.

Will snapped his head around as a troupe of musicians started to play. Fitzwalter accompanied Isabel down the dais and they began to dance to rapturous applause.

He ground his teeth together and shot up to join the circle of dancers, unable to contain himself any longer. More followed to join the group, but Will took no chances. He strode with purpose to stand beside Isabel, claiming her hand as they started the rather sedate dance, very different from the exuberant estampie that they had danced an age ago in Aquitaine.

'Is anything wrong, Will?' Isabel whispered when they partnered together.

'No, my lady. Should there be?' He noticed her stiffen as she always did when he addressed her formally. Yet it was the necessary reminder of their difference in station.

'Well, that is a relief,' she said with a wry smile. 'Although it doesn't explain your irascible mood.'

'Take no heed of me, Isabel. I have a lot on my mind.'

'What is the matter? You have been in a sullen mood ever since we arrived.'

'It's nothing.'

He reached for her, placing one hand around her waist while clasping her hand above their heads as they moved in a circular movement to the music. It was the first time that they had talked to one another properly since they had left Southampton. And also, the first time that Will was holding her this close again. It felt wonderful, despite the fact that it was not a good idea.

Yet Will couldn't resist. Being this close, holding her, the scent of her, the feel of touching her hand quickened his pulse. She looked resplendent in a deep magenta velvet dress with long fluted sleeves and square neckline that offset the silver and ruby pendant that she wore for the first time. Oh, yes, Isabel looked every bit the noblewoman that she was.

His eyes locked on to hers briefly before she swept

past him, moving to his side. They were filled with an intensity that matched his own longing. In fact, it was fortuitous that it had been broken by the movements of the dance. No good would ever come of such feelings.

By the time they partnered each other once more, Will had got hold of his wayward feelings, masking them. He knew that the only way to truly get over Isabel was to leave here as soon as he could. Yet he could not do that until he felt assured of her safety.

He turned to her. 'Tell me how you're faring?'

They parted and joined the main group, stepping up on their toes and down again, taking a step back before coming back together.

'To own the truth, I'm finding it all a little over-whelming.'

'I can imagine. And what of your reunion with your mother?'

'That, too.' She smiled wistfully. 'However, given time, I hope we shall become close.'

'I'm certain you shall, Isabel.'

'My thanks for everything you have done for me… but you need not stay here. It's clear that you do not wish to.'

'Are you wanting to be rid me, my lady?' He took her hand again, moving through the alternate couples.

'I don't believe I said words to that effect.'

'If you must know, I need to be certain of your safety.'

She smiled at him then, shaking her head. 'Really, do you think that's necessary with so many guards and knights in the garrison here?'

'Yes.'

She frowned. 'What *is* troubling you?'

'I don't know, Isabel, but something doesn't feel right

here and my instincts have never let me down before.'
He watched as she became a little pale.

She flicked her gaze to meet his. 'So that's why you agreed to stay a little longer?'

'Yes.'

'I see.'

'What is that supposed to mean?'

'Nothing, only that I now understand the brooding.'

'This is serious, Isabel,' he hissed. 'Your safety must be ensured before I can even think of leaving.'

'I think you're putting too much on all of this, but do as you wish. You're welcome to stay as long as you need to.'

'Until I know you're safe.'

Her brows furrowed. 'What is this about?'

'I don't know yet, but, when I do—' He stopped mid-sentence, his eyes fixed on the tapestries over Isabel's shoulder. 'Hell's teeth,' he muttered under his breath.

Isabel turned, darting her eyes around before meeting his gaze, her forehead creased in confusion. 'What is it? What have you seen?'

'Nothing.' He tried, but failed to keep the excitement out of his voice.

Thank God they joined the main group then, holding hands in a long line of dancers gliding together from one side to the other. This allowed for him to school his features into an expression that was hopefully a little nonchalant.

'I don't believe you.' She threw him a sideways glance. 'There's something you're not telling me.'

'Keep your voice down, my lady,' he whispered from the corner of his mouth.

'Only if you tell me.'

'Very well,' he said as the dance came to an end. 'But

not now. Meet me here before sunrise, when everyone is still abed.' He led her back to the dais and bowed over her hand before walking away without waiting for her answer, knowing it was nothing but a mistake to involve her. This was hardly a good way to protect Isabel.

Will stepped out of the shadows as he noted Isabel's tentative steps into the hall, carrying a torch and wearing the simple woollen grey cloak he had bought for her in Southampton. The hall was not altogether empty, with a few retainers and hearth knights asleep on pallets, and not exactly a place for a lady, but Will had promised to explain himself.

'You came.'

He raised a brow. 'You doubted I would?'

'I wasn't sure, but I'm glad you did.'

He had to stop himself from reaching for her. It was impossible, without an excuse such as the dance they had shared last night.

She blinked. 'So, what was it you wanted to say in such secrecy?'

How to proceed? How much to reveal and yet how much to withhold?

'It's to do with everything that happened in Aquitaine...and in La Rochelle.'

'I had wondered. Pray, continue.'

'You see, when the Templar, Phillipe de Sens, destroyed the vellum, I thought that would be the end of it.'

'As did I.'

'Precisely. There would be no reason to continue with something when there was never any hope in finding what the vellum alluded to, regardless of what I promised the dying Templar.'

She watched him for a moment before speaking. 'What did he say before he died, Will?'

He grimaced, looking away. 'Many things.'

'More than you told me at the time?'

'You were distraught Isabel, and there seemed little point in telling you all of it. However, I did tell you the main part of what he said.'

'I see.' She exhaled in obvious chagrin. 'Did he explain why, for instance, he burnt the vellum?'

'No, that I do not know. However, I believe he must have been worried that it might have found itself in the wrong hands, with Rolleston's men looking for it. Mayhap that was one reason why he did what he did.'

'He put his faith in you, however. That if you found whatever the vellum alluded to, you would hand it over to the Templars.'

'De Sens had little choice, Isabel. He made me make a solemn promise, as you know.'

She looked as though she finally understood what he was trying to convey. 'He told you, didn't he? He told you what he believed the vellum alluded to.'

'Yes.' He nodded and sighed. 'Remember when we first met him, he said that it could not be measured by any earthly value.'

'Yes, I remember.'

'By the time he was drawing his last breath, he knew exactly what that was, Isabel. An important sacred relic, stolen from the Templars over a century ago and brought to France from the Holy Land.'

'Sacred relic? I don't understand…and stolen by whom?' Her eyes widened suddenly. 'Oh…oh, heavens above…you believe that it was one of my de Clancey ancestors, don't you?'

He gave her a grim look. 'Yes, my lady. I believe it was.'

'It can't be. This is all so unbelievable.'

'Nevertheless, I'm afraid that it is true, especially now.'

'What do you mean, especially now? You know something, don't you?' When he didn't disagree, she narrowed her eyes. 'Tell me.'

'This may be dangerous, Isabel.'

'As well I know. What are we going to do?'

'You, Isabel, shall do nothing other than what you have been doing since your return, while I shall wait until I hear from Hugh.' He frowned, suddenly unsure if his old friend would acknowledge his missive.

It had more than a year since Will had heard from Hugh de Villiers, after his friend had used his prominent position to help quash his banishment. The fault in severing their ties, however, had lain with Will and he hoped he could remedy that now that he was back in England. Yet he was requiring his urgent assistance the moment he stepped foot in the kingdom. Not exactly an ideal start.

'Lord Tallany? What he has to do with any of this?'

'Nothing. I solicited his help and counsel with the anticipation of finding Rolleston here, which is why I had initially written to him.'

'But Rolleston is not here.'

'Apparently not, which is even more worrying.'

'You do not trust Geoffrey's... Sir Geoffrey's word.' *Good God! Geoffrey?*

'No, I don't and you'd do well to be more wary of him.'

'But he has given me no cause to—'

'Trust me on this, Isabel. Please.' He hadn't meant to interrupt her, but he had to labour this point.

She watched him before eventually nodding slowly. She then frowned as though she had just recalled something. 'And what do you mean by having me do nothing, while you investigate all of this?'

'Precisely that, my lady. You cannot be involved. As I said, this may be too perilous. I need to know that you're out of harm's way.'

'Do not dare to keep me out of this, William Geraint. Besides, *this*, as you call it, has been dangerous from the moment you stepped into my life.'

'That's hardly the point.'

'I'm telling you that I mean to assist in whatever it is you're doing.'

'No, Isabel.'

'Wait a moment,' she said, her eyes widening. 'You know where this relic is?'

'I had no notion of where it might be hidden. And to be honest, I hadn't thought about any of this since that night in La Rochelle. That is, until we came here.'

'Yet, you know *now*?'

'I'm not certain, but whatever this sacred treasure is, I now believe it may be here. Right here in Castle de Clancey.'

'*What?*'

Damn, but he had already revealed too much as it was.

'There something you're not telling me, Will.'

He dragged his fingers through his hair irritably. 'I said I don't want you involved.'

'And I said it's too late for that.'

'I want it noted, Isabel de Clancey, that I have warned

you. God's breath, this may be more dangerous than anything we've yet encountered.'

'Even so, we're in this together, or have you forgotten?'

No, Will hadn't forgotten anything about their journey or his time spent together with Isabel. It would be imprinted on his memory until he drew his last breath.

'Very well.' He nodded, finally acceding. Taking her by the shoulders, he turned her around to face the tapestries. 'Look. Do you see? There is a similar pattern on every one of the tapestries in this hall.'

'I don't know what I'm supposed to be looking at.'

He took the torch from her and shed light over them. 'Look again. What do you see? Look at the man in the furthest corner and see what he holds in his hand. It is small, but you can't mistake it.'

He watched Isabel before realisation suddenly dawned. 'Oh, my goodness, Will.' She snapped her head around. 'The pendants!'

Chapter Twenty-One

Isabel rushed from one magnificent tapestry to the next, trying to find the same symbolic motifs and clues. Each one depicted a different scene from the Stations of the Cross—the Last Supper, the Crucifixion and the Resurrection of Christ. In each intricately detailed narrative, it was there, included as though it had always been woven into the fabric of the story—the silver and ruby pendant.

Isabel spun around to face Will, utterly bewildered and astonished at what was and had always been here in Castle de Clancey.

He crossed his arms. 'Do you now understand why I believe this sacred relic is possibly here?'

'It all seems so incredible,' she shook her head. 'Yet the Templar Knight believed it had been stolen.'

'He did.'

'That the theft was committed by one of my ancestors?'

'Yes, I believe because of what was scribed on that vellum and the fact that the pendants have always been—'

'A family heirloom,' she muttered as she exhaled through her teeth. 'But why would anyone do that?'

'Power, greed—the same things that tempt all men.' He shrugged. 'I doubt we shall ever find out for certain.'

'In the process they put a curse on the house of de Clancey.' She flicked her gaze at him. 'We must lift it.'

'Which would mean we have to find whatever it is and take it back to Templars. The Lord Protector, William Marshal, is a Knight of the Order and could possibly help.'

'We would have to find this treasure in the first place, Will. How are we to do that?'

'I've been up all night staring at these tapestries, trying to gain some understanding.'

That made her frown. 'You haven't slept again?'

'There's much to consider.' He threw her a sideways glance. 'Besides, I've also been thinking about you and everything…afterwards.'

'As have I, but we shouldn't.' She shook her head, unable to say more.

'No.'

Isabel had been anticipating his departure ever since they had arrived. Her stomach lurched and knotted into a coil every time she considered the time when Will would finally leave Castle de Clancy, so much so that she couldn't really appreciate her reunion with her mother as well as she should. But if this was all the time she was going to have with him, then she would take it with both hands. Even this quest of finding the Templar's treasure was a welcome way for her to keep him by her side for a little while longer.

She swallowed and tried to direct her attention back to the task at hand.

'Tell me, have you discovered anything else? We

seem to have nothing more than a pair of pendants and few tapestries as our guides.'

'We have more than that, Isabel. You see, that is not all they are.'

'I don't comprehend.'

'Pay attention, my lady. There were three elements in all of this—the pendants, the vellum within...'

'And the tapestries.'

'Exactly. Each one linked to the other.' He pushed a loose tendril behind her ear, his fingers brushing against her skin briefly, sending a frisson of awareness down her spine. 'Your ancestor had an opportunity to steal an important relic either from the Templars, or from someone else. They brought it back here to Castle de Clancey and hid it so no one could ever find it or trace it back to them. They would have thought differently to you, Isabel, and believed that it was something that would protect future generations. And as a way to keep it within the family in perpetuity...'

Her head reeled. 'They had two pendants commissioned and scribed certain clues on a vellum within?'

'Precisely, then left clues as a way to find it—if there was ever need—on the tapestries.'

Something suddenly occurred to her. 'That is why Rolleston followed us, in pursuit of the pendants and the vellum. He knew about this.'

'Yes, and he may not be the only one. I would wager that this secret of the de Clancey family was only ever passed down from father to son, but then...somehow, someone found out about it.'

'Dear God...'

'Indeed.'

'But we need all three elements in finding this and we no longer have the vellum.'

'No…but I have been thinking, Isabel, that we had already uncovered all the inscriptions on the vellum. We must try to remember what was said. The rest we have found out since.'

'Would that be enough?'

He lifted his head and gave her a wry smile. 'There is only one way to find out.'

'Yes, we haven't a moment to lose.'

'Wait, Isabel.' He stilled her by the elbow. 'Dawn is about to break and the castle will be teeming with people soon.'

'When should we begin?'

'We'll meet again before sunrise, on the morrow.'

'Very well.' She nodded. 'Until later, Will.'

'My lady,' he said with a ghost of a smile. 'Remember not to talk to anyone about this.'

She gave him a speaking look before leaving.

Isabel had been impatient all day for the moment of her assignation with Will. It was astounding how much of a whirl her head had been in. She could barely eat or think about anything other than everything that they had discussed before dawn, so much so that her poor mother must have believed Isabel was hard of hearing with the amount of times she lost focus and had to ask for something to be repeated. Isabel couldn't help it, though. Much as she wanted to spend time with her mother, to renew their relationship, this issue had to be resolved before she could gain peace of mind.

Carrying a torch, she scurried down the spiral staircase from the solar with Perdu at her heel. They stepped out into the cool night's breeze, her warm cloak flapping around her legs as they rushed to the great hall.

'Isabel, is that you?'

'Yes, and I've got some exciting discoveries to share.' She hadn't seen Will all day but, strangely, had felt his presence wherever she went. He was either keeping a close watch on her, or possibly finding every opportunity to pass the tapestries as she had. She had surreptitiously studied each of them when no one was around and put them to memory.

The room was lit by her torch and the last remains of the ones left in the sconces and by the embers of the fire in the hearth. It wouldn't be long before the new day whispered through.

'Good evening...or rather, good morning, Isabel. I see you've brought our four-legged friend.' He scratched Perdu behind the ear before lifting his head. 'I have much to say to you, too.'

Her heart did a little somersault at the sight of him, clad only in dark braes and a wool tunic with a leather gambeson over the top.

'Well?' He raised a brow when she said nothing. 'What is it that you have uncovered?'

'Oh, yes, it's this tapestry here on the left. If you could kindly hold the torch?'

'My apologies, my lady,' he said with a smile, taking it from her.

'If you could hold it high, I'd be much obliged...that's it. Now do you see here...?' She pointed to the long, thin, arched stained-glass window depicted in the right-hand corner of the tapestry. 'Well, I have been pondering on this all day. It's such a small, insignificant design and yet so out of place, don't you think?'

He tilted his head as he studied it. 'I suppose so.'

'Then I realised why it puzzled me so.' She sank her teeth into her bottom lip, trying to contain her excitement. 'You see, I recognise it.'

'What do you mean?'

'The stained-glass window that you see here is a replica of the one found in the chapel here at Castle de Clancey.'

'Why would the tapestry include that?'

'Let me show you, Will, come. There's more.' She grabbed his hand as they rushed out of the hall. 'Whatever this sacred relic, I believe it's hidden somewhere in the chapel. Either that or we might possibly find more clues.'

They walked into the inner bailey and across the stone-arched bridge that separated the inner bailey from the outer one and the land beyond.

'By the way, I've been investigating what has happened to Rolleston. Despite being told that he'd suddenly left before we arrived, I've discovered that he was never actually seen leaving the castle. It's my belief that he may still be somewhere here, within these walls.' When she stopped abruptly, he held out his hand to her. 'Don't worry, I'll catch up with him soon. Come, let's get to this find of yours.'

The chapel was in the furthest reach of the castle curtain, surrounded by its own garden and a rose arbour that led to the steps of the stone building. The arched wooden door creaked open as they let themselves in. It wouldn't be long before the start of matins—they would have to gather their findings quickly.

Isabel lit all the chapel candles to provide more light before leading Will to the furthest wall in the chancel, past the altar to a tiny sliver of an arched window directly opposite, on the right-hand side. She placed the torch she'd carried into a metal sconce as Will placed his on the opposite sconce. They turned to face it. Here the glass had been split into five colours, matching exactly the same as in the tapestry.

'Do you see, Will? It's the same window.' She turned to face him. 'More importantly, this was on the tapestry depicting the crucifixion.'

'Importantly?'

'Yes, because it begs the question—why? I have been asking myself this since I found the window.'

'And have you come closer to understanding more?'

'It's just a silly notion, but do you recall what Father Gregor said when we visited him at St Savinien? That the symbols on the vellum mainly referred to the cross. Even the rose and its five petals symbolised the...'

'The five wounds of Christ,' Will muttered slowly before meeting her eyes.

'Yes, and there were five tallies marked on the vellum, resembling a cross. Do you remember?'

'I do, but what do you suppose this has to do with the sacred relic?'

'That is what I'm trying to ascertain.'

'Go on.' Will's brows met in the middle as he crossed his arms across his wide chest.

'I've been scouring the chapel for clues ever since I made the finding.'

He exhaled deeply. 'Didn't I specifically say not to do anything without me?'

'I haven't, except for only a little investigating on my own. I promise.'

'I hope so.' He exhaled deeply a second time, shaking his head. 'But I can see from your face that you've found something.'

She grabbed both of his hands and gave them a squeeze. 'I have. Come and look on the ground here in the chancel. The mosaic is inlaid here in a pattern except this one square slab near the altar. Unlike the rest, it's not inlaid. Instead, the tiles seem to be stuck on to the stone. Have a look at the centre mosaic, there is a faint marking.'

Will crouched on his knees. 'The old sign of the cross again that we found on the vellum,' he said before whistling low. 'And that oval hole beside it is a lock, if I'm not mistaken.'

'That is exactly what I thought!' She clapped her hands together.

He tilted his head back in frustration. 'That is all well and good, but we don't have a key.'

'Do we not?' She dangled a long metal key with a thick stem and lozenge-shaped handle between her fingers.

A slow smile spread on Will's handsome face, his blue eyes twinkling with a bewildered excitement.

'Where in heavens did you get that?'

She shrugged. 'Father Lambert, the chaplain here. He said as custodian of the key, he could only give it to my father's heir—namely, me.'

'You, Isabel de Clancey, are a marvel.' He cradled her head and kissed her on the lips. 'But then I've always known that.'

She touched her mouth at the unexpectedly brief impulsive kiss, which had sent a tingling warmth through her body. No, this was not the time to even acknowledge such a moment. 'Never mind that. Let's open this stone and see what hides beneath. Here, take the key.'

Will got to work and unlocked it. He grabbed the dagger attached to his sword belt and scraped the edges of the stone slab. Eventually it became loose enough for him to lift it out in one piece.

They both peered into the darkness below. Isabel

grabbed the torch from the sconce and flooded light into the hole. There was a large wooden plank with a metal ring set within the stone foundation beneath the flooring.

'It looks like a metal door knocker. And the base of the metal has the same motif, the five-petal rose, as on the vellum.'

'So it does.' Will pulled this open, revealing a dropped layer beneath, made entirely of metal. This time there was a small lozenge shape sunk in the middle. 'I have an idea what fits into this. Are you still wearing your pendant, Isabel?'

'Yes.' She took it off and passed it to Will, who removed his own pendant from around his neck and fitted them together. He then carefully inserted this into the sunken, melded shape in the centre.

'What now?'

'I have an idea.' He turned and nodded at her. 'It's been staring us in the face from the moment we discovered the vellum.'

'The cross…' she hissed, her eyes wide with eagerness.

'Exactly. It has always been about the cross and the sign in prayer.'

Will pushed the pendants up, down, left, and right, hearing a click at each point.

'In nomine Patris… Et Filii… Et Spiritus sancti.'

Finally, back to the centre, hearing the last click.

'Amen.'

This made the hinged door open, revealing a large wooden box. They both stared at it before Will reached below and grabbed it, hauling it out and laying it on the stone floor.

Isabel spread her hands on either side of Will's face,

pulling him towards her and planting a swift kiss on his lips, just as he had done only moments ago. 'You, William Geraint, are also a marvel.'

She had surprised him, but this was a night filled with surprises.

He collected himself, nodding to Isabel to remove the lid. They both stared inside at the decorative casket.

'I believe you should do the honours, my lady.' He smiled as Perdu started barking. 'Quiet, you.'

Isabel bit her lip as she pulled the casket out, staring at it in wonder. 'It's a reliquary casket and, heavens, it's astonishingly beautiful. Should I open it?'

He placed his hand over hers and shook his head. 'I wouldn't if I were you. You can imagine what it might contain.'

She nodded. 'I believe that it would be pieces of the true cross.' She leant back and frowned as she stared at the casket. 'Do you believe it is real?'

'That's of no importance either way, Isabel. The immense power that can be wielded by whoever owns it is what matters. And of huge concern. That is why it's imperative for the Templars to have it back.'

'Which they shall,' Isabel muttered.

Perdu started to bark more incessantly. 'What is the matter, boy?'

Will got up from his haunches and looked around the alter to find Geoffrey Fitzwalter, Eustace Rolleston and the pock-faced man they had encountered in Aquitaine. The three stepped out from around the shadowy pillars and moved towards them. They had a handful of men behind pointing their swords, surrounding them.

Perdu continued to bark, growl and bare his teeth.

'I'm afraid not, my lady,' Fitzwalter said, as his thin lips curled upwards.

Chapter Twenty-Two

'You!'

'Your servant, my lady.' Fitzwalter made a mock bow as Rolleston and his men laughed.

'How dare you come into my castle and its chapel in the belief that you can intimidate us in this way!'

'Oh, I dare, Lady Isabel, I dare very much,' he sneered. 'You speak with such fearless defiance behind your reprobate of a mercenary knight, but you are both outnumbered.'

'Shall we put that to the test?' Will thundered, as he drew his sword out from its scabbard. 'I see you've brought your own brand of murderous mercenaries. Ah, Rolleston, we meet again at last.'

'The pleasure is all mine, Sir William,' Rolleston scoffed.

'Lower your weapon, Geraint.' Fitzwalter brushed something off his shoulder. 'Would you want to endanger the lady's life so recklessly?' At Will's hesitation he raised a brow. 'No, I didn't think so.'

'Why?' Isabel muttered, knowing she had to keep the man talking. This would hopefully allow time for

Will to think of something in this desperate situation. Or at least she hoped that he would.

'I have waited a long time for this moment. A moment I believed I had lost all those years ago when you were presumed dead and buried…the pendants with you.'

'You knew about the pendants?'

'Well, naturally, your arrogant fool of a father was very careless about his secrets,' he snarled, throwing her a disdainful glare. 'Once I realised that both pendants had quite accidentally fallen into your possession, I had to get them back…by any means. Even if it meant orchestrating an ambush all those years ago.'

Isabel felt the warmth of Will's hand on her shoulder. 'You're quite mad,' she whispered.

The smile that spread on Fitzwalter's face made her stomach turn in disgust.

'No, not mad, merely shrewd enough to understand the true worth of what you hold in your hands, my lady. Now, if you would please hand it over?' He held out his hand. 'And get that infernal animal under control or I shall kick him to kingdom come.'

Isabel picked up Perdu and put him on the ground near her. 'Stay,' she ordered before stretching to her full height. 'Don't ever threaten my dog.'

Isabel schooled her features in the hope that she looked unafraid and assured—the opposite of what she actually felt. 'As you were saying, sir, you believed that the pendants were lost. Your hopes of getting *this* gone.' She nodded to the casket. 'Why did you remain here, Sir Geoffrey? Did you…did you have something to do with my father and brothers' deaths?'

Isabel wasn't certain that she really wanted to know,

but she must have the truth for both her mother's sake and her own.

'Your father was as indolent as he was profligate. His dissolute sons no better,' he spat. 'These lands are littered with his bastards and I can tell you that many sighed a welcome relief when they learnt of his downfall.'

Bastards?

This man was surely lying. 'It's not true.'

'Oh, but I'm afraid it is. What happened to your father and his sons was nothing short of justice.' He took a step towards them. 'Now, I shall say this one more time, Lady Isabel. Hand over the reliquary box to me.'

'No.' Will moved forward, blocking Isabel from the obnoxious toad. 'I don't think so. Come any closer and I skewer you from here to here,' he said, indicating the man's neck to his navel with the sharp point of his sword.

The short amount of time that Isabel had bought for him to come up with a solution meant that he had evaluated all their options and come up with very little. The only way out of this mess was to somehow get out of the chapel with the casket and with their lives intact.

Damn...

There were two entrances and one of them was blocked by Fitzwalter and his men, which meant their best hope was to aim for the side entrance. He jostled Isabel back and to the left of the nave, through the aisle towards it.

Slowly, oh, so very slowly, they moved back. Will surveyed every direction, noting any possible attack in his periphery.

Fitzwalter followed, prowling towards them as some

of his men splintered off, moving around to the back to block their progress.

'Have you got weaponry you can spare?' Isabel mumbled from behind him.

'Not this again,' he hissed as he surreptitiously passed his dagger to her. 'Take it, but try not to use it unless you have to.'

Their movement towards the side entrance was curtailed as two of Fitzwalter's men catapulted themselves at Will from either side of the aisle.

'Watch out, Will!'

He engaged one of them with his sword, dispatching him to the side with a handful of swipes before quickly tackling the other, who was also no match for him. 'Take care, Isabel,' he bellowed as he motioned towards the side entrance with his head. 'Move behind me.'

More of Fitzwalter's men came forward, their swords at the ready.

'This is all so unnecessarily futile, Sir William.'

'Just so. You can still do the honourable thing, Fitzwalter, and let us leave.'

'Sadly, that's not possible. Come now, hand me the casket and give yourselves up.'

'I'm afraid not, Sir Geoffrey. Sadly, *that* really is not possible either,' Isabel muttered from behind him, throwing the odious man's words back at him.

God, but Will loved her! And he would do everything in his power—even give his life—to protect Isabel de Clancey. His life was expendable. Hers was not. And the moment to prove that, it seemed, was drawing closer. As long as he could get Isabel out of this perilous situation, then that was all that mattered.

They both kept walking backwards as Fitzwalter and his men swarmed around them from every direction.

Will's eyes darted around the chapel, trying to weigh up their chances of success, but, no, it did not bode well. He still could not think of how to get out of this hole they were in. They were simply outnumbered and Fitzwalter's damned men were closing in. His heart was drumming a march. God's breath, but it had come to this…

'We're up by the side door, Will,' Isabel whispered from behind him. He could hear the little dog scratching his paws against the wooden frame.

'Good.' He maintained the positive note in his voice even though he was beginning to doubt their chances. 'See if you can open it. I'll keep them at bay,' he said under his breath.

No sooner had he uttered those words than he had to counter more strikes from sword blades from different directions.

'The door's stuck!' Isabel muttered in anguish. 'It won't open.'

'Try again,' he roared as he defended another onslaught. 'Quickly, Isabel.'

'Come now, you are hemmed in.' Fitzwalter's voice reverberated from the hallowed walls. 'All I want is the casket.'

'Is that so?' a familiar voice bellowed from the rear of Fitzwalter's barricade.

They turned to find that another set of guards had streamed into the small chapel behind their leader—*Hugh de Villiers.*

Will's shoulders visibly sagged with relief at the sight of his friend standing proudly in the middle of the maelstrom, his commanding presence creating the necessary shift of advantage.

Thank God!

Will caught Hugh's eyes and made a single nod of

gratitude, a lump forming in his throat at the expediency of his friend's arrival.

Fitzwalter finally spoke. 'Who are you, sir, and what are you doing here?' His obvious shock at this intrusion manifested in outrage. 'You are unwelcome. Take your men and leave.'

Hugh didn't look at the man, but spoke to all of them. 'I come at the behest of my friends, Sir William Geraint, Lady Isabel de Clancey, chatelaine of this castle, and William Marshal, Earl of Pembroke and Lord Protector of England. Throw down your weapons and surrender...or face the consequences.'

Will knew, from the way Fitzwalter's jaw had set, there would be little chance of that. The man would not yield and intended to fight to the death. Which meant only one thing—the unpredictability of hand-to-hand combat.

'You are surrounded by Lord Tallany and his men, Fitzwalter. Submit now.' Will was astounded by the man's singular ambition and greed. 'As for you, men of Castle de Clancey, your fealty should be to your lady here and not to this man posing as lord. He is nothing but an imposter.'

His words had the desired effect of causing a murmur of uncertainty among the castle guards.

Isabel stepped to his side, addressing the assembled group. 'I swear to those of you who return your loyalty to me that you'll receive a full pardon. Please do this. There is no need for fighting.'

Isabel's heartfelt speech gave Will ample time to motion silently to Hugh. He gave him a sign by flexing his thumb and forefinger, receiving a small nod of acknowledgment in return. Good. He understood that the most strategic way to get Fitzwalter to concede defeat was to surround him and his men. They would also have to allow them to strike first.

'Any turncoat would do well to remember that you, your family and anyone associated with you shall be wiped off the face of this earth should you decide to take that course of action,' Fitzwalter jeered. 'Is that not right, Rolleston? Le Jeniquens? Canerue?'

'You've lost, Fitzwalter. Yield and surrender.' They were outflanked and the blasted man knew it, meaning he could pose more danger than even before. Will skirted around the edge of the chapel, his sword at the ready.

'Never!' Fitzwalter lunged, engaging him with his sword. Will turned on his heel as he made a defensive swipe, using his superior height and strength to his advantage. 'I've come too far, and for too long, to yield now.'

Will knew from the clatter of movement and clashing of swords that Hugh and his men were also now immersed in the fray. He just hoped that Isabel was safe and tucked out of harm's way. 'Then on your head be it, Fitzwalter.' He scowled before stepping forward and pushing the man back with a quick succession of attacking strikes. He deflected the man's attempts, countering them with potent thrusts that Fitzwalter had difficulty matching.

Without even turning, he knew Hugh was now beside him, engaged in his own personal combat with Rolleston, who was hardly a match for his friend.

'You took your time.' Will's lips curled faintly.

'Is this the thanks I get for rushing to your aid the moment you get back to England?'

This felt a little like old times when they would fight side by side, looking out for one another in combat.

Will smirked as he lunged forward, striking Fitzwalter's sword again and again. 'I've missed you, old friend.'

'Glad to hear it.' Hugh leant back against the bench and kicked Rolleston in the stomach, winding him. 'And less of the old, if you please.'

'Well, you seem a little out of practice. I thought it may have something to do with your happy situation, which reminds me…how is Eleanor?'

Hugh grimaced as he pushed back against Rolleston's sword. 'She is with child again and plagued with the sickness curse.'

'I cannot imagine your formidable lady being cowed by any affliction.'

'Ah, but she is. Especially as your godson, William, is a handful.' Hugh shrugged. 'The little mite takes after his namesake.'

Will grinned as he swiped at Fitzwalter's sword. 'Good to know.'

Their two opponents were sweating profusely at their exertion, getting more and more fatigued during this exchange. Good. This was exactly how to wear the bastards down.

Fitzwalter stood on a step in an attempt to allow himself more leverage. The man had gumption, Will would give him that, but then he was also desperate—which made Fitzwalter all the more dangerous. He had nothing left to lose.

Will flicked his gaze around to find Isabel also doing her bit to help with the situation. Her plucky dog was valiantly defending his mistress by growling and yapping relentlessly if anyone dared come too close. Thankfully, she had sensibly stood on the sidelines and was seemingly acting only when threatened. He noticed her smack the metal hilt of the dagger he'd given her on the skull of a man who had ventured too close.

She was nothing if not brave, but Will had to get to her—she wasn't adequately protected as she continued to fend off assailants on her own—but he had to subdue Fitzwalter first. Will lunged forward, attacking him with sharp blows of the sword, but the older man managed to defend himself, even as his sword licked the side of the man's face and again his arm.

'Give in, Fitzwalter, you're not going to thwart me.'

'We'll see about that.'

Fitzwalter grabbed a small youth and pushed him out in front to act as shield before hurling the lad towards him. Will checked that he was unharmed before he pursued Fitzwalter, but it was too late. The man had taken Isabel by surprise and now held her from behind. The point of the dagger—*his* dagger—pressed into the delicate skin at her neck.

Will tried not to betray a flicker of emotion. He could not show this man how enraged he felt as his heart roared in his chest, threatening to erupt. He vowed to himself if anything happened to her… No, he couldn't think in that way. He had to keep a clear head and appear outwardly composed when what he actually wanted to do, was to tear Fitzwalter limb from limb.

'Lay down your arms!' the man screamed. 'Do it, now.'

Will turned and nodded to Hugh, his jaw rigid with tension. Only Rolleston, the pock-faced assailant and one other were left standing—the rest were either restrained by Hugh's men or had fled the scene. That meant nothing, though, as Fitzwalter had Isabel.

'We surrender.'

One by one, they slowly threw down their weaponry,

the sudden silence broken by the noise of the metal hitting the hard stone floor. 'Now, don't do anything rash. Just let the lady go.'

'All I wanted was that,' Fitzwalter said between breaths as he motioned with a tilt of the head towards the casket tucked under his arm. The other was closed tight around Isabel's neck. He stepped back, dragging Isabel with him. 'I want your word that I can leave here with a mount. My men and I should be allowed to leave the castle. Only then can you have your whore back.'

Will noticed Isabel visibly flinch at the words, but she didn't say anything, knowing as he did that it was best to hold her tongue.

'Give me your solemn word as a man of honour, Sir William.'

'You have it,' Will said quietly. 'Now, let the lady go.'

The chapel was deathly still except for Isabel's dog. It was jumping and yapping furiously, sensing that the man meant his mistress harm.

'If that dog does not shut up, I swear I shall run it through with this,' the older man hissed. 'Now get me a horse and we'll be away.'

Perdu bared his teeth, growling, and then it happened. Perdu's teeth sunk into Fitzwalter's ankle just as Isabel leant to the side and punched him in his unmentionables, the way Will had shown her. As Fitzwalter lost his grip on her she elbowed him hard in the stomach for good measure.

Will quickly pulled Isabel into his arms as Hugh and his men retrieved their blades from the ground and pointed them at Fitzwalter, Rolleston and the handful who were left.

It was over, thank God.

'Well played, my lady.' Hugh grinned at Isabel before addressing Will. 'It seems *your* lady is as formidable as mine, old friend.'

Chapter Twenty-Three

Isabel watched in bemusement as Will glared at his friend. They certainly seemed as close as brothers. And after all his difficulties of the last few years, it was good to see Will esteemed by his friend, and accepted for who he was.

Hugh inclined his head, his grin still pasted on his face, before leaving the chapel, followed by his men dragging the prisoners out.

Isabel was now once again alone with Will.

Without their quest and the mystery of the pendants to unravel, she suddenly felt shy, not knowing what to do or where to look. So she stared at her hands, instead.

Will curled a stray tendril of hair behind her ear, his fingers grazing her jaw and down the side of her neck. 'He didn't harm you, did he?'

'No.' She shook her head. 'My throat feels a little sore, but otherwise I am well.'

He hissed an oath under his breath. 'A small mercy because if anything had happened to you, I swear I would have—'

Isabel's hand reached out and touched his shoulder. 'I'm perfectly well.'

He exhaled, shaking his head as the tension faded from his eyes, replaced by humour. 'I'm glad, but, in truth, you were perfectly wonderful.' He leant forward. 'I believe you have now mastered that move, but promise me that you'll only ever use it when absolutely necessary.'

Her lips twitched. 'I promise.'

'And never reveal who taught you how to do that.'

'My lips are sealed.'

He returned her smile and for a moment they stood facing each other at the side of the aisle. After a moment Isabel broke the silence. 'Shall we go?'

'After you, my lady.' He motioned with an outstretched arm.

He took a step towards the front entrance, but she stopped him. 'The side entrance…well, it can open now.'

'Of course it can,' he said wryly, holding the door open for her and Perdu. 'Come.'

They walked out to the side of the building, to be welcomed by the glow of the morning sunrise. Isabel blinked, her eyes adjusting to the light. She breathed in the heady scent of the herbs in the garden, enhanced by the morning dew. There was sage, mint, dill, comfrey and blueish-purple-topped, spiky-stemmed, hyssop— the herb that she'd used when tending to Will's wound all those weeks ago with its blue petals that she had later scattered in the chamber after their night of intimacy in La Rochelle. She swallowed uncomfortably at the memory.

'With your permission, I'd be honoured to do your bidding, Isabel,' Will said, picking off the top of the flowering purple herb. 'I'll accompany Hugh, taking the casket, Fitzwalter and the rest of the prisoners to the Earl of Pembroke. It shall be his decision on what is to be done with them, including consigning this to the Templars.'

'Thank you.' She nodded in agreement before lifting her head. 'You have my gratitude, Will. When...' She caught her bottom lip between her teeth. 'When would you depart?'

'As soon as may be, my lady.'

'I see.' There seemed little more to say, yet so much more she wanted to.

They walked through the garden, along the path around the corner of the chapel. 'You're not coming back, are you?'

'Isabel...' He left her name hanging in the air, imbued with something akin to painful longing.

Dear lord, this was difficult.

'Come back, Will.' She exhaled a shaky breath. 'When this is all over, come back to me.'

He stilled her, grasping her elbow. 'I would want for nothing more, but you know that can't happen.'

'I begin to understand it less and less.' She lifted her head up to meet his gaze. 'Why should we not be together if we both wish it?'

'Do not ask this of me.' Her back was against the stone wall with his hands placed either side, enclosing her. 'Christ, Isabel. I'm no different to all the poor bastards, apparently, sired by your father and many men like him. I'm not fit to stand by you.'

'Would you listen to yourself!' she hissed in frustration. 'I don't care which side of the coverlet you were sired on, Will. Can you not see your own worth? Because from where I stand, it's far more than my father's, who cared little about anyone other than himself.'

'Oh, Isabel.' He cupped her cheek, his thumb brushing her skin. 'I would do anything for you, but this… us… Much as I want it, with all my heart, it cannot be.'

'Does my love not count for anything?'

'It counts for more than you'll ever know and it shall stay with me until I breathe my last. But it is not enough,' he whispered softly, tilting her head up. 'Matters of the heart cannot supersede matters to do with duty and obligation. This is the world we dwell in.'

'We can change that.'

'No, sweetheart.' He kissed her fingers. 'I wish… I wish I could be the man to deserve you, but I'm not.'

An ache formed in her throat, making it impossible to say anything.

How dare he!

How dare he believe he was not good enough for her, as though he was beneath her.

'You are a noble lady, Isabel. The chatelaine of this castle,' he continued. 'When I see you, I see someone strong, resilient, capable and, above all, kind-hearted. It has been my privilege to know you…to love you. And it's precisely because of my love for you that I must let you go. My honour demands it.'

Well…what could she say to that?

Beg him to stay? Her conscience would never permit her to do *that*. Yet she felt like shaking him out of this narrow mindset. After everything they had both been through, they deserved happiness, did they not? Despite the difference in rank between them? Isabel didn't care about that anyway. She had grown up among ordinary people—she understood them and the problems they faced better than most noble ladies. But Will did not see it that way and mayhap he never would. She realised something then…something she had overlooked until now.

She did not need William Geraint to survive. She had proven that she was more than capable to do that on her own. Isabel had survived the ambush when she had been all but a little girl. She had survived her family's abandonment, survived living in a convent and in St Jean de Cole. She had survived the journey back to England and would learn to survive this…losing Will. She would survive it even though it would take time. Even though she'd be heartsick. She knew all about difficulties in enduring and overcoming hurt. It seemed that she would have to do it again.

'Well then' she said finally, her head held high. 'There's nothing left to say.'

'You have been quiet for hours, Will. Is there something that you wish to confer with me about?' Hugh threw his friend a worried gaze as he rode alongside him.

It had been a long while since they had left Castle de Clancey. A long while since Isabel had stood on the steps of the castle keep beside her mother, looking dignified and gracious with her back straight and her gaze passive as she bid him farewell. Will knew he would never see her again and that image of her would be etched in his head for all time, along with many others that were all too painful to ponder on.

'No. It has been a tiring few weeks. That's all.'

'Either you're a good liar Will, or you're getting too old for such campaigns.'

'Perhaps I am.'

'Come now, you and I always shared everything, even our woes.'

'Did we?' Will's jaw was set so hard, it almost hurt. 'Forgive me, but I seem to have forgotten.'

He knew he was being churlish, especially as Hugh had come out of his way to help with the matter of Fitzwalter, but Will felt like lashing out at someone. Someone close at hand.

'Haven't you punished yourself enough, my friend?' Hugh muttered softly.

That got his attention.

He whipped his head around. 'What do you mean?'

'You know precisely what I mean, Will. You have not only punished yourself for what happened at Portchester, but everyone around you. Me, your family… Tell me, is it now the turn of Lady Isabel?'

'You know nothing about it.'

'Do I not? I believe I have eyes and ears and from what I saw at Castle de Clancey, I could see how deeply you both care about one another.'

'You do not understand.'

'Believe me, I do.' Hugh's voice was low, but filled with barely concealed bitterness. 'Or rather, I have been trying to for the past few years.'

'What happened at Portchester…'

'Always befalls men like us, Will. It's something we all have to live with. You were betrayed by another and yet you're the one riddled with guilt. You do your men a disservice by shouldering all the blame. Those men died in honour, protecting their King, as was their duty.'

'Yet King John believed so vehemently that the fault lay with me that he had me banished, for heaven's sake.'

Hugh shook his head. 'God rest his soul, but John was always quick to cast blame on others, rather than look closer to his circle of mercenaries. You know this and, even if it were true, which it never was, you exonerated yourself with the information you provided Marshal at the battle in Lincoln, without which we could have lost to the Barons and Prince Louis.' He threw him a glance. 'This isn't about that anyway and you know it.'

Hell's teeth!

'What I know is that this is not a welcome topic of conversation.'

'That may be so. But if this is about wanting something—or rather, someone—whom you believe you should not have... It's not true.'

'You don't comprehend. My mother—'

'She has told me everything, Will.'

'Apologies, then you *do* understand.' Will focused his attention putting his horse through its paces as he galloped ahead. Hugh soon caught up with him. 'We cannot belong to one another, Isabel and I. You must see that.'

'What I see is someone who is, and has been, unhappy for some years now.' Hugh sighed. 'Besides, if you've given her your heart in exchange for hers, then it seems to me that some part of her *does* belong to you.'

'It is not as simple as that.'

Hugh pulled the reins, bringing his horse to a halt, forcing Will to do the same. 'Life is perilous as it is, with danger and hardship at every turn. You know as well as I—as well as any soldier—how precarious life can be. One moment we're here and the next...' He clicked his fingers. 'It's extinguished. If you have a chance at happiness, even fleetingly, then grasp it with both hands, my friend.'

'I would not dishonour Isabel. I'd be no better than Geoffrey Fitzwalter in his greed—taking something that cannot belong to me.'

'How can it be, if it's freely given?' Hugh leant forward, patting his horse.

'What of duty, then, or familial obligation?'

'What of it?' Hugh frowned before shaking his head. 'I shall say this just on this one occasion, since I wouldn't want your head to become any bigger than it need be, but…you are both honourable and brave, William Geraint. You have always done your duty by this kingdom, your men and your family. I have always been proud to stand beside you…in every situation.'

Will was so surprised by this admission that he was momentarily speechless, but Hugh was not done.

'And you should never doubt a connection of the heart. It may be frowned on, with the belief that it weakens a man, but I speak from experience when I say that it is, in truth, the opposite.'

'I do not care about the accepted rule on courtly love. That is not what I fear.'

'Then what?' Hugh raised a brow. 'What are you so afraid of?'

Will blinked, not knowing the answer. What was he afraid of? He didn't know. Could it be that the circumstances of his birth meant that Isabel de Clancey was out of his reach? Was that really the reason?

'Can you not see your own worth? Because from where I stand, it's far more than my father's.'

Hugh filled the silence. 'Whatever it may be, it should not determine how you live your life. You should not care about any of it, Will.'

A slow smile quirked at the corners of his lips. 'When did you become so wise?'

'When I had the love of a good woman.' Hugh's smile turned wistful as he met his friend's eyes. 'You deserve her, Will…and I believe she deserves you.'

Could this be true? Will wasn't certain whether this was even feasible.

He had been so determined, so adamant that there

could be no future with Isabel, that he hadn't stopped to consider it. He hadn't contemplated his chances. If it was even remotely possible for him to grasp happiness, however fleetingly, as Hugh had put it, then surely, he must pursue that.

He had to find the courage to fight for that…

A steely glint flashed across his blue eyes. He turned to his friend and nodded. Yes, he would. He would fight for her if need be.

Will looked around the small yet intimate chamber within Caversham Castle, which was more a family manor than a true defensive stronghold. These were the private rooms of the most powerful magnate in the kingdom—William Marshal, Lord Protector and Earl of Pembroke.

Will knew he should feel privileged to have secured a private meeting with the older man, but also felt the stirrings of apprehension. It was Marshal's decision as Lord Protector whom Isabel de Clancey could marry. Will's whole future hinged on the success of this discussion and that was before he could even put it to Isabel.

'Ah…good. Sir William Geraint, please take a seat.' The older man limped slightly into the chamber with his hands behind his back, taking a seat behind a wooden coffer. 'I hope your journey from the Tower was agreeable after incarcerating the prisoners from Castle de Clancey.'

'Thank you, my lord, it was.'

The man might look like a benevolent grandsire, but Will was not so easily fooled. Marshal was a consummate politician—as shrewd and canny as anyone in the kingdom. Actually, even more so, since Will couldn't think of a single man in his seventieth year being able to take charge at the Battle of Lincoln, as Marshal had the previous year. No wonder there were few men whom Will admired and respected as much. Still, that did not mean that this meeting would go well for him.

'Good. The situation has resolved to a satisfactory conclusion, then.'

Not quite…

'It has, my lord.'

'Yet I believe you did not come here to discuss that matter. Would you care for some repast?' He ambled to the side table, already prepared with a jug, a few matching goblets and platefuls of sweetmeats and delicate pastries. 'Tell me, Sir William, is this unexpected visit to do with your due of silver from the Templars, which I have been informed shall be restored to you…or the Lady de Clancey?'

'Thank you, my lord,' he muttered as the older man pressed the goblet in his hand. 'And, no, I have not come about the Templar silver.'

'Ah… I see.' Marshal sat opposite him, sipping wine as he studied him over the rim of his goblet, making Will feel self-conscious, but he continued to hold his tongue. Eventually, Marshal sighed and broke the silence.

'I understand, Sir William. More than you know. And I have often thought that it is unfair that the sins of a father are often passed to their sons to bear. My own father had forsaken me to King Stephen, who threatened to have me executed, you know, when I was just a small child. A father who had claimed to be able to forge better sons from his hammer and anvil was not one whom I could depend on and so I learnt from a young age that I had to make my own way in the world, as I'm certain you did, especially…in your circumstances.'

God's breath! How the devil did Marshal know all this about him?

And he was not done talking. 'I, too, was an ambitious, landless, errant knight like *you*, Sir William.'

This was not going well at all. 'Allow me to explain, my lord—'

Marshal held up his hand to silence Will's interruption. Damn it, he would not leave until the man listened to him.

'If I could just put my case to you.'

'There is no need as I have already made my decision.'

Made his decision before Will even had a chance to explain?

Marshal continued. 'I'm not long for this world, Sir William, and the young King Henry is all but a boy. Once I'm gone, he'll be pulled in every direction by men who would use him for their own gain. I cannot allow it,' he muttered, taking another sip of wine. 'Not after everything this kingdom has been through to finally heal from all the self-inflicted wounds of these bitter battles between ourselves. I need to surround the Boy King with men I can trust and believe would serve him implicitly.'

Will couldn't believe his ears. Had the old man implied what he thought he had? 'Men like...*me*?'

Marshal tilted his head as he regarded him. 'You would never break your allegiance with the young Henry, despite his father's past transgressions in his dealings with *you*, so, yes, I believe you would serve England well, as you always have done, William.'

Will was speechless. 'Do you mean to tell me that you give me leave to court Lady Isabel?'

'With my blessing.'

It was all he could wish for, yet Will didn't want Isabel to be forced into anything against her wishes. She had been through much and endured a lot in her lifetime. It had to be her choice whether to accept him or not. She might want more time to enjoy being chatelaine or even possibly decline him after all. Either way, he would accept whatever she decided.

Besides, Will was under no false impression. He was being given Isabel's hand for his fealty to the young King, which he would be happy to swear to, but he needed some sureties.

He gave his head a little shake. 'I'm honoured, my lord, but after the trials that Isabel de Clancey has been through in her life, this can only happen if she'll have me.'

'Yes.' There was suddenly a twinkle in the old man's eyes. 'I knew I had the right measure of you. Go. And, William? My own dear lady wife is also fair and named Isabel. Good luck with your endeavours.'

Will's lips twitched as he bowed. 'My lord.'

Chapter Twenty-Four

It had been over a sennight since Will had left Castle de Clancey, but it felt far longer. In that time Isabel had made sure that she was kept busy with her new role, engaging herself in everything to do with the castle.

She liaised with the steward, met the sergeant of the garrison, and worked with the household staff to make sure of the smooth running of the castle. She engaged traders and villagers in the hope of learning more about these people—her people.

It surprised her how much her previous experiences had prepared her, in a strange way, for this role. Will had been right about that—she was more capable than she'd ever dared believe. Yes, it had been going rather well, except…except for the fact that her heart was splintering into tiny little pieces. Isabel tried to push all vestiges of William Geraint out of her head, but some days it was more arduous and painful than others.

This was one such day…

After a warming bath, she sat by the hearth in her chamber, laboriously combing through her long hair, with Perdu at her feet.

It was useless, though. Will would not be coming back.

There was sudden knock on the wooden door before it opened slowly. Isabel stood to greet her mother with a ready smile. 'Please, come in, my lady mother.'

'I hope I'm not disturbing you.'

'Not at all. Can I get you some refreshment? Some wine?'

'No, thank you, my dear. Sit, sit… It was just you didn't seem to partake in eating much earlier so I wanted to see how you were faring.' Her mother took her silver metal comb from her fingers and continued to comb her hair.

'I'm perfectly well and perfectly happy.'

'Good, good…'

'You seem distracted, Mother.'

'Am I?' She smoothed down the length of Isabel's hair with her fingers, so comforting and soothing—a mother's touch. 'It's just that I wanted to tell you once again how happy you've made me to have you back home when I… I believed you were lost to me, for all those years.'

Above all her duties, Isabel spent as much of her time as possible in the company of her mother, to become better acquainted with her after all this time apart. Isabel had told her about her life in St Jean de Cole and in return her mother filled in all the missing details about her brothers and what life had been like at Castle de Clancey. Which had, sadly, not been good.

Her mother inhaled before continuing to speak. Her hand shook as she reached out to cradle her daughter's cheek. 'We have both suffered so much pain, Isabel, but I hope that we can move forward together. I hope we can put the past behind us.'

'Yes,' Isabel whispered as her mother kissed her forehead. 'I would like that.'

'And I hope in time you'll realise how much it means to me to be reunited with you. How much peace and happiness you've afforded me at this time of my life.'

'I do and must tell you that I feel the same.'

'I'm glad. My only wish is for you to be truly happy, Isabel.'

'But I am.'

'I hope so, because that very same happiness can sometimes be much closer than you know. You just have to open your eyes, look outside and find it.' Her mother smiled as she moved away. 'And when you do, grasp it with both hands.'

Frowning in confusion, Isabel meandered to the small square window that her mother had nodded to and opened the wooden shutters. What had she meant? She turned back around to ask, but her mother had left her chamber.

Strange…

The cool air whipped through the window, reminding her that it wouldn't be long until the arrival of winter, slipping into Advent…with the joys of Christmas and Twelfth Night ready to be savoured. She inhaled the cold air into her chest.

Dusk was settling like a slumbering blanket over the vista. Though not yet. No, it hung to the daylight, causing a vivid splendour in the night sky. It was that moment in between, when night and day kissed only briefly before going their separate ways. There was something enchanting about the twilight hour, casting an alluring spell that made her wistful for things she could not have.

Isabel shuddered and was about to close the shutter again when something caught her eye in the inner bailey. There were clusters of light creating a pattern on the ground below. How odd…

What on earth could it be?

Her brows furrowed before she made the decision to investigate further. Fetching her woollen cloak that Will had bought for her in Southampton, she dashed out of her chamber with Perdu in tow. She grabbed a torch from a nearby sconce to light the way down the stone spiral staircase from the solar and hurried down. Stepping out on to the ground outside the inner bailey, Isabel rubbed her hands together, blowing hot air into them, and blinked in surprise. Small metal dishes with flat tallow candles lit a patterned path on the ground from the inner bailey through the arch and beyond. And there was more… Beside the trail of little lights was a scattering of…but, no, it couldn't be! She bent down and picked a few up, rubbing the feathery petals between her fingers before bringing them to her nose.

Hyssop petals? What in God's name did this mean?

Isabel rushed along, following the trail lit by the dispersed dishes of tallow candles, stopping only to collect more of the strewn hyssop petals. She continued along, bemused at the absurdity of it all, her cloak folded out to help collect the purple mass of hyssop, its scent perfuming the cool air. She vaguely registered that the castle was uncharacteristically quiet, without a soul in sight. That in itself should have alarmed her, but her interest was piqued far too much to stop now. With her heart pounding, she hurried along, wandering through every winding path into the outer bailey, around the castle. Eventually she reached the last few lit dishes, which came to an abrupt halt outside the entrance of the chapel.

Just then, a man stepped out from the shadow of the arched porch. A ripple of awareness ran through her.

Will?

She rubbed her eyes. Could it be?

Her stomach flipped over itself as she realised that it was indeed William Geraint looking ever so handsome in a dark blue tunic and dark braes and hose beneath a leather gambeson. He smiled, inclining his head as she approached him.

'Will?' she said in a shaky voice. 'What...what are you doing here?'

'Good evening, my lady.' His midnight-blue eyes glittered at her with such warmth that her breath stuck in her throat. 'I came to the realisation—albeit a little late—that despite your excellent progress acquiring important defensive moves, there may still be much to learn. So, I have come to offer my services.'

Her lips twitched despite herself. 'I see.'

'Indeed, and I also came to ask something else.' He dragged his fingers through his hair. He seemed a little nervous. 'You see, after bringing you back home, I felt a little lost...'

Lost?

Was it an accident that Will had used a sentiment describing her situation when he had first met her?

'I'm sorry for that. Have you resolved the situation?'

'Not quite.' His lips quirked. 'You see, I decided that I wanted desperately to come home.'

Her heart thumped even harder in her chest. *'Home?'*

'To you, Isabel,' he whispered softly, moving towards her. 'I belong anywhere you do. If…if you'll have me.'

Her knees felt weak, making standing a little difficult.

'What has brought about this change?'

'A realisation that, without you, my life is worth nothing.' He expelled a long breath. 'And I'm tired, Isabel. I'm tired of withholding happiness that could so easily be ours, if we would just allow it.'

She shook her head. 'I cannot believe this.'

'Nevertheless, it is the truth, sweetheart.'

'Is it?' she muttered, still tugging at the ends of her cloak containing the hyssop petals.

'Utterly and completely.' He edged closer still. 'You complete me, Isabel de Clancey.'

She gasped, unable to say anything for a moment, but she needed to. Words were needed here. 'As do you, William Geraint,' she murmured before a crease formed across her forehead. 'But is it enough?'

'It's certainly a foundation to build our future on.' He took a deep breath before continuing. 'I want to spend the rest of my life with you, if you'll have me. Would you do me the honour of becoming my wife, Isabel? I would pledge my life to you. And do everything I can to be the man worthy to stand beside you, protect you and love you.'

This felt so dreamlike, so unreal.

Was she, in fact, dreaming?

Before she could answer him, Isabel heard hushed voices from within the chapel. 'Tell me, are there people in there?'

'It's of no matter, my love. This is a choice for you to

make. If you decide to decline my offer, then we shall go in and attend mass as normal.'

'Do you believe that I would decline you?' She raised her brows as a slow smile spread across her face.

'This is your choice, Isabel,' he said again, evidently far more nervous than she had anticipated. 'If you require more time to consider my offer, then I'll wait. I realise that I have sprung this on you, yet I had hoped my surprise may be welcome. No matter, we'll just explain that—'

Holding the edges of her cloak in one hand, she put her finger to his lips to silence him. 'I do not need more time.' Her teeth sunk into her lower lips. 'Besides, since our family and friends are assembled here, we should really oblige them.'

'What are you saying? Do you mean that you…you accept me?'

'Yes.' She chuckled softly. 'Of course, I do.'

His shoulders sagged in apparent relief. 'Thank God, because I forgot to mention that I brought my whole family with me and they are currently waiting in the chapel. Along with Hugh, Eleanor and my young godson, William.'

She laughed. 'What would you have done if I had refused you?'

'Ah, well, I would have showered you with verses and sonnets professing my undying love.' He winked. 'Failing that, I would have wept at your feet.'

'It's just as well we have been spared that.'

'True, I'm not sure how I could provide the necessary verse to secure your hand.'

'I think you're much more capable than you believe, my knight.'

He leant forward. 'Oh, I hope so. I am going to need a lifetime to practise on you, though.' Will presented her with a bouquet of fresh and dried flowers and herbs, including long stems of blue-purple hyssop.

'Thank you, they're beautiful.'

Needing a free hand, she pulled her cloak up and watched the amassed petals rise into the air, as a sudden breeze whipped them away. The evening air, suffused in blue-purple, floated around them.

Ah, this night seemed to be filled with enchantment, after all. She reached out to take the bouquet, but noticed something dangling from the raffia string that was wrapped around the bouquet.

She held the small oval-shaped slate that bore Will's beautiful carvings as well as her own rather crude ones and flicked her gaze back to him. 'What is this?'

'You once gifted me with something precious for saving your life. I'm merely returning the favour.'

'But I have never saved your life.'

'Haven't you?' he whispered in a low timbre that rippled through her.

She stared at him, as her eyes filled with tears. 'I love you, William Geraint.' Oh, God, she mustn't weep now.

'And I love you, Isabel de Clancey.' Will removed a few stray petals from her shoulder before pulling her into his arms and kissing her with so much tenderness that Isabel almost swooned. He lifted his head and smiled against her lips. 'Come, let's go inside. Shall we?'

'Oh yes.' She beamed, returning his smile.

They entered the chapel, where they declared their solemn vows to one another, binding them together in front of their loved ones. And rather than exchange customary rings, they exchanged their pendants, signifying an everlasting love.

* * * * *

*If you enjoyed this book, why not check out
this other great read by Melissa Oliver*

The Rebel Heiress and the Knight

K